PARADE OF THE EMPTY BOOTS

PARADE OF THE EMPTY BOOTS

CHARLES ALDEN SELTZER

WILDSIDE PRESS

CHAPTER ONE

Having captured romance, only to lose it after a brief season, was worse than having no romance at all, reflected Colonel John Burleigh as he sat in an easy chair on the upper deck of the small stern-wheeler Clara Belle and tried, through the impenetrable darkness, to trace the east shore line of the Mississippi. His daughter Clara was somewhere below, probably reading—since they were grounded upon a mud bar, and there was no possibility of their getting off very soon.

Colonel Burleigh had disdained bringing a pilot along from Cincinnati—where his vast interests were—for, as he explained to a friend: "I have traveled the river so much that I know every inch of it. I expect to do most of the piloting myself. It will give me something to think about."

The present predicament of the Clara Belle only slightly annoyed him, because it had been his own fault that he had mistaken a big bend in the river for the main channel, pursuing it for miles until he realized his mistake, and then grounding the boat hard and fast at the edge of a swamp just where several miles of cypress forest concealed the Clara Belle from any steamer which might be passing.

The colonel's lost romance had begun twenty years ago. It had brought Clara and had taken away his wife, which had ended everything for him. As colonel of an Ohio regiment in the war he had thrown himself at death many times but had survived it; now he had only his daughter and his business and his memories. So now, upon this mudbank of the Mississippi, with a moist darkness crowding in upon him, and his annoyance at having made a fool of himself disturbing him more than he cared to admit, he felt that life, after all, was niggardly in its compensations.

The crew, he supposed—consisting of the wheelsman, the engineer, who was also the stoker; a Negro cook; and a mulatto boy who made himself generally useful—were asleep, for there was no sound below, and no light aboard except for the one in Clara's stateroom. The fire under the boiler had been drawn. The Clara Belle waited, dreary and dark but expectant, for the colonel had made arrangements for assistance in getting his vessel back into the main channel, and he momentarily expected a hail from the wall of blackness shoreward, where he knew there was a road leading inland.

This was the Clara Belle's second night on the mud bar. She had come in here after dusk—when she should have been at a safe anchorage, or tied up at the wharf of a town on the river—and she had stuck there in spite of all the mad churning of the paddle wheels, and there she would stay until pulled off by some outside force.

At daylight the first morning the colonel looked out upon a mile or so of brackish water stretching between the Clara Belle and a great cypress swamp, dank with a heavy mist that rose from green slime to float in weird wisps and streamers through the gray and green lacy festoons of Spanish moss.

An hour or so after daylight a punt stuck its blunt nose out of the swamp mist and came toward the Clara Belle with tentative jerks. It was propelled by a gaunt man whose garments flapped loosely about him as he wielded the long pole with which he forced his queer craft through the water. When within hailing distance of the Clara Belle he stood motionless, staring, permitting his boat to drift. He was black bearded, long haired, half wild. But when he saw Burleigh on the upper deck he called to him querulously:

"When did yo'-all git in hyar?"

"Last night after dark," answered Burleigh.

"Thet air was a mighty fool thing to do," commented the denizen of the swamp. "Ain't yo' got ary a pilot?"

Burleigh told him they had no pilot, and the swamp man sat down in the bottom of the punt, evidently to meditate.

"Yo'-all must be a passel o' damned fools," he finally said.

Burleigh admitted that he, at least, was a fool.

"Whut fer cargo yo' got aboard?" asked the man.

"Not much of a cargo. Food and supplies for ourselves," answered Burleigh.

"How yo' expaict to git outen the mud?"

"When we get someone to pull us out. How far is the next town?"

"Nigh to twenty miles. Hit air Chandler."

"I'll pay you twenty dollars to ride down there and tell them we are in trouble," offered Burleigh.

The boatman stared at Burleigh. His eyes, squinted, seemed to search the faces of the others, who were watching and listening—Clara Burleigh, who had emerged from her stateroom in morning negligee, looking very fresh and beautiful; and the members of the crew at the lower rail, aft, who seemed little interested in the conversation.

"Twenty dollars, eh?" said the boatman. "How air I to know yo' got thet much money aboard?" He smiled skeptically, slyly.

"Do you mean that you won't trust me?" laughed Burleigh.

"I don't trust nobuddy. Who air yo'?"

"I am Colonel Burleigh of Cincinnati," answered Burleigh. He couldn't afford to antagonize the boatman.

"Never heered of yo'," said the boatman. "This yere all the crew yo' got?"

Burleigh peered over the side, to see the crew at the lower rail. "That's all," he admitted.

"It'll take me a tu'lable time to git help to yo'," said the boatman.

"You mean you want more than twenty dollars?" laughed Burleigh.

"It's wuth thu'ty dollars."

"All right," agreed Burleigh. "I'll pay thirty."

"Yo'll pay it now?" drawled the boatman.

"Sure," said Burleigh. "Come closer."

While the boatman poled his craft to the side of the little steamer Burleigh went into his stateroom, to reappear almost immediately with a small buckskin bag into which, with the boatman watching, he delved, to bring forth two gold pieces, a twenty and a ten, which he placed in the boatman's extended right hand. Bright avarice gleamed in the boatman's eyes as he stared at the gold which, Burleigh decided, must seem like a fortune to him.

"Move along now," said Burleigh. "You'd best go right to the town hall in Chandler and tell them it's Colonel Burleigh with the Clara Belle," he added.

The punt was now drifting away shoreward. The boatman had pulled a leather tobacco pouch from a pocket and was depositing the gold pieces in it. He was grinning hugely. Presently he seized the pole and began to work his craft toward the swamp. Gradually he vanished into the mist.

Clara Burleigh was staring after him.

"Father," she said, "I don't trust that man. He is so greedy! Did you notice his eyes—how they stared at us?"

Colonel Burleigh laughed. "The poor devil was half starved, I suppose. He was driving what he thought was a hard bargain, possibly for more money than he has ever seen in his life. He'll be back with help before night."

But night had come again, and the humid blackness of it had rolled in upon them and over them, gradually deepening until shore line and swamp were no longer visible. The light that filtered through the margins of the drawn shades of Clara's stateroom diffused only a flickering glow upon the upper deck, yet there was enough light to reveal in shadowy outline the figure of Colonel Burleigh seated in his deck chair impatiently awaiting the arrival of the help he had arranged for.

The stillness that enveloped the steamer became the ominous calm that precedes a storm. Distant mutterings and rumblings came to the colonel's ears upon a breeze so slight that it didn't even stir the canvas canopy that covered part of the forward deck. Vainly in this quiet Burleigh strove to catch the sound of a steamer's throbbing engines, or to see the running lights of a vessel gleaming through the trees that blocked his view of the main channel, miles away.

Nothing. Nothing but the persistent diapason of night insects, the shrill pipelike calls of whippoorwills, the monotonous castaneting of tree toads and the guttural croaking of frogs in the swamps.

It was nearly midnight when the door of Clara's stateroom opened, the light from within flooding the deck behind Burleigh. Clara stood in the light, softly silhouetted. She was ready for bed.

"No signs of them yet, Father?" she said.

"No. Something has miscarried, I suppose."

"Your thirty dollars," laughed Clara.

"I suppose so," reluctantly conceded Burleigh. "The boatman said it was twenty miles to a town named Chandler. Of course they may not have had a boat of suitable draught for this mud."

Clara yawned. "Well, there is nothing to do about it," she said. "I'm sleepy. You won't mind if I go to bed, Father?"

"Good night. I'll be turning in myself if they don't come in sight in an hour."

The colonel lighted a cigar, leaned back in the deck chair and relaxed. After a while the light in Clara's stateroom went out, and the blackness enveloping the steamer seemed to descend, bringing with it a deepening silence.

Well, it was a great night to sleep, anyway, and Clara was wise in taking advantage of it. There was just enough breeze to lull one into a doze, and presently, reclining at full length in the deck chair, a pleasant drowsiness stole over Burleigh, and he yielded to it. He dreamed. The dream was so vivid that he thought he was awake and fully conscious of what was transpiring. The boatman had been honest and trustworthy after all. For Burleigh dreamed that the running lights of a steamer were coming around the bend from the main channel, bearing straight down upon his own stranded craft. He thought he could hear the slashing of the paddle wheels, the rippling of the water as it was parted by the bow of the oncoming vessel.

A series of thuds awakened him to a consciousness of danger, sudden and terrible. The rippling noises he had heard had been caused by a number of swamp punts being rapidly poled toward his vessel, and as he leaned over the side the water was thick with them, and dark forms were climbing from them to the lower deck. From bow and stern came thumps and harsh voices.

River pirates!

He started to run toward his stateroom for a weapon, realizing as he ran that he was too late. A dozen dark forms closed in about him, and he was suddenly flayed to the deck, his head and spine and legs paralyzed, dazzling white light flashing inside his eyelids. In an infernal moment before he knew anything at all he heard Clara screaming.

CHAPTER TWO

Clara Burleigh had been awakened by the noises that Colonel Burleigh had heard in his dreams. Unlike her father, she had not heard the splashing of paddle wheels; and when, disturbed and startled, she got out of her berth to lift a shade at one of the windows, she did not see the running lights of a steamer. She heard a thumping, as if dozens of floating logs were striking the steamer; she heard hoarse voices, and scuffling, and the pattering of feet, bare or moccasined, on the upper deck.

All along she had mistrusted the boatman to whom her father had given the gold pieces, and now, with a dawning consciousness of the nearness of tragedy, she swiftly slipped a lounging robe over her night garments, opened the stateroom door, ran through a short passageway, to reach the upper deck in time to see a blur of figures near the rail, to hear a thud and a savage voice saying: "That settles yo', damn yo'!" She screamed and ran toward the blur of figures, frenziedly striving to tear her way through them to reach her father, but a dozen arms seized her, held her, and raucous laughter smote her ears. Bodies pressed against her in an ever-tightening compress; heads were close to hers; she heard the heavy breathing of excitement, the voices of easy, sudden triumph. She was smothered by the weight of men crowding close to her; she was panting wildly in the grip of their arms, yet in her frenzy of anxiety she fought them desperately, crying out for her father.

"You've killed him!" she cried. "Oh! You've killed him!"

Loud laughter arose from the press around her.

"I reckon he air dead enough!" declared a voice.

She must have fainted then, for when she again became conscious she was lying in her bunk in her stateroom, which was crowded with men who were staring at her in the light of the wall lamp. They were all grinning at her; hugely they were enjoying the amazed terror in her eyes as she comprehended what was happening and what had happened. The men were of various shapes and sizes; they were tattered, unkempt, with long hair and beards, but with increasing terror she noted that their eyes all seemed to carry the same expression—an avid greediness, a cold cruelty, a gargantuan satisfaction over her predicament, of the knowledge lying naked in her eyes—that she was afraid of them. They were watching her with hawklike intensity, laughing, and she felt that while she had been unconscious they had been discussing her, looking at her. They were pressing close to her bunk, and when a man with a leering face reached out a hand to touch her bosom, which she had involuntarily covered with her night robe the instant she had returned to consciousness, she slapped his grinning face with all her strength, whereat the others roared with laughter and jibed the culprit, who scowled with rage and embarrassment.

"Yo' better keep yore hands offen her, Bill," said one of the men. "She'll be Forbush's gal, I reckin. He'll bust yo' wide open ef yo' go to monkeyin' with her. Besides, yo' got a wife and a batch o' young 'uns."

"My father!" cried Clara. "Where is he? What has happened to him?" She tried to get out of the bunk but was forcibly shoved back into it, and she sat up, staring at them helplessly.

"Thet was yore dad, eh?" said a voice whose owner grinned wickedly. "Wa-ll, yo' don't need to worry none about him. He's as dead as the rest of them."

They had killed the crew too. Suddenly realizing the truth of it all, the dread finality of it—that it was beyond her power to do anything about it—she covered her eyes with her hands to shut out the sight of the horrible, grinning faces of the fiends who had done the murders. Her crying stopped the laughter, and it trailed off to low, sober comment, some of which she heard. After a while, a long while, she looked up to see that only two of the men remained in the cabin. They were huge and powerful, and when they saw her looking at them they grinned at her hideously, with appalling significance.

"Feel like movin' now?" asked the larger of the two.

"Where am I going?" she said defiantly.

"Yo' air goin' with us. We-all air takin' yo' to the shore, whar Forbush is waitin' fer yo'."

Twice she had heard this name.

"Who is Forbush?"

The men looked at each other, grinning.

"Yo'll find thet out soon enough, I reckin," said the tall man. "I swear he'll be tickled to see yo'. Ef he ain't, then Vauchain will, or maybe Craftkin." He eyed her critically. "Yo're purty, ma'am, and them's the kind Forbush and the Leopard likes. Craftkin ain't so pertickeler." He made a gesture of impatience. "Git into yore duds," he added.

"I'll be glad to, if you will leave me alone."

"Kain't do it, ma'am." They both grinned again, horribly. "We got orders not to let yo' out of our sight, and we aim to do as we're told. Effen yo' don't put yore duds on we'll hev' to take yo' without any clothes. We'll turn our backs, won't we, Clell?" They grinned and winked at each other.

There was no help for it, she knew, so when the men turned their backs to her she swiftly slipped out of the berth and began to dress. Only once during the process did the men violate their pledge to her, and upon that occasion a small water pitcher hurtled through the air, missing Clell's head by inches. It was shattered against the wall. The next time they looked she had finished.

They took her down the passageway to the lower deck, holding her tightly by the arms, evidently divining that she might attempt to break away to search for her father, which thought was in her mind. The lower deck swarmed with dark figures which were moving about loading everything of probable value into the various punts which floated alongside. Here and there stood other men, holding pine flares which lighted the scene grotesquely. Boxes, barrels, packages, crates and the inevitable miscellany were carried over the side and loaded into the punts. Then, while one of the men held Clara, the other climbed into an empty punt, and presently she was in the punt, too, with one of the men holding her while the other poled the craft into the darkness beyond the flickering light of the flares.

Clara now cared little where the men were taking her, and as the punt moved off into the darkness she stared at the steamer, reluctant to leave her father's body, hoping wildly that he had not been killed after all, crying again, fighting the man who held her, desperately striving to leap overboard and swim back to the craft to find her father. The scarecrow forms that moved about the vessel in the light of the pine flares seemed like demons dancing in ghoulish glee over the destruction they had wrought. The punt moved swiftly into a wall of blackness, the steamer growing ever more distant, until at last Clara could see only the lights of the pine flares. The punt must have veered around a bend in the river, for suddenly the lights vanished.

A few minutes later the punt grounded upon a shallow, and her captor lifted her, swung her around in front of him, stepped off into the water and carried her up a slope, the second man following. The men had uncanny sense of direction or they were familiar with their surroundings, for they had brought her to the road that paralleled the shore line, to finally run inland—the road she and her father had seen from the steamer. She could feel its hard surface through the thin soles of the light shoes she wore.

For a time the two men stood there, holding her, seeming to listen. Then one of them called loudly:

"Forbush! Whar air yo'?"

Instantly a deep voice answered, "Here!" and Clara heard someone moving toward them. It was very still here, with the peculiar moist atmosphere of the swamp heavily enveloping her, and Clara could hear horses impatiently stamping, their hoofs thudding into the damp clay of the road.

And then she felt a new presence near her, and a deep voice, low and pleasant, was saying:

"It's Clell and Dexter, isn't it?"

"Shuah is," answered the tall man. "She's right yere." He seemed to know exactly where Forbush stood, for he pushed Clara forward, straight into Forbush's arms, which closed gently around her, and then firmly, as if to make certain that she did not escape him.

He was a big man, and powerful, for though she struggled to escape, he held her easily, laughing at her.

"There, there," he said. "Don't try to get away. You couldn't go very far, you know. There is swamp all around us, full of snakes and quicksand. Just be quiet now. No one is going to harm you."

He stood for a short space, holding her, one hand lightly brushing her shoulders and her head, as if he sought by that method to determine her height and size. Then he spoke shortly to the two men who had brought her, telling them to go back to the steamer to help the others transfer the cargo to the punts. When he heard the punt shove off he lifted Clara in his arms and began to move slowly along the road. She fought him to no avail. He carried her easily, lightly, as if she were a child. Much as she loathed him for the part he was playing in this drama of violence and bloodshed, she felt he was mentally and physically superior to the depraved, vile and unclean clan aboard the steamer. The cloth of his garments was smooth and satiny, and when she had fought him back there where he had lifted her to carry her away, her hands had come into contact with a silk stock around his neck and with a ruffled shirt bosom. Her fingers had also gripped his hair, which was thick and curly.

All her sensations were subconscious. Overwhelming everything was a sickening and bewildering knowledge of loss, which made even her capture by the uncouth clan and her subsequent delivery to Forbush trivial incidents. She had not been afraid of any of them. She was not afraid of Forbush as he swung her upward, into what, she thought, was a wagon seat, and mounted beside her, still holding her arms.

They sat there in the darkness for a little space, saying nothing. Horses were hitched to the wagon; she could hear them stamping, could hear the creaking of the harness, the tugging of the wagon tongue.

"You are trembling," said Forbush. "Let me put my cloak over you." Which he did, and drew her closer to him, without her caring. She was crying again and whispering her grief, saying over and over again, "Father, Father, oh, Father!"

"That won't help," said Forbush. "It won't bring him back. I didn't want them to do it, but they were too many for me."

There was no comfort in words, no matter how sympathetic and persuasive. She paid little attention to what Forbush said to her, for this terrible experience had dazed her to incoherence, to dull apathy. She no longer cared to know what was happening to her, around her or near her. She did not know how long she sat upon the wagon seat with Forbush holding her. She heard voices—the voices of the unclean and depraved clan, close to her and from a distance—the hateful voices. She heard punts grounding upon the shore, the rattle of poles, the clanking and thudding of collisions at the water's edge. She heard curses as men heaved heavy boxes and crates into the wagon, and after a while she saw the darkness lift as gray dawn stole into the sky. One by one, then, she made out the shapes of half a dozen other wagons with teams of horses hitched to them, strung out upon the road in front of the one in which she was sitting with Forbush. She looked up, when the light became strong enough, to see Forbush—tall, muscular, darkly handsome, his black curly hair showing under the brim of his felt hat, his white teeth gleaming, his gray eyes smiling at her. She turned away from him, shuddering at something she had seen in him, and stared back over the water at the Clara Belle. She saw tongues of flame writhing here and there, licking the rails of the upper deck, and black smoke rising to drift away in the wind. She screamed, bowed her head and covered her face with her hands. The wagons started to move.

CHAPTER THREE

Like an ocean of dusky vapor, twilight settled down over the high desert behind Brent Stoddard. He faced the purple haze of an indistinct wooded valley as he rode down a dry wash to a timbered flat. He sank into the trapped heat of the low country, where a rank, wild growth concealed him from the higher levels.

The killer had pushed his mount relentlessly, hoping, as Stoddard knew, to reach this timbered region before Stoddard's posse could overtake him, and from a distance, back there in a treeless world, Stoddard, his own horse failing, had seen the other riders and their mounts sink below the fringing treetops that marked the near edge of the wild lower country.

Stoddard's horse followed a trail no wider than a foot-path. Physically spent, the animal pushed on into the deepening purple, Stoddard sympathetically patting its left shoulder, grimly noting the quivering muscles. It wasn't his habit to push a horse inhumanely, and now a compassionate pressure of the reins brought the animal to a walk, and a stillness flowed over man and beast, enveloping them. That stillness was close. Into it, from a distance, came sound—a faint popping.

That would be Dollarbill McCarthy, who was riding the fastest horse, who owned a cold and deadly temper and a trigger finger to match it. Dollarbill could not be shaken off once he went after a man. No subterfuge deceived him. Yes, it would be Dollarbill. The other men were good, but Dollarbill would be leading them at the finish.

There was no more shooting. There wouldn't be, with Dollarbill doing it. And no need of Stoddard crowding his tired horse. The silence flowed in again with nothing to mar its perfection, and the falling shadows deepened to a murky purple, then to black with a faintly luminous star haze filtering through the treetops.

The horse, Stoddard found, dismounting and loosening the cinches, was only winded. The animal sighed with relief from the release of pressure and softly whickered his appreciation.

"He knows this country," was Stoddard's thought of the killer as he rode on again. "His heading this way wasn't an accident. There was plenty of room all around."

The killing had been done from behind, with a knife, and the victim's rifled pockets, some gashes in the flesh around his middle, together with the slashed waistband of his trousers, showed that a money belt and papers had been taken. One pocket the killer had missed. Stoddard had taken possession of a small package found in that pocket, and he now patted the left breast of his woolen shirt to make sure he had not lost it.

Killer and victim were strangers to him, and he would not know their identity until he looked over the victim's effects and until he reached Dollarbill and the posse.

An ever-widening expanse of starry blue sky showed him that the valley was broadening and that he was emerging from the timber. The carpet of cedar and spruce spikes which had deadened the beat of the hoofs of his tired horse ended, and the iron shoes were now ringing upon a rock trail. When, rounding a hill, he saw a pin point of light glowing in the wall of darkness ahead of him he knew that the race had ended, that the killer was dead or captured. The men had built a fire to guide him.

Five men, including Dollarbill, greeted him with silence, for they had seen his swift glances comprehending the tragedy. The killer's horse was picketed with the others; the killer himself, face down in the thick grass of the valley bottom, was a little distance off. Dollarbill was smoking a pipe, squatting there indolently. The men were all watching Stoddard. Their job done, they anticipated commendation, knew they would receive it. They were affectionately respectful, waiting. Even Dollarbill's bleak eyes had softened. Standing there, the firelight playing upon him, Stoddard jerked his head toward the silent figure lying in the grass.

"Any trouble with him?"

"Hardly none," said Dollarbill. "He went for his gun, but he had showed he was more handy with a knife."

Stoddard staked his horse out, returned to the fire, dropped to the grass and stretched full length, hands under the back of his head, scanning the sky.

The men had ridden long and hard and were frankly tired.

He told them that they had done well. "You search him?" he asked.

"Thought you'd like to do that," said Dollarbill. "It's him though."

"He'll be there come daylight," suggested a rider, flat on his stomach, head pillowed by an arm, his voice muffled.

They, too, would be there at daylight. They had earned a rest and they took it, leaving things to Stoddard.

A quarter of an hour later Stoddard, who had been lying flat on his stomach for a time, raised himself to his elbows. The men were sound asleep. Stoddard got up, strode to the killer, turned him over, searched him, took things from his pockets. Coming back to the fire, Stoddard dropped some papers and a money belt into the grass, sat down and inspected them. Once he got up and replenished the fire.

The killer's name was Simon Gorty. His victim's name was Pierre Villers. Stoddard separated letters and papers. The money belt, made of pliable leather with shallow pockets, was stamped with the victim's name. The pockets contained three thousand dollars in gold double eagles.

Stoddard buckled the money belt around his own waist, tucked his shirt over it. By the light of the fire he read the details of the tragedy, supplying important links from Dollarbill's previous verbal report of the killing and from his own knowledge of how these things were usually done. After all, it was simple and sordid and old. Robbery and murder. How Simon Gorty had discovered that Pierre Villers had a money belt would never be known, now. Nor was that detail important.

As marshal of Burgess City Brent Stoddard had performed his duty. Victim and killer were dead. The golden eagles and the victim's other personal property would be forwarded.

Stoddard drew up a knee, clasped his hands over it and stared into the fire. The papers he had taken from the killer's pockets were strewn about, where he had indifferently dropped them. He had forgotten. He hadn't forgotten that he was tired of all this, that for many months he had meditated resigning and that at this instant he had decided he was through.

He wasn't certain about his future. He had no definite plan of action. So far as he knew, no nostalgic yearnings possessed him. He had no home to return to; there would be no greetings, delighted or otherwise; no fatted calf. And no explanations. He was the last of his line.

He got up, threw some more wood on the fire, strode over, looked down at the dead man's face, cold humor stirring him. What had the killer planned to do with the golden eagles? Nothing now. He sat down again near the fire and found himself staring at the face of a woman. A photograph had been among the papers he had taken from the killer's pockets; he had accidentally disturbed the papers when he seated himself, and the photograph lay flat, the firelight gleaming upon it. He picked it up and swung around with his back to the fire so that the light came over his shoulder and instantly he knew that here was the explanation of the unrest that had tortured him.

It was a girl's face, and more beautiful than his dreams.

Studying the picture, he fought the pangs of ecstasy that raced through him. He fought against the awed reverence that surged over him, arraying against it the cynicism and distrust that his experiences with certain types of women had built up in him. He fought a losing battle though, for he knew that the calm, steady eyes that gazed back at him from the photograph were as honest as his own better impulses.

Something in the girl's eyes eluded him. He moved nearer to the fire, stirred the embers until a bright flame flared. Then, lying on his side, so close to the fire that the heat beat against him in a scorching wave, he sought, and found, in the eyes what he had been searching for: a gleam—a mere glint—a suggestion of mischief lying deep behind their cool, frank honesty. The discovery made her all the more desirable and appealing. Her face became animated, alive. He knew what was happening to him and with an effort he sat erect and dragged his senses back to the fire, to the sleeping members of his posse, to the dead man, the arching blue sky and the aloof stars. A guilty embarrassment surged through him.

A signature, penned upon the photograph, caught his attention, and he intently inspected it—"Marie Villers." Above the signature, "affectionately, your niece."

He carefully laid the photograph beside him, face upward, and searched among the letters and papers until he found the one he sought. It was from her to her uncle, the killer's victim, Pierre Villers.

Dear Uncle Pierre:

I shall write the good news first, then the bad, because there is so much more of the latter. I am well but very lonesome. Everything is so unsettled here, and never a day passes peacefully. Some Southern soldiers are still here. They are the last remnants of the Confederacy who refuse to give up and are pursued by scouting parties of Union troops. And there are the guerillas, and Forbush, and Vauchain's thieving, killing band. They would not be tolerated if it were not for Jim Craftkin, who supports them with his gang of ex-soldiers. It wouldn't be so bad if Father were alive; and I am beginning to believe that Father was not killed in a duel as they claim. I always thought Father's business was unencumbered, but now Asa Colder—who shot Father, as I told you in my last letter—claims that Father owed him three thousand dollars. He showed me the notes. There is something wrong, Uncle Pierre. I feel it, but I don't know what it is. Judge Marston thinks so too.

I don't ask you for money, Uncle Pierre, but I do wish you would try to come here and help me straighten out Father's affairs and, above all, help me to get at the mystery of Father's death. There are a great many things I want to tell you, but they will have to wait until I see you, which I hope will be soon.

Affectionately yours,

Marie Villers.

Stoddard folded the letter and photograph together and placed them in the inside pocket of his vest. And now he got up and walked away from the fire, to stand and gaze steadily into the southern distance where some mountain peaks caught the glow of a rising moon. He turned and looked at his riders, prone around the fire; at Dollarbill, his friend of many years; at the killer of Pierre Villers. He wondered about the killer; if the murder of Pierre Villers had been casual, or if it had been part of a premeditated plot perpetrated by the sinister forces arrayed against Marie Villers. In Stoddard's veins ran a cold fire of contempt and fury which was expressed outwardly by a smile in which there was little mirth. At daybreak he would ride south, alone, personally to deliver to Marie Villers her uncle's papers and the golden eagles which, he had no doubt, her uncle had been carrying to her.

CHAPTER FOUR

When Brent Stoddard first saw the girl she was standing, poised on a bank of the Mississippi River at the edge of a deep dark pool, ready to plunge. She was fully clothed but barefoot. She was not the girl of the photograph, not Marie Villers. And she did make the plunge into the water. A long straight dive, knifelike and deep. She disappeared. The water rippled.

Women are strange creatures, he thought. Going swimming with her clothes on. Not many clothes. A sort of wrapper, of gingham, perhaps, but not much underneath it because when she had stood poised the lines of her figure were clear. She'd need dry things when she came out, wouldn't she? No figuring women.

She came up. He thought she would swim; instead, she drew in a great deal of water and began to strangle. It was deliberate, grim. She meant to drown herself.

If he had had her on the bank now he'd have given her a rope's end upon the rounded part of her anatomy revealed most distinctly by the wind-swept garment when she had poised just before the dive. But before he could chastise her for being a fool he must get her out. There was a sound of swift unbuckling as he tossed his gun and cartridge belt into the lush grass at the river's edge, slipped off his vest containing the photograph and the letters, and, still burdened with the three thousand dollars of double eagles, went in after her.

She fought him like a wildcat, but in the end he had got her out, and now she was lying on the grass at the water's edge and he was lying beside her, holding her, to keep her from doing it all over again, and she was glaring at him from a pair of snapping dark eyes, and he was pretending to be unaffected by the torrent of epithets she was applying to him.

"Lemme up, you damn devil!" she gasped. "Don't you be a-holdin' me hyah a-lookin' at me. I ain't got hardly no clothes on."

"I'm not scandalized," he told her. "I'm not even interested, except in keeping you from making a fool of yourself."

She half believed him, for she stopped struggling and critically inspected him. She caught her breath; her eyes widened, glowed with interest. He's handsome, she thought. His dripping hair, close cut, was dark with golden-brown tones in it where the sun struck it. Dry, it would be brown. Eyes a clear blue, deep set, twinkling now with lazy, half-contemptuous amusement. A strong, lean face and a mouth as wayward as a woman's. A bronzed giant. Clean.

He saw the changes in her eyes but pretended he did not. They were the eyes of a wild, frightened young animal, bearing the appeal of unscathed and unspoiled femininity. Deep in them was the man-fear.

She would be a beauty except for her too-uptilted nose. The freckles around her eyes made them browner and gave them a penetrating, quizzical squint. She was built like a boy except for her young firm breasts and soft well-rounded throat. Her hair, brown as his own, was cascaded in wet wavy streamers over her shoulders.

"What yo' aimin' to do, stranger?" she inquired. She was rigid but momentarily passive.

"I'm aiming to keep you from doing it again."

She studied his face. She hadn't known there were men like him. She wouldn't have wanted to leave the world.

"I'm over it," she said.

"Certain?"

"Sartin."

He released her. She went to a flat rock, seated herself, spread the gingham garment out to catch the intense rays of the sun, ran her fingers through her hair in an effort to dry it and restore it to some semblance of order, meanwhile watching Stoddard, who sat down on the grass, emptied the water from his boots, placing them so that the sun would shine into them. He took off his socks, wrung the water out of them and spread them out on the grass. He picked up his hat, vest, cartridge belt and gun, laid them in the grass and stretched out beside them, face down, the sun shining on his back. In ten minutes his back was burning. He turned over and shielded his eyes with his hands.

The heat in this South country was different. Different from the dry heat of Oklahoma. He had discovered that while riding through hundreds of miles of timber and swamp land along the Arkansas River. Wilder than Oklahoma, peopled by hill folk—who peered at you like rabbits from their warrens, their noses twitching as if for a scent to identify you. A hell of a country for a white man.

The girl on the rock was drying her hair, running her fingers through it. He watched while she coiled it around her head and tucked in the loose ends.

"So you wanted to die," he said. "Why?"

"Thet's a fool question." But she answered it. " 'Cause I didn't want to live."

Certainly she hadn't wanted to give up her life because she'd seen too much of life. That would be a reason. He suspected she hadn't seen anything of life. Men would be willing to teach her, but he was certain none had. He read that in the blushes that were coming, in the way she kept pulling her garment up around her throat to cover her partly exposed breasts, in the way she shrank under his frank gaze.

"You're not so awfully old," he said.

"Seventeen."

"You live around here?"

She studied him for a time in silence.

"Air yo' one of Jim Craftkin's men?"

He shook his head.

"Or Vauchain's?"

These names had been mentioned in Marie Villers' letter to her uncle. So he was down in their country at last. And this girl feared them.

She believed him.

"If yo' ain't, I reckon I kin tell yo' what's happened. I've bin wantin' to. Yo' ever heerd of Vauchain or Craftkin?"

"No," he lied.

"Then yo' must live a long way from hyah. Whar yo' from?"

"I'm from Oklahoma."

"Yo' name?"

"Brent Stoddard. Now, yours?"

"Allie Tuttle. My pap is Bill Tuttle."

"Where's your pap now?" he urged.

"Pap was run off last night. Him and Maw."

"You mean they ran off and left you?"

"They was run off, I told yo'. Slade Forbush and some of Craftkin's scum druv' up last night jest afore dark with their wagons. They knocked Pap down and throwed him in one of the wagons; they tied Maw up and killed the dawgs and loaded all the old traps thet we didn't want into one of the wagons, leavin' the best stuff in the house. Slade Forbush locked me in a bedroom, and then they sent Pap and Maw drivin' away with the wagon of old traps. They threatened to shoot 'em if they come back or even turned to look around. The same thing hes heppened to nearly all the folks livin' in this hyah country. Craftkin is a land-grabber, and thet's the way he gits aholt of other people's property. It don't do no good to fight him. Them thet has fit has been killed."

"So your mother and father haven't come back?"

"They don't dast to. Forbush and his men would kill 'em."

Stoddard guessed that what had happened to her, following the departure of her parents, was what had prompted her to try to commit suicide. He waited, and presently she told him very frankly:

"Afteh Pap and Maw left, Forbush come into the bedroom and said I was goin' to be his woman. He was goin' to sleep with me last night. He took all my clothes but this hyah wrapper. Then he left me and said he'd come back later. I heerd him and his men drinkin' and laffin', but I got out of the winder and sneaked down to the river."

"You've been hiding out all night?"

"Shuah. You don't reckon I'd go back theah and let Slade Forbush paw me around!" Darn him, she thought, does he think I'm that kind of a girl?

He didn't. What he was thinking was that she was more vehement than seemed necessary, as if she sought to emphasize her virtue. Well, there were virtuous women. Usually you know them when you see them. Not always. He'd been fooled. But virtue militantly guarded was a new experience to him, and refreshing.

"Not Forbush." He hesitated and saw her eyes flash as he dryly added: "Nor nobody else."

"Thank yo'."

He got the impression that she valued his high appraisal of her character.

"Forbush and his men have been searching for you, I suppose?"

"I heerd 'em beating the brush half the night."

"How many of them?"

"Thar's three o' 'em. Thar was a dozen or more at fu'st. They rid away down the river road toward Chandler. I heerd 'em say they was intendin' grabbin' some other places."

Chandler was the town Stoddard was looking for. That was the postmark on Marie Villers' letter.

Their clothing was almost dry now. Allie's hair glowed duskily; she noted the whiteness of his forehead above the ring of bronze below his hatband, and his glistening, wavy, disordered brown hair, which made him seem almost boyish. But the blue eyes were hard now and coldly thoughtful. They were not the eyes of a boy.

Damned shameful treatment! After all, she was nothing but a child. Primitive, but wanting to be decent. The damned scoundrels!

"You expect to spend the rest of your life hiding out in the brush?" he asked.

"I wouldn't be hyah now if it hadn't been fer yo'."

"You can't stay here forever."

"As soon as yo're gone I'll do it ag'in."

She sat on the rock vainly trying to smooth the wrinkles out of her wrapper, watching him, blushing frequently. She was weighing her problem, he decided, and was appalled by the desperate extremity in which she found herself. Still watching her, he saw her cheeks flush crimson, yet she met his gaze steadily.

"I'd be yore woman—if you'd hev me," she said.

Poor little beggar, he thought. She's willing to accept me as being the lesser of two evils. A straight business proposition. He could take her upon his own terms. The trouble was, he didn't want her. Not that he was a saint or that she wasn't desirable, but because one night at a campfire he had studied the photograph of a woman.

CHAPTER FIVE

It wasn't a thing that could be laughed off or carelessly evaded. Desperately, Allie Tuttle was striving to avoid shame and humiliation. When a girl offers herself to you, you don't just calmly tell her that you don't want her. You tell the truth, I suppose, he thought.

"It's mighty embarrassing," he said. "I like you. I think you're a fine girl, and I'm greatly flattered that you'd select me as your man even at a time like this. But it happens that there is another girl. We've got to be loyal, don't we?" he added gently.

"Shuah," she agreed.

She was seeking protection, he thought, as, now thoroughly dry, he got up, walked to where he had thrown his gun and gun belt and his vest. He donned the vest, buckled the cartridge belt around his waist and stood looking at the girl.

There was an expression of despair on her face, of hopelessness. She'd be in the pool in another moment.

"Which way did your father and mother go?" he asked.

"Down the river, toward Chandler."

"We'll find them," he said. "I'll get my horse. He's back in the swale. You can ride behind me."

He strode away through some heavy undergrowth and then into some timber to a lowland, where he found his horse. He had left the animal there while seeking a place where he might swim and bathe, and now he mounted and rode back the way he had come. But before reaching the edge of the undergrowth he halted the horse, slipping cautiously out of the saddle, trailing the reins over the animal's head, to part the heavy foliage and peer at Allie Tuttle.

She was no longer alone. Beside her, one arm around her waist, the other gripping a long rifle, stood a tall rough-looking fellow. One of Forbush's men, evidently, and he must have thought she was alone, for he was wrestling with her, trying to force her down upon the rock on which she had been waiting, talking to her, gloating over her, while she fought him silently, tearing at his face.

"Thought you'd get away, eh?" he said. "Well, Forbush is gone, and damme if I don't . . ."

He was standing over Allie when Stoddard's bullet hit him. He slewed around, dropped his rifle, faced Stoddard, clawed for an instant at his chest near the left armpit where Stoddard's bullet had entered, then slumped forward and pitched down the steep bank into the pool, his rifle clattering after him.

Allie Tuttle had not uttered a sound, nor did she say anything when she looked at Stoddard, who was slipping a fresh cartridge into the cylinder of the huge 45 Colt with which he had killed the girl's assailant.

She ran toward Stoddard. She was trembling; her eyes were wide with shock and apprehension.

"Thet was Joe Fowler!" she gasped. "One of Slade Forbush's men. They'll skin yo' alive fer killin' him!"

"Maybe not," he said.

She was holding tightly to him; she seemed to be quivering all over, and he held her, trying to calm her. He wasn't looking at her but was watching the near-by brush and timber, and a ravine that came down from the higher country to meet the river. There had been three of the men, including Slade Forbush. With Forbush away and another of the men dead in the pool, there would be only one left, and he thought the third might have been near Fowler or had heard the thundering report of the 45.

When after an interval no one appeared he mounted the waiting horse, pulled Allie Tuttle up behind him and rode down the narrow dusty road toward Chandler.

Things had a way of happening. Situations had a way of coming, uninvited, to complicate life, to make life amusing or tragic, according to the whims of chance. This situation moved Stoddard to ironic humor. Because he had been in a certain place at a certain time he had killed a man and was carrying a half-naked girl through the wilderness—a girl who wanted his protection. Suppose Dollarbill were to see him now, and the rest of his hard-bitten riders. For that matter, suppose anyone should see him. Fortunately the narrow road was deserted, and although it wound aimlessly through timber and swamp, he passed no habitations containing people who might conjecture about his motives.

Allie seemed to be satisfied but curious.

"Yo're a fightin' man," she said. Lingeringly she touched his shoulders, his neck. "Yo' ain't takin' the killin' o' Joe Fowler to heart. Yo' don't act sceered o' whut's goin' to happen to yo' when Slade Forbush finds out who killed Fowler."

"How will Forbush find out?" he said.

"Thet's right," she answered. "I'll never tell him."

Later she pointed to wagon tracks in the road. The tracks turned off into a clearing.

"Thet's whar Pap and Maw camped last night," she said. "They ain't fer off now, 'cause the tracks are fresh."

Shortly after noon, in some timber near the river, they came upon the wagon and its two homeless occupants. They had built a small fire and were frying bacon over it, "Maw" doing the cooking while "Pap" worked with a team of crowbait horses tethered near by.

"Allie!" screamed Mrs Tuttle when she caught sight of her daughter.

"Lordy!" ejaculated Mr Tuttle.

From the saddle Stoddard witnessed the reunion, pitying them in their misfortune. For him the score was even. He had saved a life and had taken one. He would not share their meager supply of food, despite their cordial importunities, for in a breath Allie had related what had happened to her, and they were deeply grateful to Stoddard. Allie had omitted mentioning Joe Fowler. As he rode away Stoddard looked once more at Allie. She was standing near the wagon and she smiled at him, though he noted that her lips were quivering. He wondered a little.

CHAPTER SIX

Day by day as Brent Stoddard had followed the downward trend of the land there had stolen over him a consciousness of gradual change. The dry and light air of the high desert country, the iron surface of the Neutral Strip and the Panhandle seemed to belong to another planet. Blankets of ever-deepening green were the vistas that unfolded before him as he descended into a woodland world which owed its freshness and it languorous atmosphere to water.

Now, riding in the dusk upon a gumbo road that paralleled the mighty Mississippi, occasionally glimpsing lights that flickered from the windows of the town of Chandler, where he expected to find Marie Villers, he reflected upon the solemn beauty of the river at dusk. Later, when an early moon gleamed upon the smooth surface of the water, disclosing bends and bayous fringed by giant cypress trees laced with ghostly Spanish moss, he thought of other days, only a few years gone, when the river had rocked with the thunder of the guns of Confederate forts and Union gunboats.

Once, approaching Chandler, he had a clear view of the town in the moonlight. There was a wharf, fringed by some wooden buildings, probably warehouses; behind the wharf, a level thickly strewn with buildings, now dark, with streets dividing them; a square where some tall trees grew; then a high level, like a terrace, where there seemed to be dwellings; then an upland stretch where there were other dwellings, farther apart than those below; then timbered hills around which wound a road—white gravel, he thought—which gleamed like a ribbon in the moonlight.

He watered the horse from a trough in front of a saloon and restaurant at the edge of the town near the wharf. A group of loungers at the hitching rack made room for him as he tied the animal. The men accorded him a suspicious or a curious silence. They were Negroes and swarthy whites. Laborers and habitués of the water front, he supposed. They preserved their silence until he entered the door of the restaurant; then they chattered.

Inside, he sought a washroom from which he emerged, freshly scrubbed and combed, to drink and dine. From the bartender in the saloon he elicited the information that the Villers' house was in the high country behind town. You followed the gleaming road up there around the hills until at last you came to a lane at your left which took you straight to the Villers' homestead. And if you were looking for Judge Lew Marston's house you would continue on the gleaming road for another mile. It was a big house, and you couldn't miss it.

Before Stoddard set out to find Marie Villers he rode to a livery stable and sat on a bench in front of the place while the liveryman fed the horse and groomed him. Later, before he mounted, Stoddard groomed himself, knocking the dust off his clothing and shining his boots while the liveryman appraised him.

"Stranger, I reckon," said the liveryman. "And totin' artillery. Lookin' for anyone special?"

"Any special people here?" said Stoddard.

"Well, yes. Depends on what special kind you're lookin' for. If it's the law, there's Judge Marston. If it's beauty, there's Marie Villers. If it's trouble"—his eyes gleamed—"you can find that 'most anywhere. There's Vauchain's gang and Craftkin's. And then there's Slade Forbush. Only, if you won't want your trouble unadulterated, don't monkey with Forbush. He's killed more men than Grant killed at Vicksburg. Lady-killer. Slick. Fine-lookin' cuss, and knows it. If you got a good-lookin' wife you'd best keep her away from Forbush. If he wants her he'll challenge you to a duel, kill you and take her."

"Friend of yours?" asked Stoddard.

The liveryman reflected, meeting Stoddard's gaze steadily.

"Hell," he said, "you wasn't born yesterday, was you? Tell you this though. You're either a friend of Forbush, or you're makin' believe you are, or you ain't here any more."

After a quarter of an hour spent in slyly interrogating Stoddard, the liveryman stood at his stirrup grinning at him after Stoddard mounted.

"You spend a hell of a lot of your time keeping your mouth shut, don't you?" he said. "And I'll swear you don't use that there gun for an ornament either."

Well, he was learning something about Slade Forbush, and he was hearing about Vauchain and Craftkin, enough to convince him that, between them, the three rascals had succeeded in terrorizing those who knew them. He wasn't impressed by what he had heard. Every community had its bad men. The Neutral Strip had its share, and usually when you got them into a tight corner they weren't nearly as bad as they might be. Their exploits were exaggerated; the legends that surrounded them were colored by repetition.

At the crest of the rise above town he came upon the lane that had been described to him and he followed it between two rows of arching trees—magnolias—which, judging by their size, had been there for half a century. The bright moonlight disclosed broad acres of cultivated land, orderly gardens, patches of timber, a gray stone house with gravel walks around it; several stone outbuildings and in the distance other buildings—no doubt the Negro quarter of another day. The Villers, he perceived, had been planters.

Well, here he was. Soon he would be face to face with the original of the photograph, and now a doubt of the wisdom of his quixotic mission assailed him. A photograph. Merely a photograph. Hm, a photograph. In many cases photographs flattered the originals. After all, what was facial beauty compared to beauty of character? His romantic impulse had brought him this far, and of course he'd see her and turn over to her her uncle's belongings. What he would do afterward depended upon—upon any foolish whim that might strike him. He reached a turn of the lane that brought him to a rear veranda and a lighted window, and he became aware of a Negro—evidently a servant—standing in an open doorway, watching him.

"Yas suh," responded the Negro in reply to his question, "dis yere am whar Missy Villers lives. But she ain't hyah now, suh; she's gwine to a pahty down to Judge Marston's house. Ah don' 'spaict she'll be home much afore midnight. Judge Marston's house is right down the road, suh—to yo' left, suh, aftah yo' go out of the lane. Yo' won't miss it. If yo'll listen yo' kin hyah 'em."

At the junction of the road and the lane Stoddard halted the horse and sat listening. A big party, judging from the laughter. A party. Bad news would spoil it for her, yet he had no right to withhold it from her.

Once again, this time where the drive leading to the Marston house intersected the white gravel, he halted, reluctant. He decided he would not interrupt the party, for his news wasn't that important. He would get as close to her as possible, though, without making himself conspicuous, for he wanted to see her tonight, if only from a distance. Tomorrow he would get the interview he sought; would be able to talk to her, to bring his dream to reality. Now, no longer reluctant, he rode down the driveway, past flanking rows of carriages and horses, to a row of hitching posts where many horses were tethered.

The house was one that harmonized with Judge Marston's profession. Dignity, simplicity and a tranquil atmosphere in spite of the party. An old colonial mansion with an overhanging roof, supported by tall columns, forming a great veranda. All painted in spotless white which glowed in the bright moonlight. Wide stone steps, with a runner of velvety carpet covering them, joining the carpet on the floor of the veranda. Perhaps a score of guests were there. Three great swinging lamps, suspended from the ceiling, made the veranda light as day, and the brightly animated faces were sharply scrutinized by Stoddard as he stood motionless beside his horse at the hitching post while he searched for the girl of the photograph. He saw her presently. She was facing him, seeming to look straight at him. Surrounded by beautifully gowned women and well-groomed men, she made a picture that stirred in him a sudden breathless longing—a longing that shamed him, that made him conscious of his drooping vest, his woolen shirt, his somewhat threadbare corduroy trousers, his scuffed boots, the spurs at his heels, his unshaved face. He might have had himself shaved in Chandler had he not been so eager to meet his lady. He was a capable and efficient town marshal, a rider of broad experience, a fighting man who had never known fear, and yet at this moment a wave of trepidation swept over him, a stealthy embarrassment, a dread of having all these people watching him—as they would—had he held to his original determination to appear before her. He congratulated himself.

But already he had attracted attention. Several men, grouped upon the lawn at the edge of the veranda near the steps, were looking at him, were discussing him. They were perturbed over his appearance among them, yet, being gentlemen, they were reluctant to appear inquisitive.

And now occurred a curious phenomenon—the always strange spectacle of a crowd staring at a common object of interest. A few of the guests on the veranda had observed that the group on the lawn were staring concertedly in a certain direction and, themselves becoming curious, they also stared. Presently all the guests were looking at Stoddard.

This was unexpected, and Stoddard, caught, refused to make himself more ridiculous by retreating. He stood there, slowly drawing himself erect, enduring a silence which had fallen like a stroke. He felt the absurdity of the situation—the utter and complete absurdity of it—yet, now that it had occurred, he was determined to see it through. Always master of himself in a crisis, he met the concentrated gaze of the guests with outward calmness, an unsmiling and dignified calmness which should have won him the respect of the assembled company.

Instead, a ripple of laughter greeted him. Polite laughter. Of all laughter the most biting. Expressing the insolence of indifference, searing its victim with the bitter stigma of social inferiority.

Stoddard, coldly determined to see the situation through, was keenly observant. Not all the guests laughed. There were some among them whose lips tightened as they watched Stoddard, and who frowned with disapprobation. The group of men on the lawn in front of the veranda had not changed position, though all were looking at Stoddard. One, a tall young man, broad of shoulder, slender, built like an athlete, with a stern and manly face, was faintly scowling, as if he deprecated this manifestation of ill manners. Stoddard caught the flashing light of his eyes and smiled at him. Then he looked again at Marie Villers. She wasn't tall, not as tall as he had thought she would be. Her head would just about reach his shoulder.

A queen. Her royal diadem a wealth of golden-brown hair framing a white placid brow. Her eyes, seeming to gaze into his inquiringly, held in real life the mischievous glint he had detected in the photograph. Yet they were proud eyes, thoughtful eyes, with depth and clarity and wisdom. She was leaning forward a very little, slightly resentful, he thought, over this unexpected disturbance, for her lips were pressed tightly together and her head was disdainfully raised, revealing the white smooth column of her throat. The silence became a hush.

Of all the people there, Marie Villers seemed least interested in the intruder. He was a stranger, uninvited, unwelcome. His calm self-possession she tried to interpret as impudence but failed because deep in her consciousness lurked a disturbing conviction that the man was merely master of himself. The disdain she felt, and which the guests and Stoddard saw, was for herself—that she should be aware of an inward start upon meeting the stranger's gaze, that she had felt her pulses quicken at sight of him. Against the dark green background of the foliage, with the moonlight gleaming upon him, he was formidable and romantic. Yet because he had startled her so, she must humiliate him. She laughed also, a rippling, mocking, lilting laugh directed at Stoddard but expressing contempt for her own disturbed emotions.

Many of the guests laughed with her. The tall stern-faced young man in the group of gentlemen on the lawn did not laugh. Instead, his dark eyes flashed, and he stood rigid, watching Stoddard. He stepped forward, stood in front of him.

"Can I help you, sir?" he said. "You see," he added apologetically, "so few of the people here have ever seen a cowboy."

"You've made me feel better," smiled Stoddard. Not even now would he retreat, though he could do so without enduring further embarrassment. Nor—even though he was grateful to the stern-faced young man—would he explain that he had not intended to interrupt the party. He permitted the tall young man to glimpse the badge pinned to his vest inside.

"Official duty, sir?" asked the tall young man.

"A message to Marie Villers. Perhaps not important enough to justify this sudden appearance, but one she ought to get."

"Certainly, sir. I'll take you to her." He urged Stoddard ahead of him, across the lawn to the steps, past the group of men who were still watching him, with greater interest now—a patriarchal gentleman with the profile of a patrician smiling at him—and up the steps to the veranda—ladies and gentlemen making way for him; and across the veranda to where Marie Villers stood erect, her eyes flashing. Stoddard was calm and steady, though now acutely conscious of his shabby garments, even aware of a slight odor that accompanied him—the odor of horses and saddle sweat—to the lady of the photograph, whose proud eyes were swimming with disdain.

The stern-faced young man bowed gravely, with a hand upon Stoddard's arm.

"A messenger in boots, milady," he said.

The lady's gaze roved up and down Stoddard, from dusty boots and spurs, over faded corduroy trousers, broad leather belt—studded with cartridges; upon the huge gun in its black worn holster; over his worn woolen shirt, his open vest, the scarf at his throat, to his virile brown hair, short and tousled, glistening with moisture from the heat of the lamps and the humid atmosphere, and from his racing, tingling blood, which had never been as warm as now. When at last, in the hush which had fallen, she looked into his eyes, there were many there who observed that she seemed to catch her breath with a slight gasp. But Stoddard, returning her gaze with all the steadiness he could summon, could see only cold disdain in her.

"A messenger," she said finally, repeating the words of the stern-faced young man; "A messenger in boots, to disturb my party. Would not your message keep until morning, sir?"

"It would," confessed Stoddard. "Yet I thought——"

"If you were a thinking man you would not have come here tonight, sir!" she said scornfully. She drew herself up, haughtily arrogant. "Begone, sir," she ordered. "And if your message is of any importance you may bring it tomorrow."

Stoddard stood very still, looking at her. He saw none of the others. So that was the kind of girl she was, he thought. Well, then, that was the kind she was. That was settled. She was still looking at him, and the guests were laughing and talking, watching him with sidelong glances, enjoying what they thought was the putting of an uncouth intruder into his place. But Stoddard accepted the girl's rebuke gallantly. Still standing rigid, he swept his broad-brimmed felt hat around, held it over his heart, and then bowed gracefully to her. For an instant, as he straightened, he saw the stern-faced young man smile approvingly. Stoddard's spurs jingled musically in the sudden silence as he walked across the veranda and down the steps to the hitching post where he had left his horse. He stood there reflecting.

Aristocratic women are hardest to understand. The least human. The more primitive the woman, the easier you get along with her. Drag a primitive woman out of a pool and she wants to marry you. Try to perform a service for a well-bred woman and she rebukes you, unheard. To hell with women! Well, he'd ride back to Chandler, stop at a hotel overnight, and in the morning he'd send Pierre Villers' personal belongings to the girl. He'd keep her photograph, though, for no other reason than that looking at it would help him to keep his self-esteem in hand.

He had untied his horse and was stroking the animal's head when he became aware that the tall stern-faced young man was standing near him, watching him.

"Pardon me, sir, I'd like to shake hands with you," said the young man. "Damme, that was as fine an exhibition of gentlemanly self-restraint as I have ever seen! My name is Evan Weldon. I hope you will not have a poor opinion of our hospitality because of this incident. You will find the men less whimsical than the ladies."

"I hadn't planned to stay long enough to inquire into that. But thank you for your sympathy, sir. My name is Brent Stoddard, and I'm glad to know you." They shook hands.

"I'm here as Judge Lew Marston's emissary, Mr Stoddard. The judge witnessed your—er—ah—unfortunate encounter with Miss Villers, and begs the honor of a meeting with you in his den—where there will be no ladies. You won't refuse, sir; the judge is greatly interested in you and declares you would not have appeared here without good reasons."

CHAPTER SEVEN

Judge Lew Marston's den was in the rear of the house, on the first floor, and when the door was closed, as it was after Stoddard and Weldon entered, the noise of the party was completely shut out.

Judge Marston was the patriarchal gentleman Stoddard had seen on the lawn. You knew he was a gentleman when you stood looking into the keen, calm eyes with their kindly, appraising gleam as he shook hands with you firmly, warmly. You felt he liked you, thought Stoddard, though for what reason you couldn't guess. The judge was sixty perhaps, and you knew that his fine old head, with its wealth of gray hair, was occupied by a brain that was in the habit of thinking. He reminded you of Calhoun, or Jefferson or Jackson, as he invited you to be seated and took a chair opposite you, and you were instantly at ease. Stoddard observed the quiet deference of Weldon's manner, and he did not take a chair until after the judge was seated.

"Mr Stoddard—Judge Lew Marston," said Weldon. The judge acknowledged the introduction, adding: "It gives me pleasure to extend to you the hospitality of my house, Mr Stoddard. You are a brave man, sir."

"I do my best, Judge."

"Your best was admirable, sir. I watched you. A fine performance, sir. Not once did you show the white feather. You brought Marie Villers important news. Yet you intended riding away without telling her. After she embarrassed you by laughing at you before her guests, you declined to humble her publicly. That is true, isn't it?"

"I did not blame the lady, Judge. She was frightened by my appearance. A desert scarecrow."

"But she doesn't frighten so easily, Mr Stoddard. She was startled. Thrilled, sir. She laughed to conceal it. That was why I sent Evan Weldon after you. Tomorrow, alone, she will treat you differently."

"Tomorrow I shall be on my way back to where I came from," said Stoddard.

"Tomorrow morning, after you have shaved and made yourself presentable, you will call upon Marie Villers," said the judge.

"What makes you think so, sir?"

"I saw you watching Marie Villers. You love her. You were disappointed in her, but you did not lose hope. I think even Slade Forbush could not drive you away. That is true, isn't it?"

Evan Weldon smiled at Stoddard. "You will not be the first who has lingered near her," he said.

"She has treated them all alike until now," said the judge.

Why are these men so interested in me? thought Stoddard. They're gentlemen; they are trying to be polite and courteous. Yet they have some purpose which they have not yet divulged. They are not mind readers, and they can't know what I think. Yet the judge is right. I did think of leaving here, but I knew I would stay. I intend seeing her again.

"Probably you think it strange that I am taking an interest in you," said the judge, as if he read Stoddard's thoughts. "But it isn't strange. I am Marie Villers' guardian and I am interested in every young man who looks at her. Men—especially a man like you, Mr Stoddard—do not play the role of uninvited guest without some good reason. Undoubtedly your reason is a good one."

"You remind me of my plain duty," said Stoddard. "As the lady's guardian, you are entitled to my confidence." He drew the package of papers from the inside pocket of his vest, placed it on a table at his elbow; stood up, unbuckled his cartridge belt, removed it and placed it on the table, together with the big Colt in its black leather holster. The money belt containing the three thousand dollars in gold double eagles followed, but not until the gun belt and gun were again around his waist did Stoddard empty the money belt of its contents, the judge and Evan Weldon watching him in silence as he stacked the gold pieces in gleaming columns. Then he told them the story of Pierre Villers' murder, the subsequent killing of the murderer and the finding of the letters and papers. He did not mention the photograph. He'd keep that. He did not tell them of his quixotic impulses, but he frankly answered Judge Marston's questions.

"Dollarbill McCarthy," mused Judge Marston. His eyes gleamed. He sighed. "A fighter. A dead shot. The West has some picturesque characters. A cognomen 'Dollarbill' symbolizes an incident in Mr McCarthy's life, I presume."

"Dollarbill McCarthy is a hard-money man, sir. He once killed a man because the man offered him a paper dollar which Dollarbill refused to regard as money."

"Men have been killed for less in Mississippi recently," said the judge. He studied Stoddard's face. "As peace officer in the Neutral Strip you had no sinecure. The Neutral Strip has produced more desperate outlaws than any other section of the country."

"With the exception of Mississippi, sir," said Weldon.

"Yes," sighed Judge Marston. "The war did that to us. There exists a state of affairs which we all deplore but which, so far, we have been unable to clarify. The war ruined the South, sir. It has left us staggering in chaos.

Our problem is one of reconstruction, of striving to regain a perspective in which law and order will assume their proper proportion. To some degree you have the same problem in the West—in the Neutral Strip. How do you handle it?"

Stoddard tapped his holster, and the judge smiled.

"That's the way our fire-eaters plan to work it out," said the judge. "I may secretly agree with them, and I do, but I represent the law here and I may not allow my prejudices to interfere with justice. You are not interested, of course, because you are a stranger here, but if you stay here only a few days you should be warned. During the war a colony of riffraff from Kingston and other West India ports settled near the delta swamplands of New Orleans. They were a nondescript lot, mostly French and English. They had been pirates, blockade-runners, thieves of high-handed caliber. Murder was their trade, and for some months they ruled the New Orleans water front. A troop of Confederate soldiers ran them out of New Orleans in the spring of 1865. By stages the colony moved up-river to a spot near Greenville, some distance south of here. They lived by thieving from plantation owners and by piracy on the river. They are now ravaging this section and have become so bold and rapacious that they are threatening the very foundations of our social life. No man's life is safe. His property vanishes overnight."

Stoddard thought of Allie Tuttle, of how Forbush and his men had taken possession of the Tuttle property after dispossessing the owners. The judge had not overstated the situation. Only Allie Tuttle's courage had saved her from becoming a victim of Forbush's brutality.

"I have two reasons for burdening you with our troubles," continued the judge. "The first is that you are an officer of whatever law there is in the Neutral Strip, and as such you may be able to advise us. The second reason is that you are interested in Marie Villers, whose fortune and perhaps future life are involved. I know you are interested in her, because you personally brought her uncle's belongings. You could have forwarded them."

The judge had been examining the package of papers brought by Stoddard. He had them spread out upon the tabletop and now he looked at Stoddard, faintly smiling.

"Marie told me she had sent her Uncle Pierre a photograph of herself with her last letter to him. The photograph isn't here. Do you know what became of it?"

The sly old devil, thought Stoddard. He still remembered his own youth, and he was able to distinguish between warp and woof in the fabric of life and human nature. And he knows I won't lie about it, thought Stoddard. He was caught. The judge had leaned back in his chair and was studying

Stoddard's face. Even Weldon could not hide his broad grin with the hand he had placed over his lips. His eyes gleamed with delight and approbation.

"It is a common contagion, I assure you, Mr Stoddard," he said. "I carried her picture myself, close to my heart, until—until I was certain there was no hope for me."

"It's the first time I've been that kind of a fool," confessed Stoddard. He looked at the judge. "Am I to understand that there was a time in your life when you treasured a photograph, Judge Marston?"

"We all carry them, sir," laughed the judge. "In our pockets or in our memories. Take the romance out of a man and he becomes a clod. I congratulate you, sir."

When Marie Villers had rebuked Stoddard, he had thought it was all over. It was not all over. With her it was all over perhaps. But not with him. He would stay near her until he won her or until there would be no further use of his hoping. Judge Marston continued:

"You have read Marie's letter to her Uncle Pierre. It was your duty to do so, of course. And you know she mentioned Vauchain and Craftkin, and Asa Calder—the man who killed her father. These men have a great many followers. They are powerful, cunning and unscrupulous. They pack the juries and obstruct justice. Yet they are not nearly so dangerous as Slade Forbush. It is Forbush you will have to be careful of, if you stay around here. Forbush is a swaggering soldier of fortune. He maintains the outward appearance of a gentleman. He dresses the part. He is a gambler and a libertine. If the husband of a woman he wants objects to his attentions to the wife he challenges him to a duel and kills him. If there is no husband, so much the worse for the girl." Judge Marston hesitated. His cheeks paled; his eyes grew bleak. "Now he has turned his attention to Marie. She despises him, yet he persists. He is here tonight, Mr Stoddard, and when Marie rebuked you his laughter was loudest."

CHAPTER EIGHT

Language was invented for the purpose of expressing thought. The greater a man's vocabulary, the greater his potential facility of expression. Judge Marston was a learned man, with a judicial temperament, who knew that words could also be used to conceal one's thoughts. So Stoddard reflected, through a silence into which came the muffled vocal murmurings of the merrymakers.

The judge had said either too much or too little. Too much if he had misread Stoddard's character, too little if he was trying to enlist Stoddard's services against the sinister forces arrayed against law and order.

"This talk with you has restored my failing courage," the judge said. "It has revived my faith in men. These stacks of gold pieces did not tempt you, and the sight of a woman's photograph sent you upon a dangerous mission. I am indebted to you, sir. Captain Weldon and I were beginning to feel that chivalry and honor were dead. Now we feel there must be other men in this country like you."

His fine old eyes were glowing with gratitude.

"But you must leave Chandler," he added.

"He should, but he won't," said Evan Weldon, smiling at Stoddard.

"He must leave," insisted the judge. "They'll kill him!"

"Damme, I should like to see them try it!" said Weldon.

"You seem excited, Captain," reproved Judge Marston.

"I am, sir. I am more than excited. I am delighted."

"Why, sir?"

"Because until a moment ago I did not recognize our guest as the famous peace officer who met and killed Blondy Antrim, the most deadly gun fighter the West has known."

He arose and bowed to Stoddard. "I read an account of that battle in a New Orleans paper, Mr Stoddard. Antrim had terrorized the Southwest, and they sent you after him. You met him in the open and beat him to the draw. It is an honor to know you, sir."

The judge peered hard at Stoddard, his eyes gleaming. "And I have been trying to frighten you," he said.

Once again Evan Weldon tried to conceal a smile by placing a hand over his mouth. He knew what lay behind Judge Marston's tentative explorations into sentiment, he knew that he was merely soliciting Stoddard's aid while pretending to discourage him, while warning him of the possible dangers he would face. Weldon knew it and now he knew that Stoddard knew it, for the puzzled expression in Stoddard's eyes had given way to comprehension.

The judge perceived what was happening and was embarrassed but resolute, and his gaze was unwavering.

"Please accept my apologies, sir," he said. "I hope you will believe me when I say there was no deception intended. What I have told you is the truth. It was merely a question of how to present the situation to you. We were aware that money would be no inducement to you and so we sought to enlist your sympathy. I had no right to do it, sir. We are in desperate straits but we have no right to suggest that a stranger should sacrifice his life in our behalf." The judge lowered his head and looked at the tabletop. Stoddard and Evan Weldon exchanged glances. Stoddard smiled.

He was not thinking of Judge Marston and his problems but of Allie Tuttle and the girl whose mocking laugh had stirred him so deeply. He stood up and began to restore the stacks of gold pieces to the money belt. That done, he buckled the belt around his waist; then replaced the letters and papers in the pocket of the vest, the judge watching him curiously, Evan Weldon confidently.

"I'm afraid we've bungled this affair," said Weldon. "Judge Marston has not been entirely frank. The fact is, Mr Stoddard, both the judge and myself admire you. We admire you too much to have you stay here to risk your life. But now that you know the danger, we are hoping that you will stay in spite of it."

The two men were facing each other, and now their eyes met—Evan Weldon's still confident, Stoddard's coldly quizzical.

"What would you do if you were Stoddard?" said Stoddard.

"I'm afraid I'd think the judge and myself were two fools to expect you to stay," grinned Weldon.

"This would be a sad world if it were not for the fools in it," said Stoddard.

CHAPTER NINE

When Stoddard rode through the streets of Chandler the next morning he was conscious of the attention he attracted, of the stares that followed him as he rode to the livery stable, to be greeted by the liveryman who had conversed with him the night before. The water front was buzzing with activity. A river steamer was tied there, smoke curling lazily from its stacks, Negro stevedores loading merchandise into its bowels. Carts and drays were rattling over the cobblestone street that paralleled the docks; merchants were opening the doors of their stores and exposing their wares to the view of possible purchasers. The early-morning activity was confined to the water front. The larger business buildings, fronting upon streets that rose gradually from the water's edge, were quiet, and the streets deserted. Beyond the business buildings Stoddard could see a large frame structure set deep behind trees and shrubbery, its terraced grounds overlooking the river. A sign across its front identified it as a hotel. The Planters' House. Crowning a knoll and facing the square was the courthouse, a squarely built stone structure with an overhanging roof and wide porticos. Signs above doorways and in the windows of office buildings—all of them old and weather beaten—Stoddard read as he stood in the doorway of the livery stable thinking of the previous night's experience. The sun was hot; mist from the river was sweeping in, its vapory streamers licking the streets and the buildings. Musty odors from bales of goods and casks on the water front mingled with an indescribable stench that rose from the wooden planks of the wharf and the cobblestones. The dwellings upon the high terraces back of town escaped the town's odor and its heavy atmosphere. Serene in their isolation, they accentuated the vast gulf between business and aristocracy. Yet one supported the other.

Leaving the livery stable, where his horse was to be groomed and fed, Stoddard sought a barbershop and, afterward, a clothing store. After buying what he wanted he selected a traveling bag which seemed suitable, packed his purchases into it and went to the Planters' House where he registered, calmly enduring the polite scrutiny of the clerk, and was assigned to a room, where he bathed and arrayed himself in his new clothing, which was practically the same as that which he discarded.

The change was a concession to necessity. Gun and cartridge belt were in their accustomed places, and he did not neglect to remove the rawhide thong at the bottom of his holster and tie it to the new trousers. His new garments did not appear new; when he stepped out upon the street in front of the Planters' House he seemed merely clean and comfortable. He found the post office and stood at a desk in its lobby inditing a letter to Dollarbill McCarthy.

"I am in Chandler, Mississippi," he wrote. "I have found Marie Villers, who wrote the letter to her uncle, Pierre Villers, which I showed you. I would not say that her reception of me was enthusiastic, but she's an aristocrat and probably spoiled, so I don't feel as bad as I might. She's in trouble, though, and I'm intending to stay here for a while to see that nothing happens to her.

"Things are about as bad here as they are in the Neutral Strip, but the folks here don't do as much about it as we do. I have met a Judge Marston, who is a friend of Marie Villers, also a young man of about my age, named Evan Weldon, who is still a friend of hers, although she jilted him. These two men want me to stay here to help them clean up the gang which is bothering her. Evan Weldon is organizing all the young men in this part of the country who have been robbed of their ancestral lands by the outlaws. The judge says the regular law is powerless to deal with them and that a new day will not dawn for the South until the people awaken to a sense of their responsibilities. The new organization will be called the 'Riders.' Evan Weldon will be the boss rider. He is a good man. Before they told me that they were getting ready to fight the outlaws I was of two minds about the situation. I want to stay here to help keep the women out of trouble—especially Marie Villers and another named Allie Tuttle—but maybe I wouldn't have agreed to stay if Judge Marston and Evan Weldon hadn't shown fight. Nothing has happened yet except that on the way here I had to kill a man because he was deviling a woman.

"I'll write you again, later." Signed "Stoddard."

On the street again, he returned to the livery stable, to find his horse ready. He mounted and rode down the cobblestone street to a gravel road that presently undulated into the hills leading to the Villers' home. He had left the money belt in his room at the Planters' House and the three thousand dollars in double-eagle gold pieces was in his pockets. Riding around a corner which was occupied by one of the larger buildings, he saw a sign over a doorway: "Asa Calder"; and below it, "Attorney at Law"; and farther below, "Real Estate." Calder, Weldon had told him, was suspected of participation in the profits of the lawless enterprises of Craftkin and Vauchain and Forbush. Vauchain was known as the "Leopard."

Stoddard expected to meet Asa Calder. But not now. There would be no point in his meeting the man until he learned the details of the quarrel which had resulted in the killing of Marie Villers' father. He did not know how he felt about meeting Marie. Two forces were at work in him—reluctance and eagerness. He wondered how she would receive him, wondered whether, if she rebuffed him again, he would tell her some of the things he had been thinking. Her mocking laugh had penetrated deeper than he had thought, but when, after a period of waiting on the broad front veranda of the Villers' house, Marie Villers appeared in the doorway, he had no thoughts at all. The bow he gave her was involuntary, a tribute.

He had made no mistake about her height. Her head reached a little above his chin. She was slender, with splendid shoulders and a perfect figure. Her hair was almost dark, and the gold in it was dusky, though there was no suspicion of red. When she turned her head from him to dismiss the Negro servant her eyes were thoughtful. Perhaps she was thinking that he was a fool for seeking her out after his rebuff of the evening before. Whatever she thought, he was aware that his heart thumped heavily and he clenched his teeth to keep it from jumping out of his mouth. She was sweetly beautiful when you looked straight at her, but her profile! Delicate as roses, patrician, perfect, completely pure, even to the lovely, stubborn chin.

"So you came again?" she said, her tone implying that she had expected him.

Well, she had recognized him, at any rate, in spite of the several days' growth of beard he had worn.

"Yes," he answered. "I'm here again."

"Your business with me is important, I presume. It must be, since you have appeared twice without being invited." Her chin was tilted proudly; her gaze roved over him and back again to his eyes, into which she looked steadily.

"That depends upon how much you thought of your uncle, Pierre Villers." She was a thoroughbred, he thought. She was curious, startled, yet quietly attentive.

"How can that possibly interest you, Mr . . ."

"Brent Stoddard," he supplied.

"Mr Stoddard," she finished.

"Of the Neutral Strip," he added.

"Very interesting, Mr Stoddard."

Judge Marston had been mistaken, thought Stoddard. In fact, when the judge had told him that Marie Villers had been thrilled at sight of him and had laughed to conceal her emotion, he had mentally disagreed with him. The judge had been mistaken, just as he himself had been mistaken in women many times. The only thing you knew about them was that they knew about you—what you were thinking, what your feelings were. You didn't even know when they were really angry, or whether their proud disdain was a subterfuge adopted to hide another emotion which they didn't want you to see.

"Yes," he said. "I have been wanting to tell you that your uncle, Pierre Villers, was murdered in the Neutral Strip."

Brutal, he thought vindictively. But she deserved it. It would shake her out of that studied arrogance. She'd cry out now, she'd show some emotion, and then he could talk to her.

She didn't cry out, she made no sound at all, but stood watching him. She had gone a little pale, and there was a fleeting shadow in her eyes to show that the news had hurt her. Otherwise she was calm.

"How do you know?" she asked.

Now her lips had tightened a little, which made her more beautiful than ever, and Stoddard regretted his vindictiveness.

"I saw him afterward. My men captured his murderer."

"Oh!" The exclamation was almost a cry of pain, and Stoddard's face whitened. You don't want to hurt a woman, especially a brave one. Even if she has treated you contemptuously.

"Who was the murderer?"

"A man named Simon Gorty."

"Oh!" she exclaimed again.

"You know him, eh?"

She nodded. Her face had grown whiter.

"Someone from around here?"

She nodded again.

So the murder had not been a casual one, reflected Stoddard. The murderer had known about the money belt.

There was no hint of arrogance in Marie Villers' manner now. She was merely a beautiful woman overcome by tragedy, helpless, mutely enduring.

"One of Craftkin's men or Vauchain's?"

"No," she said. "Asa Calder's."

She was staring at him now, a question in her eyes.

"How do you know about Craftkin and Vauchain? You are a stranger here."

"I found your letter to Pierre Villers in the killer's pockets. I read it because it was my duty to do so, and because I didn't know what to do with the three thousand in gold that I found in a money belt around Pierre Villers' waist."

He began to empty his pockets of the gold pieces, stacking them carefully into little columns upon a rustic table near him; she watching him in silence, shrinking a little, her face whiter than ever. This indeed was proof that the terrible news was true.

After stacking the gold pieces, Stoddard took Pierre Villers' papers and documents from his vest pocket, together with Marie's letter, and placed them upon the table beside the gold. The photograph was not with the papers. He'd keep that. In later days, perhaps, he'd compare it with his memory of the original.

She had stepped back a little as Stoddard had been stacking the gold coins, and she now stood against one of the jambs of the big doorway, her hands folded in front of her, her head bowed a little, as if crushed and somewhat bewildered. Stoddard stood silently looking at her.

CHAPTER TEN

The trouble with women of Marie Villers' type was that you could never tell how deeply they were hurt. If you were an enemy you could get no satisfaction out of mentally injuring them, for they were too proud to exhibit grief in your presence. Only a friend could offer sympathy, and that only in moderation. When you add beauty to pride, breeding and courage you have a devastating combination, thought Stoddard, who stood watching as she conquered her emotion. And then she began to ask questions about her uncle. To the final ghastly detail. And when the story was finished her eyes flashed.

"I should like to thank your friend, Dollarbill McCarthy," she said. "When you return to the Neutral Strip I wish you would send him to me."

"That would make the time of Dollarbill's visit very indefinite," he said.

"Do you mean that you are not going back there right away?"

"That's it. You see, I rather like this country."

She was suddenly serious, very thoughtful, and her brows contracted a little as she appeared to study his face. The experience was delightfully thrilling to Stoddard, and he hoped, watching her eyes, to see them fill with a certain unmistakable expression. Interest. They did not. Instead, they gleamed with curiosity in which there was disdain and mockery, and he observed that her final glance, before she dropped her gaze entirely, lingered upon the cartridge belt at his waist and the black leather holster at his hip, out of which peeped the stock of the huge weapon he carried there.

"You are some kind of an officer of the law in the Neutral Strip?" she asked.

" 'Some kind' is correct, Miss Villers."

"You are capable and efficient, I am sure." Her voice was gentle, patronizing, even slightly mocking, as if politeness demanded that she approve of him.

She looked at the stacks of gold pieces on the table and then at the letters and documents beside them.

"Where did Mr Dollarbill McCarthy overtake my uncle's murderer?"

"On the Cimarrón near the Arkansas."

"How far is that?"

"Several hundred miles."

"And you rode all that distance just to deliver this money and the papers to me personally?"

He assured her that he had acted in the line of duty.

"Thank you," she said. "It was a dangerous journey, with the country full of Indians and outlaws. Your duty would have ended if you had forwarded my uncle's personal effects by express, wouldn't it?"

Judge Marston had asked him practically the same question, or had suggested it. Certainly he could not confess to Marie Villers that her photograph had lured him, nor could he tell her that the reading of her letter to her uncle had aroused the latent chivalry in him.

"I'd been in a dry country so long that I wanted to see water," he explained.

These were polite questions, involving nothing more than casual interest on her part, and he was bound to answer them or be considered uncivil, yet the deepening gleam in her eyes troubled him.

"Is the West so very dry then?"

"Dry and hot."

"Yet you stayed there—how many years?"

"I didn't mention," he said. "Ten years," he added.

She was making him feel like a pupil being questioned by a teacher. Why? He could not tell. The disdain was still in her eyes, but there was something else there too—something quietly and calmly meditative, curious, speculative.

"Mr Stoddard," she asked, "was the Neutral Strip for the North or the South?"

"Both. It had no government. It went like Texas, yet there were plenty of Northern sympathizers."

"And you, Mr Stoddard," she said quietly, "were you a Northern sympathizer?"

"I was never able to decide."

"But you did decide finally?"

"No."

"But you had to fight on one side or the other."

"I took no part in the war, Miss Villers."

"But you were old enough to fight."

"I was eighteen when it began." He was now twenty-eight, but he didn't tell her so. She was making him feel much younger.

"Eighteen," she said coldly. "A great many Southern boys were fighting at that age. Many of them were killed. Thousands were wounded. You must have had a good reason for not fighting, Mr Stoddard." He saw contempt dawning in her eyes.

"If you had sympathized with the South you would have fought for the South," she said. "You must be a Yankee." The stubborn chin went slowly up, her eyes darkened with cold steadiness, and she laughed as she had laughed the previous night when she had insulted him in the presence of the guests.

"Yankee!" She exclaimed. She used the word as a scathing epithet.

Pale, rigid, square of jaw and tight of lip, Stoddard stood, stern and cold. He saw her right hand, suddenly clenched, accidentally touch a column of the gold pieces and send them clinking to the floor. Still a gentleman in spite of it all, he stooped to gather the fallen double eagles, and as he bent over to retrieve one that had rolled almost to Marie Villers' feet the photograph in his inside vest pocket slipped out and fell, face upward, upon the floor. He did not at first notice it, and when he did finally pick it up it was too late. She had seen it and now she was laughing at him; scornfully, proudly, mocking him:

"I think I understand now why you came here, Mr Stoddard."

There were several other gold pieces upon the porch floor, and Stoddard picked them up, aware that Marie Villers was standing there watching him. Then he heard the rustling of her skirts and he was alone on the porch, her photograph in his left hand. He saw her standing in the subdued light of the room beyond the front door, her head erect, her body rigid, her eyes flashing. Deliberately he placed the photograph into the pocket of his vest, bowed to her and strode down the steps, across the lawn, to his horse.

CHAPTER ELEVEN

Of course Judge Marston and Evan Weldon did not question Stoddard regarding the result of his visit to Marie Villers. It is to be doubted that they even knew he had made such a visit, for during the days that followed Stoddard made no mention of it, and the judge had not even seen his ward. With another young lady of her own age she had boarded a steamer for Vicksburg. Moreover, Stoddard had witnessed her departure, for he had seen her step out of the Villers' carriage, sedately arrayed for traveling, to be personally escorted aboard by the young captain of the steamer. Stoddard was near enough to see the captain's face, which he distrusted. The young woman who accompanied Marie Villers was Anne Randolph. Stoddard had heard Marie Villers mention her name to a young gentleman—an aristocratic gamecock who came to the dock to see the girls off. And Marie Villers saw Stoddard. He became aware of that when, happening to glance toward him—where he stood in front of the livery stable waiting for his horse—he saw her straighten haughtily and thereafter completely ignore him—even when, after mounting his horse, he rode down the cobblestone street on his way to the Planters' House.

He was in a black mood all day. The town had lost its charm and was more desolate than the hard surface of the Neutral Strip. Even the luxury of the lobby of the Planters' House irked him. He kept remembering the scorn in Marie's voice when she had called him "Yankee." He had not thought it possible that any woman could make him feel so miserable. Once, after her departure down the river, he stood on the terrace above the broad expanse of water, which had become dismally bleak. He felt he would have gone back to the Neutral Strip that night had he not met Asa Calder. He was still on the terrace and at that moment engaged in wondering how long the young captain of the river boat had known Marie Villers, when a voice, Southern, lazily drawling, reached him.

"Picturesque, I grant you, Dalrymple, but rawther absurd. The gun and the cartridge belt, suh, and that outlandish rigging. I have seen him several times, riding about town. I presume the gun would frighten some people."

"But not you, Asa Calder," a second voice said. "You have used them too often to be frightened by seeing them."

"I do not set myself up as a duelist, Dalrymple," disclaimed Calder.

"Have it your way, Asa," said the other. "I don't dispute you. It is too dangerous."

Stoddard turned to look at the "dangerous" man. He saw first the gentleman's polished shoes, then his peg-legged dark trousers with their wide knees; then a heavy watch fob dangling from the pocket of a white waistcoat, above which was an expanse of shirt bosom and a ruffled stock. Then a long broadcloth coat with square shoulders, narrow waist and wide flaring tails, the lapels faced with dull satin binding which ran into a fluted collar. The gentleman also wore a bell-crowned beaver hat whose curved brim accentuated the narrowness of his face, giving him a hawklike appearance, the comparison rendered more startling by a long high-bridged nose and a wide thin-lipped mouth. His age, Stoddard decided, was about forty. He was black haired, and his face, though clean shaved and powdered, was swarthy. Had he been looking at Stoddard at this moment, Stoddard would have called him to account for the insult, but he had now turned and was walking along the veranda with his companion—a small negligible-appearing man—and Stoddard conquered the cold rage that had flared in him. There was no hurry. Calder would keep.

The following evening, in response to a note from Judge Marston, Stoddard again rode the white gravel highway that led upward to the judge's house. The judge, Evan Weldon and a stranger were seated upon the big veranda, and Stoddard was made to feel welcome. The stranger was James Galt, a young man of about Weldon's age.

"One of our fire-eaters," whispered Judge Marston when he introduced Stoddard. Galt was as tall as Stoddard, with cold, clear dark eyes. He was friendly but not effusive.

"The judge and Mr Weldon have told me about you, sir," he said. He had been doing field work for Evan Weldon, traveling about the country to get information about the men who were threatening to destroy the social order of the South, and he had come to report.

"It is baffling, sir," he told Weldon. "I am afraid the fight will be a long one." He drew a sheaf of papers from a pocket and spread them upon a porch table. "These reports of outrages committed by Vauchain, Craftkin and their followers come from widely separated parts of this state, and from northern Alabama and southern Tennessee. The outrages include plain robbery, attacks upon women, the seizure of lands—often whole estates, sir!—the theft of deeds to property from courthouses, arson and murder. Members of our organization have investigated a great many of these crimes, and we are convinced that Vauchain is directing the whole miserable enterprise. It is difficult to get any direct information about him or his band of desperadoes. Victims are warned not to talk. We all know Vauchain. He is a wild animal, gentleman, nothing less! We can't catch up with him. He moves with incredible swiftness. He is here, there and everywhere, leaving a trail of violence and bloodshed behind him. The pirates of the Spanish Main were gentlemen compared to Vauchain!"

"They must have a place, more or less permanent, where he and his leaders meet," suggested Judge Marston.

"We haven't been able to find it," answered Galt. "But no doubt there is such a place. If there is, it must be deep in the swamplands or in a wilderness section not yet explored."

Galt and Weldon began to speculate upon the probable location of the Vauchain rendezvous, and for a time the judge and Stoddard listened to them as, with a map spread before them, they sought to trace wilderness trails that might be used by the outlaws.

When Stoddard caught a peculiar gleam in the judge's eyes, accompanied by a slight motion of the head, he left the table and strode down the veranda steps to the grounds, with the judge following. Under a giant cottonwood they halted.

The judge seemed elated.

"They are serious," he said, nodding toward the two men on the veranda. "The organization is already large and is growing. The governors of half a dozen states and all the local peace officers have tacitly agreed to permit the Riders to exercise police powers. That means, sir, that killings by the Riders will not be officially investigated. It means that the courts will not issue writs against the Riders unless a violation is so openly flagrant that honor would demand legal interference. Decency will yet prevail, Mr Stoddard. Men like Vauchain, Craftkin and Forbush . . ." he hesitated, slowly adding, "and Asa Calder must be ah—er—eliminated from our social order."

And now Judge Marston abruptly changed the subject. Humor glowed in his eyes.

"My ward has gone down-river, to Vicksburg, for a visit."

"Yes," said Stoddard.

"You knew she had gone?"

"Yes."

"Do you know why, sir?"

"No; she did not consult me, Judge Marston."

"But you delivered her uncle Pierre's personal property to her. And she thanked you by calling you a 'Yankee.' She hates Northerners and thinks that any man who did not wear a Confederate uniform—if he was old enough to fight—is a Yankee. It is time to forget such distinctions, Mr Stoddard. The South can nurse its wounds without rancor. I speak of the men, Mr Stoddard. The women—who bore the burden of the terrible disaster—will not forget nor forgive so easily. You have seen that. And yet my ward ran away to Vicksburg because she is afraid of you." He laughed. "You will not understand that until you know more about women," he said.

The judge grew serious again.

"Your continued presence in town has caused tongues to begin to wag," he said. "A great many people in this state carry guns, but they are not as conspicuous as yours. Nor are they as large." The judge tapped the holster at Stoddard's hip. "That weapon is the size of a siege gun. It looks dangerous. But how about accuracy, sir?"

Stoddard smiled.

"You have confidence," continued the judge. "I have caused it to be known that you are here in pursuit of a fugitive from the peculiar justice of the Neutral Strip. But beware of Asa Calder and of Slade Forbush. They are deadly—particularly Asa Calder. Witnesses who saw him kill Leslie Villers—who, by the way, got his Christian name from an English mother— say that Leslie was dead when the word to fire was spoken.

"That murder was deliberate. Asa Calder appeared in court after Leslie's death and produced notes and mortgages against the Villers' property. The notes and mortgages were so obviously forged that I dismissed the suit, thereby making an enemy of Calder. Now Calder claims to have other notes. He is persistent and determined."

And now the judge began to speak of trivialities, and so, as they began slowly to walk toward the veranda to rejoin Weldon and Galt, Stoddard gave some thought to the two major subjects of the judge's conversation. Asa Calder and Marie Villers. Violence and romance. Death and life. Stoddard understood violence, because he had experienced it. Romance was a mystery to him. He felt its nearness, but it eluded him.

CHAPTER TWELVE

The river was the artery which gave Chandler life, and Chandler's water front was the pulse of the town's commercial activity. Travel up-and down-river was attended by very little ceremony but with the usual display of interest by those who, for some reason or other, remained in town. It was known that Marie Villers and Anne Randolph had taken the packet to Vicksburg, and people understood Judge Marston's interest in the arrival of steamers from down-river, since it was whispered that the judge's ward had not announced the date of her return. A stranger's interest in the river, particularly his interest in the arrival and departure of all steamers, passenger or freight, was bound to arouse speculation, so that whenever Brent Stoddard appeared upon the water front, as he did several times a day and often at night, he was accorded the attention of all those people—and there were many—who had heard rumors of the significance of his presence in town. The habitués of the water front—workers and loungers—and the small merchants whose shops were near were certain that if they watched Stoddard long enough, and vigilantly enough, they would one day—or night— witness the apprehension of the fugitive he sought. They did not know that Stoddard was haunting the water front in anticipation of the return of Marie Villers, that she was the fugitive he waited for.

Nearly two weeks had passed since the night of Marie Villers' party at Judge Marston's house. And Marie had been away a full week. There was no outward sign of the decadence of the social order, no visible evidence that depravity and violence and murder lurked under the smooth surface of everyday monotony. Judge Marston continued to preside in his courtroom; there were no reports of the activities of the Riders; the aristocrats on the heights back of town and in the country beyond amused themselves as usual; the businessmen and the small merchants were interested only in their daily balances and mild pleasures. Perhaps they were indifferently conscious of the sinister influences at work around them, or perhaps they were not even interested.

The liveryman was interested in Stoddard. This morning there was unusual activity along the water front. A freight boat was in and being unloaded; a New Orleans packet had touched the wharf for a brief stop; the packet from down-river was shortly due. Asa Calder, accompanied by several gentlemen, was in the steamship company's dock office. There were rumors of important improvements. A new wharf perhaps, or modern slips, to facilitate the loading and unloading of steamers.

"You-all like the watah, eh?" said the liveryman to Stoddard. "You shuah keep a-lookin' at it."

"It certainly is wet, after living in a dry country," said Stoddard. He had come down from the Planters' House an hour before. He had been watching a punt that was being poled down the river toward town. The craft was skirting the swamplike shore, where the water was shallow.

"Looks like a woman," said Stoddard. He pointed, and the liveryman stared.

"Sho' 'nough," he said. "Got a sack of somethin' in the bow. Swamp trash, I reckon. They don't often come that way," he added. "And usually the men do the totin' into town. They'll ride a bag of bones or drive a broken-down wagon with crowbait horses. Nobody knows where they come from or where they live."

The liveryman continued to talk about the swamp denizens. He may have talked of other things, but Stoddard was paying no attention to him. He was watching the progress of the punt along the shore; particularly he watched the figure in the stern, standing, poling the queer-looking craft. When the punt reached the piling at the east end of the wharf it veered so that it came alongside. The woman—for it was a woman—dropped the pole, gripped the stringer at the wharf's edge and began to pull the punt along the wharf toward some steps that led down to the water—a landing place for small boats.

By the time the punt reached the steps Stoddard was at the edge of the wharf, for as the woman had drawn the boat toward the landing place her face had appeared above the edge of the wharf and he had recognized her as Allie Tuttle, the swamp girl he had rescued from drowning.

He reached down, grasped the bow of the punt and drew it toward him, to see that what he and the liveryman had thought was a sack of something salable was in reality a man—a man so dirty, so emaciated, so hollow of cheek and eye, that he resembled no living thing that Stoddard had ever seen. But his eyes, unnaturally bright, implored Stoddard.

"Help," he whispered.

"Sure," answered Stoddard pityingly. "You're in the right place." He tied the painter of the boat to a ring in the wharf and found that a crowd of people had collected near him.

"Lend a hand here, some of you," he said, and two Negro dockmen leaped forward to assist him. They got the man out of the boat and laid him upon a bale of goods upon which someone had quickly spread a blanket. Draymen were leaping from their vehicles; merchants from the stores were leaving their places to satisfy their curiosity; even Asa Calder and his gentlemen were sauntering up; and while Stoddard was inquiring for a doctor, feeling the man needed immediate medical attention, a packet from down-river whistled warningly and headed for her landing place.

Stoddard and Allie Tuttle had exchanged glances of recognition while the girl had been steadying the punt as Stoddard and the Negroes had lifted the man out. The girl had smiled at Stoddard, but with the smile had come a shake of the head, which Stoddard had interpreted as pity for the passenger she had brought. She was now standing near the man on the bale of goods, stroking his forehead, encouraging him in a low voice. The man was shoeless, hatless. He wore trousers which were caked with mud and filth. Upon them were splotches of green slime which had dried in poisonous-looking patches. The trousers were tattered and frayed, and the shirt was without sleeves—they, Stoddard decided, having been torn off. The green slime told the story of his having been in a swamp.

The crowd had been chattering. Now it was silent; sensing tragedy. A doctor bent over the man, applying restoratives; Asa Calder and his gentlemen had forced their way to a point near the bale of goods, risking their immaculate clothing in the press of bodies. There were women there, too, and the down-river packet had discharged its passengers, who stood on the outer fringe of the crowd, watching and listening.

When the stimulant took effect the man on the bale of goods became suddenly, passionately vocal. He sat up on his bale, stared around him and began to mutter incoherently about river pirates, a steamer that had been burned and looted, about his crew having been murdered, about his daughter having been carried off into the wilderness, about his being in a swamp for ages, about his thirst and hunger. The crowd stared at him, unable to glean anything from his incoherence. Not understanding, the people became skeptical, doubtful. They had heard of no such tragedy. They had seen no sign of a burning steamer. None had been reported. So the people chattered, yet they were still interested. It was Asa Calder who expressed what a great many of the people were thinking. He smirked at the gentlemen with him. "His whisky must have been potent," he said. "It is a miracle what happens when one indulges through a long period. Most of them see white mice and pink elephants." His lips grew hard; his eyes glittered. He spoke to a group of Negroes standing near, his voice curt. "Take him to jail until he sobers up."

The people muttered approval. They were uncertain. If there was no tragedy in this situation they had been fooled into betraying curiosity, and of course a great man like Asa Calder would know what was best for the stranger. They expected the Negroes to obey Calder's orders and were amazed when the black men, moving forward, halted and stared at Allie

Tuttle, who was suddenly standing erect, rigid, white of face, defiant, her eyes flashing. She looked at all the people, but she spoke to Calder.

"He ain't drunk!" she declared. "He's sick. Me an' my maw an' pap hev' been takin' care of him fo' more then a week. He's been out of his haid, but he ain't drunk, an' yo've got no right to put him in jail, where he'll likely die!"

The people became silent. Here was direct evidence, which seemed authentic enough.

Asa Calder straightened and glared at Allie Tuttle. His voice was poisonously hateful, but his laugh expressed contempt unutterable.

"Swamp strumpet!" he said.

"Yo're a liar!" shrieked Allie Tuttle. "I'm decent! Ef yo'-all was a *man* yo' wouldn't say thet, an' ef I was a man I'd tear yore heart out!" In a transport of rage she tried to reach Asa Calder but found Stoddard calmly holding her.

"All right, Allie," he said. "The gentleman has evidently mistaken you for what he thinks is a kindred spirit." He smiled into Asa Calder's eyes, and the laughter of the people caused Asa Calder's face to mottle and redden; and as Calder stood uncertain, glaring at the grinning crowd, Stoddard spoke low to a cab driver and the Negroes who had received Calder's orders, telling them to take the swamp victim to the Planters' House. "You go along with them, Allie," he added, "to nurse him."

The Negroes and the cab driver sprang to obey, for the quiet big man in the picturesque clothing of the new West exuded confidence and authority, and his personality enfolded them. Besides, they knew Asa Calder and were pleased that the stranger was bold enough to countermand his orders. Some of them lifted the swamp victim—Allie Tuttle helping them—and were carrying him toward the cab—which stood at a little distance—when Asa Calder moved in front of them, blocking their way. He stood so close to them that they could move no farther. His face was as white as his ruffled shirt bosom, and his thin lips were tight with the cold rage that glowed in his eyes. His gentlemen were watching him curiously, and the faces of the people were filled with sudden resentment, for the big man from the West was championing the weak.

Accident or design had placed Asa Calder close to Stoddard, who had been leading the way from the bale to the cab, and the two men stood chest to chest, so close that their thrusting chins almost touched. This was a clash of wills, and the people crowded closer, eager to witness the outcome. The passengers of the down-river packet and its crew—even to the young captain who had greeted Marie Villers so warmly when she had boarded his vessel a week ago—were there, and each instant the crowd was being augmented by other men and women who, passing, had been attracted by the disturbance.

"Give way, sir," said Stoddard.

"No!" Calder's voice came through gritted teeth. "You may take your slut with you to the Planters' House, but the man goes to jail!"

Now Calder was forced to turn away from Stoddard, for Allie Tuttle had thrown herself at him and was clawing at his face with her hands, and Calder, not daring to hit the girl, was awkwardly fighting to evade her, attempting to hold her, to shove her away from him. The crowd laughed in high glee when Calder's ruffled shirt bosom came away in Allie Tuttle's clutching fingers, and several voices cried "Shame!" when Calder, finally yielding to the rage that seethed in him, shoved her so viciously that she fell, in a sitting position, to the planks of the wharf. Instantly, his face white with fury, Calder wheeled upon Stoddard.

"You damned upstart cow-flunky!" he cursed and struck Stoddard's face with his open hand.

Even as the people gasped, before Calder could withdraw his hand, there was a thud as Stoddard's right fist, driven with tremendous force, struck Calder's chin. Calder's head snapped almost to his spine, and his body went up and back, to crash into his gentlemen, sending them reeling, to come to rest at last, face downward, upon the wharf, where it stretched, limp and lax, while the gentlemen stared horrified and the crowd yelled its approval.

CHAPTER THIRTEEN

It was easy to classify the people. The morbid-minded ran toward the fallen Calder, interested in seeing how badly he had been hurt, hoping to learn details that would enable them to graphically relate to less fortunate friends the story of his downfall. The romantic, the hero-worshipers, lingered near Stoddard. They watched him help Allie Tuttle to her feet; they saw the swamp girl throw her arms around his neck and hold tightly to him as if for support, and some of them observed that both her hands patted his head and his shoulders caressingly. But Stoddard, chivalrously assisting Allie, was thinking little of her. He was watching as much as he could see of the prone Calder, remembering that in the duel with Marie Villers' father Calder had shot before the word had been given. He was also watching Calder's gentlemen, to see if any of them contemplated interfering in their companion's behalf. And when he saw they were interested only in Calder he led the way to the cab and helped the Negroes place the swamp victim into it. Allie Tuttle got in also, and the cab whirled away, its wheels rattling over the cobblestones. Turning away from the cab, Stoddard looked straight into the eyes of the young captain of the steamer that had taken Marie Villers to Vicksburg. The young captain smiled, spoke.

"Permit me to congratulate you, sir," he said quietly.

Stoddard bowed, smiled. Over the young captain's head he saw Judge Marston's carriage moving away, and a face in the window nearest him caused his heart to swell with heavy ecstasy. So she had returned in the packet that had taken her away! She was looking straight at the young captain and himself, and her stubborn chin was tilted disdainfully. Of course he could not know what Anne Randolph had been saying to her at that moment.

"Your wild Yankee is a *man*, isn't he?"

"He isn't *my* Yankee!" declared Marie. "I do not like him."

Anne Randolph meditated. "Well," she said, "I don't know. I feel sorry for him. For Asa Calder will probably kill him. And he *is* brave, Marie."

"Let's not talk about him, Anne," said Marie.

"Of course not, honey." But one could think about him, decided Anne. Indeed, one could not help thinking about him, after having seen him knocking Calder down and thereafter standing there, submitting—though somewhat indifferently—to the caresses of the swamp girl. In fact, somewhere inside Anne Randolph was an obscure feeling that she was not exactly pleased over the spectacle the swamp girl had made of herself—publicly too—and she wondered how much of Marie's dislike of Stoddard had been inspired by the scene. But Marie was silent during the drive to the Randolph house, where she took leave of Anne, and she was still silent as the carriage rolled homeward, though her eyes were flashing with ominous lightnings.

Standing at Stoddard's side as Stoddard mounted his horse, the liveryman watched Calder's gentlemen leading him away and then turned to Stoddard, who would not leave the scene while his enemy remained.

"Yo'-all has shuah done busted yo'self into trouble, Mistah Stoddard," he said. And then he found himself attempting to analyze Stoddard's smile.

"He cert'nly ain't scared none," he muttered to himself as his customer rode away toward the Planters' House. "An' I'm shuah hopin' he c'n shoot as well as he c'n hit. He'll need to."

At the desk in the Planters' House the clerk told Stoddard that he had assigned the swamp victim to a room adjoining Stoddard's, and that he had given Allie Tuttle the one next to that.

"The gentleman claims he is Colonel John Burleigh, of Cincinnati," said the clerk. "Is that true?"

"We must accept his story as the truth until we find it isn't," said Stoddard. "But who is Colonel Burleigh?"

"A nabob who is reputed to own half of the No'th," smiled the clerk. "I have had one of the pahtahs give him a bath and put him to bed, suh. I have also sent him a doctah. The doctah is with him now, suh."

Allie Tuttle was also with Colonel Burleigh. She had bathed, and combed her hair, and the matron of the hotel had provided her with a change of garments, so that when Stoddard saw her bending over Colonel Burleigh he was startled into staring at her. She was as fresh and vital as when he had pulled her out of the pool two weeks ago. Burleigh was conscious.

"He's had a touch of swamp fever," the doctor explained to Stoddard. "But he is nearly over that. What's bothering him now is exhaustion and a sort of hysteria resulting from his experiences prior to his exposure. There isn't any doubt that he is entirely normal mentally and that he remembers clearly everything that happened to him. I should think his story would deserve investigation. He has a bad head wound which is nearly healed."

Coherently, but with passionate sincerity, with concern and anxiety in his eyes and manner, Colonel Burleigh related his adventure with the river pirates, and with equal sincerity, but more calmly, Allie Tuttle told Stoddard how she and her father and her mother had found Burleigh lying half in and half out of the water at the edge of the swamp near where, in the wilderness, the family had driven to escape the persecutions of Forbush and his men. They gathered from Burleigh's babbling that he had been in the swamp for about a week, where he had jumped from the deck of his burning vessel after lying for some time in a semiconscious state, listening to the marauders killing his crew and carrying off the steamer's cargo and bearing his daughter away, while he had been unable to move because of the paralysis that had seized him.

"Paw found this in one of his pants pockets," added Allie, and she gave Stoddard a gold hunting-case watch which Stoddard opened after reading an engraved inscription: "From Mary to John." Inside the case was a faded miniature photograph of a young Union officer whose features were undoubtedly those of Colonel Burleigh.

"Where did this happen, Colonel Burleigh?" asked Stoddard.

"At a big bend on the east shore of the river," answered Burleigh. "The man in the punt said it was about twenty miles from Chandler. There was a road that led inland beside a swamp. They had wagons. They took Clara with them. I saw her on a wagon seat while I was swimming toward shore." Colonel Burleigh began to sob, and while Allie Tuttle was soothing him Stoddard left the hotel and went straight to the courthouse, where he told Judge Marston of the tragedy.

Judge Marston's face grew gray and grim.

"If I am not mistaken, this will be the final major outrage committed by those scoundrels!" he declared. "The Riders are organized and ready. Two hundred men, in units of twenty, are scattered over the northern section of this state, awaiting word to go into action. They will operate singly or in groups, as necessity seems to demand. They will haunt every village and hamlet. They will even become inhabitants of the suspected country and will identify themselves with every social group, no matter how vile. They will acquaint themselves with the occupants of every homestead or estate which, either by force or cupidity, has been seized from the original owners. Once there is proof of guilt, the Riders will act. The miscreants will vanish, not to be seen again. Only their boots will remain, to warn potential offenders."

"Their boots?" smiled Stoddard, puzzled.

"Their boots, sir!" grimly repeated the judge. "Every time a rider brings retribution to a desperado he will take possession of his boots and set them in a public place, properly placarded with the desperado's name."

"But suppose they don't wear boots, sir?" asked Stoddard.

"Their moccasins then!" answered the judge. "Or their socks, sir! Or anything else they happen to be wearing on their feet at the time."

"Such a scheme ought to be effective," soberly commented Stoddard. "But am I to take Asa Calder's boots after I have killed him?"

The judge stared. "Are you intending to kill Asa Calder?" he asked.

"I'm afraid Mr Calder will force me to do so. You see, you have a somewhat ridiculous custom in the South, sir; and I suppose, since I am in the South, I shall have to conform to it. It is a cumbersome and lengthy ceremony, I understand. You affront a man, and he slaps your face with a hand or glove, thereby challenging you to a duel. Immediately afterward he sends a friend to you——"

"Damme!" ejaculated the judge impatiently. "What in the devil are you driving at?"

A door behind Judge Marston opened and closed. He heard the double click of the lock and turned swiftly to see Evan Weldon standing in the room. Weldon nodded to the judge but he was looking at Stoddard. Obviously he was striving for calmness and not succeeding very well, for his eyes were bright, his cheeks pale, and he was breathing fast, even though he sought to mask all this with a smile.

"You're here, eh?" he said, as if relieved. "I've been looking for you. I went directly to the Planters' House. They said you had gone out, and I thought you had come here. I heard about it from Marie Villers. Already Slade Forbush has been to the Planters' House looking for you."

"Calm yourself, young man," growled the judge. "Why should Slade Forbush be searching for Mr Stoddard?"

"Undoubtedly Forbush is acting as Asa Calder's second," said Weldon.

"Lord!" exclaimed the judge, beginning to understand. He stared hard at both men, reprovingly at Stoddard.

"I had been trying to get at it," reminded Stoddard.

"You haven't heard?" asked Weldon.

"What?" said the judge.

"That on the dock, just as the down-river packet landed, and in the presence of a crowd of people, Asa Calder slapped Mr Stoddard's face and was instantly knocked unconscious. The town is in a tumult, and nearly everybody thinks Calder got just what he deserved." Weldon looked at Stoddard. "Have you told Judge Marston about Colonel Burleigh, sir?" And then, despite Stoddard's affirmative nod, Weldon told the story all over again, and the judge listened, his gaze on Stoddard, as if studying him. At the end of Weldon's story the judge stared for a long time out of a near-by window.

"Mr Stoddard," he finally said, "I am distressed over this situation. I feel guilty. I had no right to send for you that first night, no right to attempt to persuade you to remain in Chandler to help us fight our battles. Sir, when the certainty of tragedy confronts us we remember that our emotions sometimes drive us to indiscretions which we later regret. You are facing death. I beg of you to leave this place immediately."

"Death is always beside us, sir," said Stoddard, "but that is no reason why we should run from it."

CHAPTER FOURTEEN

Asa Calder's gentlemen had taken him to the steamship company's dock office, where, while concluding their talk with him regarding the improvements they contemplated, they expressed their sympathy. A crowd of people lingered upon the wharf, their imaginations inflamed by the violence they had witnessed. The more bloodthirsty peered into the windows of the dock office and did not desist until the agent drew the shades. The last of Calder's gentlemen to leave the dock office was frankly merciless.

"Egad!" he exclaimed. "The ruffian! You'll kill him, of course."

"Never doubt that," said Calder.

On his way to his office, following the departure of his gentlemen, Calder several times thoughtfully caressed his chin, where Stoddard's fist had landed. There was a lump there, and an abrasion which bled slightly, and Calder dabbed at it with a handkerchief, the malignance of his thoughts bringing a scowl to his lips.

Entering his office, in the rear of which was a suite of rooms in which Calder lived, he immediately walked to a wall cupboard and took down a black case containing two pistols, which he fondled gloatingly. Restoring the pistols to the case, he went into a lavatory adjoining the office and, standing before a mirror, examined the abrasion on his chin. Re-entering the office, he stood in its middle, facing the front windows, and twice horizontally extended his right arm, watching it for tremors. It was steady. Five minutes later, while he was seated in a chair staring at a case filled with dust-covered lawbooks, he answered a knock on the door with a curt "Come in", and a man, arrayed like one of Calder's gentlemen of the dock office, entered and closed the door behind him.

"Hello, Forbush," said Calder. "I expected you last night."

"Delayed," explained Forbush, smiling.

"Where's Craftkin?"

"I left him in the Planters' House bar. The man's getting to be a tank. He'll be here directly."

Forbush walked to one of the front windows and stood looking down into the street, and Calder gave the man's back his grudging admiration. Tall, broad of shoulder, imposing, his dark curly hair clinging close to his well-shaped head, Forbush was a man to command attention in any group. He had a way about him, too, reflected Calder; natural mannerisms that were as distinguished as his appearance. Everything he did was graceful, even the way he accepted deference from those who thought they were inferior. The grossness in him, with which Calder was familiar, was glossed over with surface gentility and culture.

When he finally turned from the window and dropped into a chair his face was expressionless except for a certain quiet intentness of gaze. One could never know what Forbush was thinking about.

"I'd like to represent you in your meeting with Stoddard, Calder," he said.

"Oh, you've heard about it?"

"I've heard nothing else. And there's that bruise on your chin. He hit you hard, eh?"

"A strong-armed fool," scowled Calder. "He'll pay for it."

"They usually do when they clash with you," laughed Forbush. "But be careful, Calder. This man Stoddard has nerve. But I had already told you that, I believe."

"Nonsense!" scoffed Calder.

"He shot Joe Fowler through the heart," said Forbush. "Clem Buel claims he did it from about forty yards. Fowler was dead when he hit the water. Stoddard didn't even look at him after he fell—so Buel says."

"Why didn't Buel do some shooting? Seems he did a lot of looking," said Calder.

"Buel told me his rifle wasn't loaded. He and Fowler weren't expecting to see Stoddard. They were looking for Allie Tuttle. And when Fowler saw her he didn't see Stoddard."

"Evidently you didn't impress Allie Tuttle as you have impressed some women," smiled Calder. "She climbed out of the window of her house to escape you. You're losing your appeal, Forbush."

"Perhaps. There's bound to be a failure now and then. However, she's still here, I understand. I'll see her again after you kill Stoddard. By the way, one must admire the man's judgment. She's a pretty piece of baggage, and he took her to the Planters' House. That's nerve, Calder, nothing less. A surprising man, and a bold one. Marie Villers' nigger—Ben—told me Stoddard was making headway with Marie, the morning he stacked the gold pieces on the table, until she found he was a Yankee."

Calder frowned. "It's odd that he should have come here; that he was romantic fool enough to be lured here by a girl's photograph. Not one man in a thousand would be harebrained enough to do that."

Forbush laughed. "Such things do happen, though, Calder. I admire the fellow for the romantic impulse which you condemn. A beautiful woman does things to a man."

"You've done worse things to Marie Villers' nigger," said Calder. "How did you prevail upon him to tell you what he has told you?"

"The niggers think freedom gives them license to betray their employers," laughed Forbush. "Besides, I convinced Ben that my only purpose was to ascertain the progress I was making with his mistress. He thinks he is aiding and abetting a romance."

"So Simon Gorty had to kill Pierre Villers in order to get the gold," said Calder reflectively, staring into space. "And a member of Stoddard's posse, known as Dollarbill McCarthy, killed Gorty. Stoddard brought the gold to Marie Villers, with a letter she had written to Pierre. See how things go, Forbush. If she hadn't sent her photograph to her uncle, Stoddard would not have come here. He wouldn't have been on the dock when Allie Tuttle brought Colonel Burleigh in, and I could have sent Burleigh to jail, where he would have died as an inebriate. My killing Stoddard won't shut Burleigh's mouth, nor Allie Tuttle's."

"After you've killed Stoddard I'll take care of Burleigh and Alice Tuttle," said Forbush. "The girl has spunk, Calder. They tell me she made you mighty uncomfortable there on the dock." He laughed at the look in Calder's eyes.

"Bah!" said Calder. "I didn't bother with the girl any more than I had to. She's swamp trash," he added vindictively, as if to assure Forbush that he did not agree with the latter's appraisal of the young woman. "I was after Stoddard. You know that. He's too deep in my affairs, and he's been swaggering around town for more than a week, displaying that big gun. He annoys me, and I'm beginning to believe that he has other business here, aside from his mooning around after Marie Villers."

"You're not as young as you were, Calder," laughed Forbush. "You don't remember your ancient ardors."

"He may be an impetuous, reckless fool," declared Calder, "but she's given him no encouragement. She's been away to Vicksburg for a week. Besides, he's a Yankee, and she doesn't like Yankees. I tell you, he's here for some other purpose. There's been a change in this town during the last week or so. I can't describe it, but I can feel it. There's an undercurrent of excitement, as if something unusual is about to happen. There have been many strangers in town. There's something stirring. I've an idea that the authorities know something about what happened to the Clara Belle. You bungled that job, Forbush. If Burleigh lives he'll go straight to the governor with his story."

"Burleigh won't live long after you kill Stoddard," promised Forbush. "He's got a mighty thick skull. A dozen of the men swore he was dead when they set fire to the steamer. She was burned to the water line. The crew went with her. There's no evidence of violence. Even if Burleigh should talk, no one would believe him. People would want to know how the steamer got so far away from the main channel."

"Where is Burleigh's daughter?"

"With Vauchain."

"Up there?"

Forbush nodded.

The men exchanged glances. Forbush smiled shallowly; a tinge of white appeared around Calder's lips and nostrils. "You took her there?" he asked.

If Forbush was aware of the contempt in Calder's voice he gave no sign. "You don't kill women," he said.

"Sometimes they're better off," commented Calder. "Pretty?" he added. Forbush nodded. "So much the worse for her," said Calder. "He can't keep her there forever," he added, as if uttering an afterthought. "The swamp will get her."

Forbush regarded Calder with a gaze which was curiously speculative. He spoke softly: "If I didn't know you so well I might think you had grown fainthearted since I talked with you before. Or perhaps," he added, his voice becoming gently insinuating, "the thought of your coming meeting with Stoddard is bothering you."

Calder glanced sharply at his confederate, to see that he was blandly smiling. There was a contradiction between the smile and the insinuation, and Calder tried, unsuccessfully, to define it.

"What the devil do you mean?" he asked. "Are you trying to unnerve me?"

"As if that could be done!" smiled Forbush. "Long ago you established yourself. You are experienced enough to face a gun without flinching, and you ought to be able to discuss possibilities with calmness."

Calder sat very still, staring at his friend. "What are the possibilities?" he said.

"They are few but important. For instance—your indigestion. Qualms in a man's stomach at an early hour of the morning might affect the steadiness of his arm. Your gun might misfire. Your ears might be laggard when the word is given. A gnat might fly into your eye as you press the trigger. Stoddard might escape all these."

"Damme!" angrily ejaculated Calder. "This is a hell of a time to speak of such things!"

"They must be spoken of," said Forbush with steady implacability, "because they are things that a man about to fight a duel always thinks of. I've thought of them, Calder. You've thought of them. Usually they don't happen, but they might. If one of them happens there's an end to thinking of them."

"You're right, Forbush," smiled Calder. "Those are the things that a careful man guards against."

"Certainly," said Forbush. "Just as he gets his affairs in shape in case one of the possibilities might occur."

"You are right again," agreed Calder. "There's a division due, isn't there? I always suspected you had ice water in your veins. Now I'm sure of it. I'll give you a check for your share of the loot to date."

Forbush smiled and walked to the front window, where he stood looking down into the street and over the roofs of the buildings while Calder wrote. Pocketing the check, Forbush placed both hands upon Calder's shoulders and shook him gently from side to side.

"I'm off to ask Stoddard to name his seconds," he said, "I understand you did the challenging, and so, of course, Stoddard will name the weapons and the terms. You'll fight him tomorrow morning?"

"And kill him," replied Calder.

"You will, of course," smiled Forbush and took leave of his friend. He walked down the street toward the water front. With purposeful step he turned a corner and kept on down the sidewalk.

"These things must be thought of," he said, as if he still talked with Calder. Then he entered a bank, had Calder's check cashed, stuffed the currency into a pocket, emerged from the bank, walked down the sidewalk to another bank about a block and a half distant, entered and deposited the currency to his own account, remembering that checks, deposited on the day preceding a man's death, are sometimes the objects of unusual scrutiny and may be returned if they have not passed the clearing house.

CHAPTER FIFTEEN

The morning was not yet spent, and Forbush, walking along the water front, not noticing how people stared at him as he passed, made his way slowly and thoughtfully toward the Planters' House. Just as the serene and smiling face of nature gives no hint of storms to come, so there was no visible sign in the town to indicate that tragedy hovered near. Yet as Forbush moved toward the Planters' House, Asa Calder, one of the pistols from the black case in hand, was leveling it at various objects in his law office and at himself in the mirror in the lavatory, intently peering at the steel ring of the weapon's muzzle, observing that his hand was not as steady as usual. But steady enough, he grimly assured himself. He could not understand Forbush—not quite. There had been other duels, and Forbush had been calmly confident. This time . . .

Damn it! All this talk about possibilities. And a settlement before the meeting with Stoddard. "These things must be thought of," Forbush had said. That was true of course. Always, on the day preceding a duel, Calder had thought of them, but never as he was thinking of them now, with a chill of apprehension running down his spine. He walked to the front window and stood looking out over the roofs of buildings at the calm surface of the river, and into the bright sunlight that flashed upon the green countryside.

The same sunlight was engaging Judge Marston's attention as he sat in his office staring out of a window after Stoddard and Weldon had left him, and after Weldon had agreed—nay, volunteered—to act as Stoddard's second. There had been some talk between Stoddard and Weldon about the "conditions" of the duel. Stoddard would use the weapon in the holster at his hip. He had another, exactly like it, which Calder might use. Or Calder could use another of his own choice. "A rifle, if he wishes to," said Stoddard.

Judge Marston found himself wondering about Stoddard and about the new West out of which he had come. A rough, grim country which, as Judge Marston had seen, had produced a man who was chivalrous enough to risk his life because of a woman's photograph.

While Forbush walked toward the Planters' House, and Asa Calder fretted in the seclusion of his law office, and the judge thoughtfully considered Stoddard, Marie Villers, who had gone over to Judge Marston's house to tell him about her trip—and to tell him of the disgraceful scene she had witnessed on the dock—was seated in a chair at one end of the big veranda of the judge's house impatiently waiting for Weldon and Galt, who stood at the bottom of the steps on the front walk, to finish their whispered conversation. Previously she had told Weldon of the incident of the water front and had watched him as, pale and startled, he had ridden away to tell Judge Marston what had happened. But now, returning, Weldon had been accompanied by Galt, both riding, and a Negro boy was holding their horses as they talked together at the bottom of the steps.

"That's what has happened," said Weldon, apparently concluding his recital. "I believe Colonel Burleigh's mind is wandering somewhat, as it would be, if those things really happened to him. But he sticks to the story that the Clara Belle was looted and burned by pirates, and his daughter carried away. We are going to investigate. Select men who know that country, preferably those who have lived around there, whose families are the victims of Vauchain's depredations. They will be vindictive, but that's the way we want them to be. Have some of them verify Burleigh's story about the steamer. If it's been destroyed by fire Burleigh's story is probably true. Have your men trail the wagons Burleigh talks about. On one pretext or another they must get into every house in the back country; into every crossroads store and Negro shanty. They must mix with the plantation laborers. They must trace the Clara Belle's cargo. Whenever they are certain that they have come into contact with one of Vauchain's desperadoes they are to keep after him until they get a chance to kill him secretly. Take as many men as you can handle, and if you get into a tight spot send word to me and we'll put the entire organization on the trail."

"All right, sir," said Galt; "I'll have thirty or forty of the men in that section before dark."

Galt mounted his horse and rode away, and for an instant, as Weldon turned toward her, Marie studied his face.

"Trouble has come," she said and held up an admonishing finger as she added: "Don't try to pretend to me, Evan Weldon. I know all about the Riders. The judge told me."

"I swear you wheedled it out of him," declared Weldon. "The judge is clay in your hands, to be molded according to your moods. I am glad you refused to marry me. I would have been spoiled by now."

"You are already spoiled, sir." Her eyes were flashing spiritedly, but her defiance was not entirely genuine, Weldon decided.

"What has spoiled me, Miss Villers?" he asked mockingly.

"Your association with that Yankee, Stoddard."

While Marie sat very still, gazing, apparently, at the trees between the house and the road, Weldon mounted the steps, crossed the veranda and seated himself upon the rail in front of her, whereupon she transferred her gaze to him, and he smiled very faintly.

"You don't like Stoddard?"

"I detest him!"

"Strange," said Weldon reflectively. "You and I are invariably at odds. I like Stoddard and consider him a gentleman."

"Does a gentleman permit a swamp girl to caress him in public?" she asked.

"I hadn't heard of that," said Weldon. "Did you see it happen?"

"I did." Scornfully. "I was standing on the dock with Anne Randolph and Captain Harding of the packet Louisiana."

"And what form did her caresses take?" He observed that Marie's cheeks had reddened. Wisely he did not permit her to see his eyes, which were full of knowledge.

"She embraced him lovingly. It was very brazen, Evan. The people laughed, as they had a right to do. The people know there is something between them."

"That something is gratitude on the girl's part," said Weldon. "He had saved her life—saved her from drowning—from suicide. It was when he was on his way here. It happened near Allie Tuttle's home, after she and her parents had been dispossessed by Vauchain's men. Stoddard rescued her and took her to her parents. Naturally, when she saw him again she was delighted. And he could not publicly rebuke her—no gentleman would."

"Perhaps you are right," she said, looking past him and speaking coldly. "And being a gentleman, of course he took her with him to the Planters' House."

Weldon answered very gently: "That was because Burleigh needed a nurse immediately." He now told her of Burleigh's experiences with the river pirates, and she sat pale and quiet and attentive until he finished.

"Poor Colonel Burleigh!" she said then and sat quiet and attentive again. And then added, almost whispering: "Poor Clara!"

They were bound to find her, Evan Weldon declared. The Riders now had something to work on, and their energy and ingenuity would be definitely applied to the task of rescuing her and exterminating Vauchain's band; and he explained that he would have gone with Galt if Stoddard had not asked him to act as his second in his duel with Asa Calder which, Weldon was certain, would take place the following morning. "I don't know, though, I think I would have stayed even if he had not named me. Marie, Stoddard is a very courageous man."

Weldon was now doing the looking, and Marie's glance had dropped to her hands, which were in her lap, the fingers slowly clenching. She had grown very pale.

"They are to fight—tomorrow morning?" she said in a curiously small voice.

"I'm almost certain of it," said Weldon. "Stoddard expects it, and Judge Marston. Asa Calder will not delay matters, you may be sure. He will be more deadly than ever." He hesitated, studied Marie's pale face, dropped his gaze to her clenched hands, shook his head as if puzzled, and continued, a trace of emotion in his voice: "I feel guilty about this, and so does the judge."

"Why?" she asked, startled into looking up at him. Her eyes were pools of wonder shadowed by anxiety.

"Because the judge and I prevailed upon him to stay in Chandler and help us fight Vauchain's gang."

"Oh!" she exclaimed, staring at him. "You asked him to stay?"

"Yes. And if Calder kills him we shall be to blame."

Of course Weldon was sincere. He had always been sincere. One could depend upon him to express his feelings with entire frankness. "And if Calder kills him!" This portion of Weldon's sentence was a dozen times mentally repeated by her.

How completely men accepted the conclusions of their reasoning! If Weldon and the judge had been able to see in Stoddard's eyes the things she had seen—which they apparently had not seen—or if they had been able to peer for an instant into a certain pocket of Stoddard's vest, they would not now assume the responsibility of Stoddard's continued presence in Chandler.

They knew nothing about the photograph, of course, she was certain. Nor would they know about it through her telling them. She knew that if Calder killed Stoddard she alone would be to blame. Not directly, of course, but the shadow of her nearness to the tragedy would always be over her.

"Must they fight?" she asked. "Isn't there some way to stop it?"

Weldon shook his head. "Stoddard has been publicly challenged. Calder has been publicly humiliated. I'm afraid nothing can be done."

"Stoddard could go away," she suggested.

Weldon smiled. "You don't know him," he said. "He isn't the running kind."

She smoothed a refractory flounce in her skirt, and Weldon was amazed to discover that her hands were shaking a little. She did have capacity for deep feeling after all. He had wondered, for his own courtship had ingloriously failed. He was just not the man, that was all, and he had been sensible enough to know it.

Was Stoddard the man? He hoped so. Stoddard would be a perfect mate for this aristocratic, spirited girl, who had so courageously endured the calamities that had eddied in the wake of war. His stern face softened as he watched her, and, watching her, he shook his head again in wonder for the depth and the mystery of woman's emotions.

"Of course I know you don't like Stoddard," he said. "You've told me so, and I believe you. But, after all, he is a man, Marie, a brave man, even if he is a Yankee. And he has done you a service in bringing your uncle Pierre's things to you. The judge has invited him here tonight, and I hope, because he is Judge Marston's guest——"

"That I will forget he is a Yankee," she interrupted.

"Yes," he smiled.

"You are right, Evan," she said. "I shall try to forget he is a Yankee. And I shall try to remember that he is a brave man. Allie Tuttle was brave too. She was magnificent, Evan, for she had the moral courage to let them all know that she loves Stoddard."

Was this mockery? Weldon did not know.

CHAPTER SIXTEEN

Perched up on its bluff above the river, its white walls and wide cornices outlined against a background of walnuts, oaks, hickorys and persimmons, the Planters' House was visible for miles up and down the river. Jefferson Davis had once enjoyed its hospitality and had passed a pleasant hour or two under the canopied green of the trees, where he had been heard to remark that never should the wild grape be stripped from the tree trunks, because they gave a graceful touch to the woodland, softening the rugged austerity of the great trunks around which they twined. Sam Houston had paused there long enough to praise the great magnolias and to admire the silvery-gray boles of the dogwood trees, whose pure-white flowers appear early in the spring, although at the time of Sam Houston's visit the white blossoms had given way to reddish-purple berries. The portals of the Planters' House had been hallowed by many illustrious gentlemen and beautiful, gracious women, and the Union officers who had been swept down the river, accompanied by a thundering flotilla, had not desecrated the place, so that there still lingered around it the mellowness of age and the calm atmosphere of Southern chivalry and dignity.

Inside was the quiet of plush and velvet, the richness of satiny silver and glittering glass, of old linen and fine tapestries and paintings, and a pervading aroma, like the musty bouquet of some fine rare old wine.

Colonel Burleigh knew nothing of all this. In a room off the great plush-carpeted hall on the second floor he had suffered a relapse which had dulled his senses to everything but his torturing dreams.

Allie Tuttle's dreams had only begun. The luxury of the Planters' House was to her a fairyland through which Stoddard, the king of romance, moved. During Stoddard's absence, and while Colonel Burleigh slept, she had tiptoed about the room, marveling at the softness of the carpet, examining the pictures upon the walls, peering admiringly at the draperies of the windows, enjoying the solitude of the room in which she, temporarily, was queen. The door of the room, leading into the great hall, was open, and several times Allie timidly approached it to gaze down the grand stairway into the palm-dotted lobby. More often she stood in front of the mirror in a big dresser, critically and wonderingly—and with some approval—gazing at her reflection. Astonishment was one of the expressions in the eyes that looked back at her. Was she *that* pretty? Or was it merely that the dress the matron had given her made her appear so? Pretty or not, she was a swamp girl, a being who was somehow inferior, and member of a clan which was despised by the quality folk she always saw from a distance. They and their luxurious life represented the unattainable. The Planters' House—this sudden and unexpected glimpse of paradise on earth—made her more conscious than ever of her inferiority. It increased the shame she felt over offering herself to Stoddard. Almost—if Stoddard had accepted her—she would be what Asa Calder had named her.

"Darn him!" she said defiantly to the mirror. "I'd ruther be Stoddard's strumpet than Asa Calder's wife!" And she stared, amazed and perplexed over her feelings, at the crimson tide that rose to her cheeks.

And there, returning from Judge Marston's office and from a talk with Evan Weldon, Stoddard found her and laughed at her, thinking she was admiring her new garments. She had been so interested that she had not heard him enter the open doorway.

"Satisfied?" he said.

"No."

"You should be."

"Shucks, yo' air jest tryin' to be nice to me. I ain't purty and I look like the devil in this yere dress. I ain't fitten fer sech things."

"It's just a matter of getting accustomed to them," he said, "and of learning how to live up to what they represent."

"I don't think that's so," she disagreed.

"Why?"

"Folks that wear nice clothes ain't always decent. Thar's Forbush. He looks like a gentleman. He don't live up to his clothes. And Asa Calder!"

"I'm afraid you've got me there," he said earnestly. "I suppose I should have said 'As a man thinks, so is he.' "

"Yo' think right," she said with devastating frankness. "I expaict thet's the difference. I offered to be yore woman, and yo' wouldn't hev me. Thet was right. Forbush wanted to take me without askin'. But thet don't explain it either. I think right, but I ain't nothin'. And clothes don't make me feel no different."

"Well, they make you look different," he argued gently. "That ought to satisfy you until you learn the rest of it—which you never will, any more than any of us will learn it. But if you keep right on thinking right you'll come pretty close to being what you want to be."

"Wishin' don't do no good, I expaict?"

"Hardly."

"The day yo' fished me out of the water I was wishin' yo' wouldn't find my pap and maw," she confessed. "That didn't help. Yo' found 'em. And when yo' rode away, after we found Pap and Maw, I was wishin' yo' would stay with me. That didn't happen. I reckon yo' air right. Wishin' don't do no good. Do quality folks do any wishin'?"

"Of course."

"Do yo' do any wishin'?"

"Certainly."

"What fer?"

He drew a deep breath. He was thinking of Marie Villers. "What I wish for I can't have," he said.

"Me neither." Abruptly she turned from him and walked to a window, where for an instant she gazed down upon a vast bed of rhododendrons, their rubberlike leaves gleaming with satiny smoothness in the sunlight. Stoddard had gone to the bed and was studying Colonel Burleigh's face. The colonel was asleep. Allie Tuttle moved to the big dresser and gazed into the mirror again. She saw her eyes, filled with cloudy wistfulness and resignation. Tight-pressed lips, betraying rebellion of spirit which, as she continued to look at them, softened to waywardness and finally to a smile which she presented to Stoddard when he turned from the colonel's bedside to look at her.

"You air wishin' fer a woman," she said, "Ain't yo'?"

"There's no use denying it," he said, amazed.

"I knowed it," she said, her smile fading a little, the wistfulness in her eyes deepening to anguish—which he did not see. "She was on the dock theah, standin' with another girl and Captain Harding of the Louisiana. It was Marie Villers. Shucks, she was jealous! She saw me huggin' yo'."

"She would, of course," he said, ruefully smiling. "It was a free show, and she saw it, all right. But look here, Allie. You know the hugging was all one sided, and that between us there is no nonsense."

"Sartin." She paled.

"She wouldn't understand that of course," he said, as if to himself.

"A woman knows when another woman loves her man. I'm sorry I done it. It'll make her jealous."

He shook his head. "It won't," he said. "She doesn't like me, Allie."

"Yo' think thet?" she asked. She turned quickly that he might not see the agony in her eyes. With her back to him she said: "She air jealous of yo' because she loves yo'."

"You're wrong, Allie. She hates me. She hates me because I'm a Yankee."

"An' loves yo' 'cause yo're a *man*."

Stoddard was moving toward the open doorway and did not hear the sobbing catch in Allie's voice. In the great hallway, opposite the door toward which Stoddard was moving, were three men—two white men, apparently gentlemen—whom Stoddard did not know, one tall, the other as tall but stoop shouldered, and a Negro porter. The porter and the tall man were supporting the other man, who was very drunk—so helplessly drunk that his eyes were closed as he swayed on rubbery legs as the porter and the tall man sought to maintain him in an upright position.

"Lawd, Mistah Stoddard!" apologized the porter as Stoddard reached the doorway. "I'se shuah sorry I'se distuhbed yuh, suh, but Mistah Craftkin has drunk hisself 'most to death, and we's gwine take him to a room."

Craftkin!

Stoddard heard Allie Tuttle cry out gaspingly and he saw the tall man gazing past him at the girl, his eyes flashing a message of desire to her. Stoddard heard the rustle of Allie's skirts as she fled, and the tall man's gaze, now mocking and mildly derisive, was upon Stoddard. It was an alert, roving gaze. It went from Stoddard's head to his boots; it paused at the wide cartridge belt and the heavy gun in the black holster, lingered for a probing instant upon his eyes, and dropped to the carpet as he bowed and released the stoop-shouldered man to the care of the porter, who staggered down the hall with him.

The tall man, who was Forbush, smiled at Stoddard. An expansive smile which narrowed and grew sly and subtle with the growing conviction that Stoddard was on the point of guessing his identity. Stoddard had not seen him before, Forbush was certain, but Stoddard had probably heard of Craftkin from Judge Marston, and probably Marston had described both Craftkin and himself. And also, there was his glance at Allie Tuttle, and if Allie had told Stoddard of a certain experience she had undergone, why of course Stoddard, reading his eyes, would suspect. Forbush was never forthright. His profession forced him to employ various artifices of speech and manner, so that now he became suave and blandly polite.

"I am distressed, sir. I assure you that this disturbance was unintentional and unfortunate, and yet it provides me with an opportunity to discuss with you informally a subject which, from its very nature, becomes formal and awkward. I am Slade Forbush, sir; and my friend, Asa Calder, has sent me to represent him in the inevitable meeting which will occur over that deplorable incident on the water front this morning. For a meeting is inevitable, is it not, Mr Stoddard?"

"As inevitable as Mr Calder's death tomorrow morning," said Stoddard.

"Ah!" softly breathed Forbush. Although he strove mightily to control himself, his muscles stiffened and he became straight and rigid. For his senses had been rocked, not entirely by Stoddard's words, but by what he saw in Stoddard's eyes.

Yes, Calder's death was inevitable. There in Calder's office Forbush had had a presentiment of it. Out of that presentiment had come his words of warning to Calder. Warnings about "possibilities." His own dark thoughts. His sudden determination to arrange a division of spoils prior to the proposed encounter. His words: "These things must be thought of," which he had mentally repeated many times while walking from Calder's office to the bank. Yes, Calder would die tomorrow morning. Forbush's presentiment went beyond that. It reached out into the future, into the time that would come after Calder's death. Strangely, he was not concerned so much about the killing of Calder as he was about how the killing would be accomplished. This man Stoddard had killed Joe Fowler on the morning he had kept Allie Tuttle from drowning herself. Clem Buel, Fowler's confederate, had witnessed the killing, which had been done with a single shot at a distance of about forty or fifty yards. The bullet had gone into Joe Fowler's heart. Stoddard's nerve was "cold." It could not be shaken. He had not flinched under Marie Villers' rebuke when, with all the people looking at him, he had smilingly bowed to her. He had knocked Asa Calder down. And now, standing in the doorway, he was coldly predicting that he would kill Asa Calder. And so Forbush found his thoughts involuntarily groping into the future, to the day when he would supersede Calder and thus become involved in future trouble with Stoddard. Decidedly, it would pay him to watch Stoddard, to search for a weakness in him.

"You are sure of yourself, sir," he said.

"Yes," said Stoddard. "I am sure of two things. The first is that I shall kill Calder. The second is that if you molest Allie Tuttle again I shall kill you. That's plain enough, isn't it?"

"Quite," said Forbush. A whiteness appeared around his lips and nostrils. A sudden coldness stole over him. However, he managed to hold his eyes steady. He was in the grip of a powerful fascination. Stoddard's eyes were frosty; the straight lines of his lips seemed not to move as words came through them:

"Right now, for what you have already done to her, if you're ready!" he challenged.

Calder had said that Forbush's veins were filled with ice water, and at this moment it seemed so, for the blood had drained from his face, and the smile he succeeded in summoning was stiff and shallow.

"The Calder matter is what I am here to discuss, sir," he said.

"Of course," answered Stoddard. The right corner of his mouth twitched downward with contempt. "Mr Evan Weldon is acting for me, Forbush. Good day, sir."

He backed into the room and closed the door.

Turning, he looked for Allie. She had not gone very far. She was in a corner of the room, between the big dresser and a window, flattened against the wall, her hands behind her. She had fled from Forbush, yet she had not moved out of hearing distance of his voice. Her face was white, her pallor banishing the normal tan of her skin. Yet she seemed strangely calm and resolute, like some wild thing, cornered but unconquered.

Stoddard suddenly realized the depth of her fear of Forbush. He knew now why she had tried to drown herself. While talking with her, after pulling her out of the pool, he had attributed her attempt at suicide to emotional hysteria, brought on by the calamity that had overtaken her parents and herself.

"He air gone?" she whispered, stepping away from the wall. She breathed more regularly, fighting off her fright, the color coming back into her face, the wild light in her eyes dying out. She came close to Stoddard, staring at him wonderingly.

"I heerd what yo' said to him. I knowed yo' meant it, and he knowed yo' meant it. I'm thankin' yo'. But I don't want to cause yo' thet much trouble. Ef Forbush tries to take me ag'in I'll kill him. Ef he takes me and I don't kill him, I'll kill myself."

"Forbush won't bother you again, Allie," he assured her, and his thoughts went back to the morning he had rescued her, when her protestations of virtue had seemed to him to be somewhat overemphasized. But nothing could be more convincing than a determination to kill in order to preserve virtue. "Poor little beggar," he thought, "how she cherishes her only possession!" And he remembered other women he had known who had not considered virtue so valuable. He had wondered why she was keeping her hands behind her, and now he seized her shoulders and gently, but quickly, turned her around, to see a revolver gripped tightly in her right hand. Still gently holding her, he removed the weapon from her hand and held it in the palm of his own, she intently watching him.

"Where did you get this, Allie?"

"Colonel Burleigh had it when Pap found him. I hid it in the pocket of my dress."

"You intended to kill Forbush if he came into this room?"

"Sartin. I won't let him tech me ag'in."

He laid the weapon on the dresser top and gazed out of a window, his back to Allie. He did not tell her that the weapon was rusted to uselessness, that it would not fire. He was strangely awed. From the first he had pitied her, and now the emotion had deepened. When he finally turned he saw her standing near the foot of Colonel Burleigh's bed, watching him. He thought he saw dark apprehension in her eyes as he turned. But they were clear enough now, and steady.

"Yo're goin' to fight Asa Calder tomorrow mornin'," she said. "I heerd yo' say so, to Forbush. Don't think of no women while yo're fightin'."

CHAPTER SEVENTEEN

Dr Buchanan, the physician summoned by the hotel clerk to attend Colonel Burleigh, had spent most of the afternoon with his patient, making various tests; probing, examining, observing; with Allie Tuttle assisting. Dr Buchanan's gravity of manner, his negative head-shakings, revealed, even to the girl, that Colonel Burleigh's condition was far from satisfactory. In the end, after dusk, when the lamps were lighted and a mist from the river was stealing in, Dr Buchanan stood looking down at his patient.

"I'm afraid he's in for a long siege. A paralysis, affecting both legs, induced by swamp fever or by that blow on the head." He pointed to a formidable array of medicines he had prepared, telling Allie to administer them according to directions. "Be with him as much as you can," he added. "Be within call all the time. If he awakens send for me instantly. Don't let anyone disturb him."

Thus was Allie Tuttle's sojourn in paradise to be prolonged. To the swamp people a physician was a magician, a godlike being whose word was law. And so, even if Allie had meditated returning to the swamp—which she had not—she would have obeyed Dr Buchanan.

After the doctor went away she closed the door leading into the hall, locked it and seated herself in a chair beside the small table upon which the doctor had left various bottles and boxes, arranging them in order. A subdued knocking at the door interrupted her and she ran to it, opened it slightly, gasped a startled "O-o-oh!" and stood staring at Stoddard, who was there, dressed in new garments for his visit to Judge Marston's house, smiling at her. At first her face whitened, but instantly a tide of color swept into it, betraying sudden and complete embarrassment, and with it startled incoherence.

"Good Lord," she exclaimed, "I thought it was a—a—gentleman!"

"And it isn't," he said, entering and closing the door.

She had retreated from him, her embarrassment deepening. Her cheeks were flaming; she had pressed both hands to her throat; her eyes were alight with mingled admiration and amazement. He saw them become distressingly wistful, then staringly fearful, and she suddenly sank into a chair and began to cry.

He stood looking at her, puzzled.

"Why are you crying, Allie?" he said sternly.

"Yo' air a gentleman," she sobbed more violently.

"And you don't want me to be a gentleman?"

"Y-y-es-s."

Bewildering. Startled at first, because she had mistaken him for a gentleman, she became grief stricken in acknowledging the fact. He would never understand women. He sometimes wondered if women understood themselves, if they were able to unravel the cross threads of their emotions.

To Allie Tuttle it was all simple enough. Appalling. He looked like a gentleman. He *was* a gentleman and therefore as unattainable as the other gentlemen whom she had always seen from a distance. Paradoxically, while considering him as possessing all the attributes of a gentleman, she had hoped he would not betray the outward graces of the type. For that would make him more attractive to other women—to Marie Villers perhaps.

She suddenly stood erect, smiling at him through her tears, pretending relief as she moved farther away from him.

"Yo' mighty near skeered me out of a year's growth," she said. "I knowed yo' was a gentleman right off, but what skeered me was thet I thought yo' was a strange gentleman."

She was still palpitant with emotion, he observed, but there was no mistaking the genuineness of her smile, so that he could not think of doubting her. However, she seemed suddenly more shy, more reserved, more timid, somehow remote, as if she had withdrawn the natural charm she had previously exhibited to him.

She told him about the doctor's visit, about his verdict. And while she talked to him he was aware that she was inspecting his new garments, the apparel which at that period was popular among gentlemen—polished shoes, dark peg-legged trousers with wide knees, a white waistcoat showing an expanse of ruffled shirt and a white stock, a long broadcloth coat with square shoulders, narrow waist and wide flaring tails, the lapels faced with dull satin binding which ran into a fluted collar.

The phenomenon of her sudden burst of emotion partially explained, he was indifferent to the rest of it. He did not like to have women cry, but now that she had stopped it was evident that, whatever the provocation, the mood had passed. Strange thing to cry about though—surprise and fright. But when he left her, a few minutes later, he was wondering why, after crying, she had suddenly become so solemn.

Seated in Judge Marston's carriage, which had been sent for him, he was thinking of Forbush, wondering about the destructive fury that had been seething in him when he had threatened to kill the man should he again molest Allie Tuttle. It was not his custom to threaten people, and he had no thought of enacting the role of protector of a swamp girl's virtue, particularly when that virtue was so easy that it had been offered to him gratuitously. He was certain that his hatred of Forbush had been aroused by Judge Marston's statement that Forbush was paying attention to Marie Villers. Beneath this conviction persisted a recollection of Allie Tuttle's emotional outbreak. Somewhere in all this was an obscure significance to which his senses could not, or would not, become attuned.

CHAPTER EIGHTEEN

Evan Weldon and Judge Marston greeted Stoddard at the steps leading to the veranda of the judge's house, and there, with the great porch lights shining upon him, Stoddard bowed formally to Marie Villers, who came to the door upon his arrival. She was in white, something simple and soft and satiny—but not as white and smooth as the skin of her partially bared arms and shoulders. Her hair Stoddard would long remember, and her eyes, too, for in them was something he had seen in Allie Tuttle's eyes when, upon opening the door of Colonel Burleigh's room in the Planters' House, she had retreated from him. Amazement and startled embarrassment. No panic, however. Merely a smile and bow, acknowledging his own, and she turned from the doorway, leaving him with Judge Marston and Evan Weldon.

Amazed, standing at a little distance, Evan Weldon had witnessed the meeting. Marie, prepared by Weldon, had appeared in the doorway ready to be gracious to the judge's guest. Startled by what she had seen, she had fled.

Weldon had also been startled, and the judge. The judge was beaming as he talked with Stoddard, but Weldon was critically watching Stoddard, alert to find a flaw in him, in the garments he wore, or in the way he wore them, or in his behavior in the new role he was playing.

"Egad," he thought, "he's perfection! His tailor is a genius. But what a model to work on!"

Mystification was mingled with Weldon's approval. Men become gentlemen through careful rearing or through association with other gentlemen. Above all, a gentleman has, whether inherited or acquired, certain distinctions of appearance which only dignity of thought can create. And where, reflected the mystified and delighted Weldon, in the rough, grim West could Stoddard, wearing a gun and knowing how to use it, have acquired the graces he was now displaying?

Later, in the great dining room with Marie sitting opposite Stoddard, Weldon was conscious of the girl's guarded scrutiny of the guest, and at the conclusion of the meal he saw in her eyes a puzzled gleam. She, also, was mystified. Disturbed, too, for when, afterward, they went to the veranda, she glanced at Weldon as if wondering if he had seen what she had seen. It was not until Weldon and the judge had quietly withdrawn from the veranda that Marie spoke to Stoddard.

"You look less warlike tonight, Mr Stoddard," she said.

It was her way of letting him know she was aware that he had discarded his cowboy regalia for the garments of a gentleman.

"It is a concession to custom," he said. "I was becoming an object of curiosity."

"That is true," she answered, and by the slight smile she gave him, a thinly disdainful smile, he knew that she was numbered among the curious. Even now he saw her glance linger for an instant upon his coat, at the hip, where, if he had been wearing a gun, there would be a noticeable bulge.

"I left it at the Planters' House," he said, answering the question in her glance.

"To be worn again tomorrow morning," she suggested. "Or perhaps you will use a different weapon?"

So she knew! "Perhaps," he said. "I understand Forbush and Weldon have arranged the conditions."

"You haven't inquired?"

"No."

His apparent indifference nettled her. She could have understood him if he had betrayed some slight nervousness or tension that would have manifested itself in irritability, sullenness or laughter. But so far as she could see, he had not changed from the day he had stacked the gold pieces in front of her, and so she knew that his steady calmness was not assumed, that he was not worried over the outcome of tomorrow morning's encounter.

Her thoughts raced back to her first meeting with him, when from this same veranda she had seen him standing on the lawn in the light from the ceiling lamps, the dark foliage behind him, a romantic and formidable figure in his picturesque garb; seeming, to her startled senses, to have suddenly stepped from another world. Now he was here again, a gentleman. Undeniably a gentleman. Moreover, a handsome gentleman. Yet strangely, as she looked at him now, the sensations of her first meeting with him were revived. The quickened pulse, a sudden confusion of her senses through which flashed a dismayed realization that this man was master of himself and would, if she did not repulse him, ultimately become *her* master. She had promised Weldon she would be gracious to him, but she knew graciousness would lead to surrender. And she would never surrender to a Yankee.

"You like to fight, don't you?" she said.

"No."

"Yet you have fought."

"Yes."

"And you will fight Asa Calder tomorrow morning?"

"Certainly."

"You will be careful, won't you?" she almost whispered. Strange. She did not want Calder to hurt him, yet she herself wanted to hurt him, to punish him for forcing upon her the startling fact that she loved him, that she did not want him because he was a Yankee, and that she was jealous of Allie Tuttle.

"I may promise that, I think," he said. He was thrilled over her sudden concern; his hopes were aroused by the absence of disdain in her voice, in her eyes, in which he was certain he saw real anxiety or apprehension.

"Please do," she insisted. "And you must remember that when Calder fought my father, he fired before the word was given."

"Yes," he said; "I'll remember that."

She moved to the rail of the veranda and stood there, almost breathless, confused by the tumult of emotion her whispered words to him had evoked.

"Do you still have my photograph, Mr Stoddard?" she said. Firmly, she thought. But she was not quite convincing. He had detected a significant hesitation in the question. He was master of himself, but he could be stirred by hope.

"Yes," he said.

"You have it with you now?"

"Yes."

She had only wanted to know if he still treasured it. If she now permitted him to keep it she would tacitly confess interest in him. She turned to see him standing close, smiling at her, and only her knowledge that he was a hated Yankee kept her from answering his smile. He looked very handsome, standing there, steadily watching her.

"It was intended for my uncle Pierre. You have no right to it. Please return it," she said.

Once more he detected a hesitant pause between her words and he slowly shook his head.

She said tauntingly, "Yet you look like a gentleman. Are you one?"

"Perhaps not. But I think a gentleman may treasure a photograph."

"And will return it when requested to do so."

He sighed—smiled. But he made no effort to return the picture.

Now as these two faced each other in a clash of wills the girl once more felt the unyielding quality of the man. True, he was romantic. Deeply disturbing was his appeal to the wildly turbulent longings which frequently seized her—emotions which had not responded to the gallantries of half a dozen unnamed young gentlemen or to the serious courtship of the stern-faced Evan Weldon.

Yet as he stood there faintly smiling, confident that she did not really wish him to return her photograph, she was remembering certain incidents of the past. She would never forget them. The terrors of the invasion of the South by the Northern armies, the destruction the invaders had accomplished, the desecration of peaceable homes, the cruelty, the relentless and ruthless slaughter. These things were her memories, shadows of the past which could not be forgotten. Standing close to her was Stoddard, a vital and attractive figure, yet foreign and strange against the background of the life she had known. Her own war sacrifices, which were many, she could have forgotten, but she could never forget the victims of the horrible conflict: the young men she had intimately known; friends and acquaintances, schoolmates whose bodies had been blasted by Northern gunfire. Randy McMillan's empty sleeve; David Elliot's legs—both gone—which, she vividly remembered, had been long and straight. Keene Abbot's face, mutilated so that she did not recognize him; Oran Stillwell's wounded spine. Oran had always made her think of a bird with a broken wing. The widow Seeger's two sons, Will and John, human wrecks who had dragged themselves home from a Northern prison camp, racked by lung trouble. They lived in the back country, their mother supporting them. At Vicksburg, at Gettysburg, at New Orleans, at Richmond—over the entire South—were scattered the dead and the maimed. And into the South's atmosphere had swept a shocked silence—the silence of surrender and defeat, a still shuddering horror over the price the South had paid for its devotion to a principle.

It was hard for her to understand how the people of one section of a nation could engage in war against the people of another section. None of the arguments she had heard had explained it or would ever explain it to the people of the South. Yet out of the confusion and chaos one truth had gradually developed. That slowly but inevitably the national character had become divided by an invisible line drawn across the states, separating the North from the South, and that out of this division had grown two national characters, each separate and distinct, Puritan and Cavalier, the Stern and the Gay.

Because he was a Yankee Stoddard brought these memories vividly back to her. And because they came, and would not be banished, even though she tried not to think of them, they became a barrier against which her emotions beat in vain. And after he left her, to face Calder in the duel which would take place the next morning, she sat for a long time in a chair on the veranda, crying, hoping he would kill Calder.

CHAPTER NINETEEN

The dueling ground selected by Evan Weldon was half an hour's drive down-river at a place called Council Grove, to Stoddard merely a name, but to Weldon and Forbush and Calder and Chandler's citizens a rendezvous which in years gone by had been the scene of peace conferences between white men and red. It was where, Weldon told Stoddard, Asa Calder had killed Marie Villers' father.

Judge Marston's carriage drew up at the front door of the Planters' House shortly before dawn, Weldon in the front seat with the driver, Judge Marston occupying the rear. When Stoddard appeared, as he did almost instantly, the judge and Weldon alighted to greet him and changed places when they re-entered the carriage. Stoddard was dressed in his cowboy clothing, with a gun in the big holster and another, exactly like it, stuck muzzle first into the waistband of his trousers. He smiled faintly at the set, grim faces of his friends, causing Weldon to remark: "You have slept well, at any rate. I wonder if Calder did." As the carriage left the Planters' House Stoddard saw Allie Tuttle at a window. Her face was pale, but she smiled and Stoddard answered. At the edge of town, upon a terraced street in the residential section, the carriage stopped to take in a black-garbed man who had been waiting on the porch of a house and who was introduced to Stoddard as Dr le Cler. As the doctor seated himself he glanced sharply at Stoddard, who was facing him, and smiled approvingly.

"You look fit," he said.

The carriage rolled up the wide undulating roadway back of town, went past the Villers' house and the judge's and then sank to a low country where tall trees arched over and a mist from the river floated in to dampen the gumbo road. After several miles of weaving and turning through the timber they surmounted a knoll and there was Council Grove, and in it an empty carriage and some riderless horses. Near the carriage stood a group of men talking. They were facing the Stoddard party. Behind them, through the trees, flowed the turgid waters of the Mississippi. The grove was ominously quiet and solemn, as all such places should be, and the faces of the men who gathered here were solemn, too, as if the reputation of the grove affected them. Asa Calder was there striding back and forth at a distance; and Forbush, who did not take his gaze off Stoddard; and two other men, friends of Calder.

All were gravely polite, and they spoke in hushed voices as they gathered together to complete the final details of the coming tragedy. It seemed that, after all, Forbush was not to be Asa Calder's chief second. The change had been made at the last moment by Calder himself, just as the carriage carrying him and his party arrived at the grove.

"Marblay will act as my chief second," said Calder, looking straight at Forbush. "If you acted for me I should be continually thinking of your damned 'possibilities.'" Which proved, of course, that Calder was even then thinking of them.

And now Forbush stood in the background of the group listening. But he heard very little. He was intently watching Stoddard, and often as he stood there his right hand came up and meditatively caressed his chin. A duelist himself, he was more interested in the principals than in the conditions under which they were to fight. Conceding neither principal would fire before the word was given, the victor would be the man with the coldest nerve and the surest aim. Calder had lost his nerve. The suggestion about "possibilities" had affected him as Forbush had known it would. Calder had not known about Forbush's ambitions. Now he suspected, yet the prospect of Calder's death was not affecting Forbush as it should. Yesterday, facing Stoddard in the Planters' House, a fearsome sensation had crept over him, and with it had come a stealthy curiosity, an insidious urge to watch Stoddard carefully in the hope that the man might betray a fault which, later, he might turn to his own advantage. His own conduct while on a dueling ground awaiting the word had always been a matter of great interest to him. Witnesses to the killings he had perpetrated had frequently complimented him upon his complete lack of nervousness. Yet sure as he had been of himself, he knew that he had always been nervous. And he had always been able to detect signs of nervousness in an adversary. A pallor or a twitching of the lips. A rapid blinking of the eyes, an uncontrollable impulse to walk about or to impatiently move the feet or hands. Stoddard did none of these things. He had given Evan Weldon the guns he had brought—huge weapons with highly arched stocks and long barrels—and now, while awaiting the completion of the details, he was standing near the judge's carriage talking with the judge's Negro coachman. He was actually smiling at something the coachman said.

"Of course, as the challenged party, my principal has the choice of weapons," said Weldon. "He chooses those to which he is accustomed." He held the two huge weapons out for inspection. "They are identical. Mr Calder may have his choice of them."

"Egad!" ejaculated Calder's chief second. "They are as big as siege guns!"

"And as deadly," Weldon assured him.

"But they are strange to us, sir," protested Calder's second, who was Marblay.

"But no stranger than yours to my principal," said Weldon.

"It is a terrible weapon," mused Marblay. "I've not seen its like."

"A Texas pistol," said Weldon. "It is called the 'Peacemaker.' A single-action weapon of 45 caliber. The cylinder holds six cartridges, but at each shot the hammer must be lifted by using the thumb. It is the same as the ones you have, sir, except that it is of larger caliber."

"Mr Calder's weapons are 32 caliber," said Marblay. "The recoil of your principal's weapons would disconcert Mr Calder should a second shot be necessary."

Weldon smiled. He said evenly: "The meeting may be avoided by an apology, sir."

Marblay flushed. "I am certain my principal will make none," he said. "May I permit him to inspect one of Mr Stoddard's weapons?"

He talked with Calder and returned to the group to announce that with Mr Stoddard's permission his principal would use one of his own weapons. Now Weldon approached Stoddard to make known Calder's request. Stoddard nodded as he continued his conversation with the coachman. Forbush's face grew as white as his ruffled shirt bosom. The man was an iceberg.

As finally Stoddard walked to the group and stood in front of Weldon, accompanied by Calder, Forbush again watched. Once more he marveled. Calder was pale, with lines around his mouth, but Stoddard's color was the same as when he had been talking with the coachman, and a trace of a cold smile seemed to lurk about his lips.

"Gentlemen, you are to stand back to back," instructed Weldon. "You will then cock your weapons. You will each take ten steps forward as I count. At the word 'ten' you will halt. Your weapons shall be at your sides, the muzzles pointing downward. As you stand in that position, your backs to each other, I shall begin to count again. I shall count one—two—three. At the word 'three' you will turn and fire. If a second shot is necessary you may fire at will—if your opponent is still standing. That is the agreement."

As the men stood back to back where Weldon placed them, the gentlemen attending them ranged alongside, Stoddard's friends on one side, Calder's on the other. Forbush moved closer to Stoddard than to Calder, for it was Stoddard in whom he was interested. Now, if Stoddard had a weakness, Forbush would detect it. But there were no signs of a break in Stoddard's calm naturalness. He stood at ease, with a sort of lazy grace, in sharp contrast with Calder, who was stiffly rigid, his shoulders square. When Weldon had placed the men back to back there had been an instant when their bodies had touched. Immediately Stoddard moved away from Calder, and by that action Forbush judged Stoddard's contempt of his opponent.

The big gun—the Peacemaker—in Stoddard's right hand seemed to dangle from his fingers, so loosely was he holding the stock, while Calder's knuckles showed white with the firmness of his grip. Intently Forbush watched both men as, at the word from Weldon, they cocked their weapons. A flick of the thumb, a metallic click in the silence, and the hammer of Stoddard's gun had been raised as it still dangled at his side, while Calder lifted his weapon breast high and used both hands. The difference in technique of this simple operation startled Forbush. Somehow Calder's method seemed awkward and antiquated. Moreover, Calder's way of cocking his weapon was also Forbush's way. A trifling thing, but it gave Forbush a creepy feeling of inferiority, for it emphasized Stoddard's familiarity with firearms.

Forbush had killed many men in duels and he was cold to the prospect of witnessing Calder's death, so that he was able to watch this scene in comparative calm, to observe and comprehend the significance of every move and action; yet when at last under Weldon's direction the principals began slowly to walk away from each other, Forbush was not thinking of Calder at all but only of Stoddard. The figures of all the other men faded from the scene; they were there, acting their parts, but he did not see them. True, he was curious about Calder; he knew Calder would not fight fairly, that he would shoot before the word was given. He had always done that and he would do it this time. Calder was tricky, but after today he would cease being anything.

Forbush was fascinated by Stoddard's method of handling his huge weapon. He still held it loosely as in response to Weldon's slow counting he stepped away from his opponent, and when ten such steps had been taken, and Weldon paused before beginning anew, Forbush, his gaze upon Stoddard with a fixed concentration that excluded all else, saw Stoddard's fingers close upon the stock of the big gun. So far there had been no flaw in Stoddard's manner or movements. There had been no jerky motions; his muscles seemed to flow to his bidding. There was no sign of excitement in his eyes, no passion, only intent alertness.

Weldon's pause grew long. Someone breathed heavily, stiflingly, and Forbush's muscles leaped convulsively as the word "One" came from Weldon's lips, and Forbush realized that it was his own breath he had heard. He saw Stoddard's knees bend a little. He wondered at that, nursing a furtive hope that this was the weakness he was looking for, but when he observed that Stoddard's shoulders had dropped slightly, he knew that the man's muscles, as alert as his mind, were preparing themselves for a sudden turning of his body.

"Two!" called Weldon.

There was a slithering sound as Weldon's voice died on the word, a concerted gasp of astonishment. That would be caused by Calder, turning before the final word. But Forbush did not look at Calder, for Weldon's startled voice had explosively called "Three", and Stoddard was moving. A flowing muscular motion, coordinated and instantaneous. As he turned to face Calder the big gun swung around, came to a sudden stop at his hip and crashed thunderously from that position, belching fire and smoke from his waistline up to Calder's chest. Then Forbush saw Calder—saw him as the heavy bullet from Stoddard's big gun tore into him. Calder's body jerked convulsively and he pitched forward, face down, into the grass of the grove, his pistol popping futilely and harmlessly as his dead finger pressed the trigger.

Forbush stood staring, listening. Evan Weldon stared at Stoddard, who stood there quiet, the big gun dangling from his fingers.

"Damme," gasped Weldon, "he turned before I gave the word!"

CHAPTER TWENTY

Calder's seconds as well as Stoddard's, and Dr le Cler, had seen that Calder had sought to take unfair advantage of his adversary. Calder's gentlemen were crestfallen as they, together with Stoddard's friends, gathered near Calder as Dr le Cler turned him over upon his back and deftly closed his staring eyes. Chief second Marblay's face was flushed with embarrassment; he did not look at the other gentlemen. But he spoke to Weldon.

"I'm sorry, sir. I had not anticipated this. I did not think it of Calder. He was a damned coward, sir. Believe me, sir, when I tell you that if I had known what was in Calder's mind I should not have acted as his second."

Weldon bowed politely, grimly. "It would have made no difference if Calder had anticipated still another word, Mr Marblay. He made the mistake of underestimating his opponent, as did we all. We have witnessed a demonstration of a new shooting technique—a new style of fighting."

"Also a superb exhibition of marksmanship," interjected Dr le Cler, looking up. "The bullet went straight through Calder's heart. He never knew what happened."

"What did happen, sir?" asked one of Calder's friends. "I saw it, of course. I saw Calder turn before the final word, and he should have got in the first shot."

"Calder was merely old fashioned, sir," said Weldon. "He followed a dueling code which has been in effect from the time firearms were invented. Progress killed him. Calder could not hit anything unless he deliberately aimed his pistol. He thought Mr Stoddard would also have to deliberately aim. The old code is outmoded."

The gentlemen were astounded. They stood, now, looking at Stoddard, who was removing the spent cartridge from the cylinder of the Peacemaker and inserting another. Forbush stood a little apart, still watching Stoddard. He had sought weakness and had found perfection, and the shock of his discovery had drawn the blood from his face, which was gray. Stoddard had holstered the big gun, and Judge Marston and Weldon were crowding around him and congratulating him. The Negro coachman of Judge Marston's carriage was grinning broadly, and as Weldon gripped Stoddard's right hand he saw that a change had come over Stoddard. In his eyes was the steely cold of the fighting man and a glint of machiavellian and swashbuckling humor. A devilish gleam, thought Weldon.

"Egad!" ejaculated Weldon. "You are meditating mischief."

"I'm thinking of symbols," whispered Stoddard. "Symbols of war."

"Damme!" exclaimed Weldon, baffled.

"And of challenges to the enemy. In less than an hour the country will know what has happened to Calder, and people will wonder what boots he wore in walking to his death. By inverting them, according to the plans you have laid for his swamp henchmen, we shall declare open war. It's time, isn't it?"

Weldon stared. "Damnation! An idea!" he whispered delightedly. "Stoddard, I knew mischief was breeding in you." He turned to Judge Marston, who had been standing near, mystified by this whispering; spoke rapidly to the judge, whose eyes leaped with interest. Standing together, the two watched Stoddard, who strode to where Calder was lying and called sharply to the judge's Negro coachman.

"Jabe! Come here!"

Jabe's grin faded, but he answered obediently: "Yas suh."

"Remove Mr Calder's boots," ordered Stoddard as Jabe came up.

"Wh-a-at?" gasped Jabe.

"His boots, you black devil. Instantly!"

It was in the minds of Calder's gentlemen to protest, for they stirred nervously, sullenly, but when Stoddard turned a cold eye upon them they permitted Jabe to remove the boots, which he did, fearsomely.

The faces of Calder's gentlemen, including Forbush, betrayed blank stupefaction as they watched Jabe, still pursuing Stoddard's orders, carry the boots to the judge's carriage and deposit them therein. Stoddard bowed stiffly to the gentlemen and turned to Forbush, who continued to stare at him. Stoddard did not look at Forbush, but it appeared that he critically studied Forbush's boots, turning his head this way and that, as if estimating their size and quality. Forbush's gray face grew grayer. And then, abruptly, Stoddard turned from him, joined his friends and walked with them to the carriage, not looking back.

Not until they were on the road and well on the way to the judge's house did anyone speak to Stoddard.

"Sir," said Weldon then, "permit me to compliment you on your choice of boots. I venture that Forbush is at this minute shaking in his."

CHAPTER TWENTY-ONE

Singularly, although age and senility enveloped it all, a primitive atmospheric aura hovered over the land—over the swamps, out of which floated the odor of dead frogs, fish and snakes, bearing a suggestion of the malarial gloom of their depths; over bog and morass and swale and into fertile lowlands where the white cotton blossoms nodded serenely out of reach of flood waters. It went into the hills and beyond them into far reaches of country; indeed, they went together: ancient nature, primitive atmosphere and primitive man—nature hard, secret, darkly threatening; man hopefully founding his habitations. Along a gumbo road, at night darker than dark and wriggling like a huge water moccasin bellying across drift silt, could be found man's handiwork—shacks, hovels of cypress logs, rough hewn, with slabs of cypress for their roofs. As if to mock man's efforts, desolation had crept upon these shacks. Forlorn things, sagging and dilapidated. Dozens of these hovels dotted the landscape. They were in ravines, upon hillsides, upon islands in the swamps; here and there a few of them were crowded together, forming a settlement. The nucleus of such settlements was always a store—a structure not more pretentious than the hovels surrounding it, but stocked with sufficient goods for the community's needs.

The road, narrow, its surface rubbery to the naked feet of a bearded man who was walking upon it, wandered away eastward from the great bend in the river where the Clara Belle had grounded. The road was not always a road. Many times, between the man and the river, it became a quagmire, or a morass, or a bog, depending upon how deeply the water from the adjoining swamp had overflowed it during the last rainy period. The man had emerged from a dull wall of timber skirting the swampland. Wisps of green slime clung to his toes as he strode along the road, and after a while the slime dried into a gummy mass which he removed with his fingers. His garments flapped loosely as he walked, carrying an empty sack over his shoulder.

Still about two miles from the nearest settlement, which was known as "Yancy's", he turned from the road into a hard-trodden narrow path which led into a swale and thence to a hillside where in front of a particularly squalid shack a man—his counterpart—was leaning against a rotted paling of a tumble-down fence. Behind the shack a slatternly woman in a faded calico dress was chopping wood with a rusty ax, while near her some scraggly chickens hopefully scratched and fluttered. A razorback hog in a pen raised his head at the visitor's approach, and some thin angular shoats took fright and plunged into the shelter of some chinaberry bushes. A hound dog, lying at the feet of the man at the fence, cocked a knowing eye at the man approaching his master; a slab-sided cow with a flabby udder and a sullen, apathetic mule with washboard ribs missed a mouthful of browse in their interest.

" 'Lo, Clell," greeted the man at the fence.

" 'Lo, Dex," said the visitor.

The woman gave them an incurious glance as she picked up an armful of wood and carried it into the house, while the owner of the shack led his guest to some rickety wooden steps at the front door, where both men seated themselves in lazy, ruminative fashion. The sun was high over the great swamplands, and the overhanging mists of early morning were clearing away, changing the dull tones of the timber, bringing a delicate green sheen to the cypress fronds weaving a maze of crisscross limbs against the sky.

"Goin' to Yancy's?" asked Dex.

"Yup."

"What fer?"

"Pervisions."

"Ain't bin in yere fer over a week, hev yo'?"

"Nope."

"Money run out yit?"

"Not yit."

"Sho. Ef hit was only a mite yo' shore hev hung on to hit. Ef hit was a lot yo' ain't squandered none. How much did Burleigh give yo' fer sendin' help to him?"

"Mighty little."

"Yancy was sayin' he changed a twenty-dollar gold piece fer yo'. Yo' call thet little?"

"I'll bust Yancy's face offen him!" threatened Clell.

Dex grinned slyly. "Yancy didn't say nothin'," he said. "But yo' gittin' mad proves yo' got thet much outa Burleigh." He eyed Clell reprovingly. "Yo' didn't even fetch a bottle of likker."

Clell grinned as if relieved. "I air aimin' to buy likker. I'll buy hit at Yancy's effen yo' come along with me and fetch yore mule to tote my pervisions back to the boat."

"Hit air a barg'in," said Dex. He roused himself from the stupor into which he had apparently fallen, got up, yawned, stretched himself and went to the rear of the house, to reappear presently leading the mule by a halter. He stopped at the front door and bawled: "Yo' wantin' ary thing down to Yancy's, Em?"

The woman appeared in the doorway, to glare suspiciously at both men. "Yo' kin git a sack of corn meal and some salt," she said. "But effen yo' come back yere stinkin' o' likker and shootin' off yore gab I'll peel yore hide offen yo'!"

Clell and Dex and the mule drifted down the path leading to the road. They talked as they walked, but suddenly into their voices had come an undertone of concern. Not concern over what Em had said, however, but over something which they had not dared to discuss within hearing distance of the woman.

"Hev yo' heerd any more?" asked Dex as they reached the road and began to walk along it toward Yancy's, leading the mule.

"I hev. Las' night jest afore dark I was asettin' back thar on the road by them big syc'mores, dryin' my boots, when Forbush come along on thet big bay of hisn which he keeps at Kello's place. He was headin' fer up thar, whar the Burleigh gal is. Hit's sho 'nough true. Calder's daid. Forbush was kind of skeered like, seems. While we was talkin' he seen my boots. He jumped so thet he darn near fell offen his hoss. 'Hell and blazes!' he said, not bein' able to see very good in the dark, 'What in tha hell hev yo' got thar?' My boots, I sez. 'Yore own boots or somebody else's?' he asts. 'Put tha damn things on!' he told me. Fust time I evah heerd of a man gittin' skeered of a pair of boots, and I laffed and tol' him so, sayin' thet ef hit wasn't fer wearin' boots, the cottonmouths would hev had me afore now. 'Thar's somethin' wuss than snakes wrigglin' around this kentry now,' he sez. 'They're men. They kill yo', take the boots offen yo', turn 'em upside down and stick 'em—one or tother of them or both—on stumps of saplin's, or fence palin's, or somewhar whar they kin be seen right off, puttin' a sign on 'em which tells the man's name, an' adds thet the river pirates hev to git out or die. Underneath it sez, 'The Riders.' "

"Thet means us," said Dex.

They walked slowly, their faces lugubrious.

"Calder was kilt two weeks ago, fightin' a dool with a feller named Stoddard," said Clell.

"The feller thet kilt Joe Fowler!" said Dex.

"The mornin' efter tha dool Calder's boots was stickin' on tha co'thouse fence in Chandler, with a sign on 'em like what I've tol' yo' about. But no Riders kilt Calder. It was Stoddard. And Forbush sez Stoddard is still hangin' around Chandler, and thet it couldn't hev bin him thet kilt all the others and hung their boots up."

"Others!" exclaimed Dex, his mouth opening and staying open.

"Six more, 'cordin' to Forbush," said Clell. "One up on the Yallobush, one at Big Crick, two at Yazoo Pass, one near Black Bayou an' one at Victoria."

"I ain't seen no Riders," said Dex, staring fearfully back.

"Ner me."

"It must be Riders, ef the signs say so," reflected Dex.

"I reckin. What I say is thet I ain't seen no Riders."

" 'Pears nobody ain't seen none," said Dex. Both men stopped and stared into the timber. "No Riders could hide up thar," Dex added.

They turned to stare up the swale past Dex's shack and beyond, where a wavering ridge threaded the lowlands and finally vanished into infinite space. "They could hide up thar," said Clell. "But thar'd be tracks. I ain't seen no tracks."

"Thar ain't no Riders around yere," said Dex. "Nobody's bin kilt yere."

They moved on down the road, discussing the sinister news.

"Effen my boots is anywhar, I want to be in 'em," said Dex.

"Them thet was kilt was all with us the night we burned the Clara Belle," Clell stated solemnly.

"How did the Riders know how to pick out the ones they kilt?" asked Dex.

"I ast Forbush thet. He didn't know," answered Clell. "Thet Burleigh man didn't see nothin', 'cause he was layin' on the deck with his haid busted. The gal seen somethin', 'cause most of us was in her room, lookin' at her. But she ain't tol' nobody what she seen."

Half a mile from Yancy's timber and swamp and road bulged north to encroach upon a level formed by the floor of a ravine between two flat ridges. Ravine and level were covered with a rank growth of native Mississippi bottom trees and brush. Here, because the rays of the sun had not yet penetrated, reigned a sepulchral gloom. Swamp water licked at the edges of the road, dampening it. The mule halted to test the swamp water. Before drinking he wisely pawed the earth at the water's edge and stared down into the water, fearing the dreaded cottonmouth.

"How was they kilt?" asked Dex, pursuing a thought which had remained with him.

"They was shot."

"Then they was found o' course."

"O' course. They wasn't fer from their boots."

"Seems . . ." began Dex. His mouth popped open; his eyes bulged. He was staring at the rank bottom growth that fringed the north side of the road. "What's them?" he gasped.

Clell also stared. His muscles jerked; his lips worked soundlessly.

Two sycamore saplings, not more than an inch in diameter, growing side by side, had been broken off about a yard or so above the tips of the lush green growth around them. Upon the boles, inverted, their soles and heels facing the sky, were two leather boots, worn and scuffed. Suspended from the boots by a piece of rusty wire was a slab of cardboard such as might once have formed the lid of a box. Upon this was written in crude but legible black characters the words: "Jim Nailor. His boots. River pirates, get out or die! The Riders."

Shortly, at Yancy's, two shaken creatures in loose, flapping garments were standing at the plank bar drinking great quantities of vile swamp whisky. Although the day was comparatively cool, they were perspiring freely, and they stared at each other with bright questing eyes in the depths of which lurked haunting terror.

CHAPTER TWENTY-TWO

The appearance of Asa Calder's boots upon the courthouse fence, fronting the square, where they were seen and inspected and commented upon, startled Chandler's best citizens into the realization that finally something was to be done—indeed, was being done—about the river pirates and the other desperadoes. That Calder had been associated with the evil element had long been suspected, for as a lawyer Calder had often appeared in court to defend accused members of the swamp clan and various criminals of the water front. Often he had quarreled with Judge Marston, and once, shortly after he had murdered Marie Villers' father, he had been heard to threaten the judge with a like fate. Friends of Marie's father had agreed with Judge Marston that various notes and mortgages, presented at the trial, involving the Villers' property were forgeries. Seizures of the titles to homesteads and estates were defended by Calder, who in court had produced deeds to the disputed properties, which the victims of the seizures declared were stolen. It was suspected that the juries which invariably returned verdicts for Calder's clients were heavily packed with Craftkin's friends—Craftkin, known land-grabber, who always claimed the titles. So when Calder's boots appeared upon the courthouse fence, together with the printed warning, there were grim smiles and congratulatory whispers exchanged by the best citizens, while among the worst citizens lurked a disturbing presentiment of further trouble.

Stoddard, still staying at the Planters' House, was accorded flattering attention, which he ignored, together with hostile surveillance, which amused him.

Colonel Burleigh had regained consciousness, to find that his legs were paralyzed, even though his mind was unimpaired. His torture over the fate of his daughter continued. Listening to him, with Evan Weldon standing by, Stoddard told Weldon of his determination to search for the girl.

"I know how you feel, sir," said Weldon. "But please don't try it. The country into which they have taken her is nearly all swamp. You would get lost in there and you would never get out. We have two hundred men in there now, and every man knows the country. They will break up Vauchain's clan if they have to kill every member of it. Already reports have been drifting in to me. They are making progress. They have traced some of the Clara Belle's supplies, which were widely distributed. In one week they have killed half a dozen of the swamp men. They are patient, thorough and merciless, for they are all people who have been dispossessed by the outlaws and they are merely taking their revenge, which they have a right to do. They will find Clara Burleigh, if such a thing is possible."

"If the devils haven't killed her," groaned Colonel Burleigh.

"I have hopes that they may be holding her for ransom, sir. They have spies here in town, and everything that happens is reported to Vauchain. I feel that the story of your rescue has reached Vauchain, and as he is known to be a mercenary creature, there is a chance that he may spare her the fate other women have suffered at his hands."

Colonel Burleigh writhed, and Stoddard, who could not bear to witness the man's agony, turned away and went to a window, the very window through which Allie Tuttle had smiled at him on the morning he had left the Planters' House to go to the dueling ground. Allie had been at the same window when he returned, and had smiled at him again, knowing by his appearance that he had been the victor. She had not been visible to him when he reached his room that morning, but when, after discarding his cowboy clothing for the garments which had so startled her, he returned from breakfast to find her in his room, she was ecstatically hugging the big gun which she had taken from its holster, holding it tightly to her breast, her cheek caressing it, her hands fondling it. She heard him at the open doorway and quickly hid the weapon in the folds of her dress, to gaze at him defiantly, though her face was crimson.

"What were you doing with my gun, Allie?" he said, trying to be severe.

"I were huggin' it."

"Why, Allie?"

"Because it killed Asa Calder—the derned devil!" She dropped the gun upon the bed and fled from the room, fearful that if she stayed he would see the truth in her eyes—that she had not caressed the gun because it had killed Calder, but because it had kept Stoddard from being killed.

Unobserved, because she was concealed behind a giant honeysuckle vine which twined around one of the heavy columns of the Villers' veranda, Marie saw the Marston carriage as it went to the dueling ground, and for an hour she stood there almost motionless, awaiting its return. When she saw it again, with Stoddard in it, talking animatedly with the others, and Jabe grinning broadly, she sank into a chair and sat there trembling. Later that day, when she learned from Evan Weldon the details of the duel and the grotesque incident of Calder's boots, a pulse of vindictive triumph shot through her, but she said quietly: "I must thank Mr Stoddard."

"We must all thank him, I think," said Weldon.

"Yes," she whispered. Her eyes baffled Weldon. In them was something clouded, quiet, intent, remote, as if some thoughts of hers, half formed, were troubling her. She was wondering about Stoddard.

"Evan," she said, "do you know why he killed Calder?"

"Because Calder challenged him."

"Not because of what Calder did to Father?"

"No, Marie."

"I am glad of that," she said.

The half-formed, nebulous thoughts had become whole and crystal clear. If she loved Stoddard she wanted to love him because of himself. Nor was her decision weakened by the fact that after his duel with Calder her friends had accepted him and did their best to entertain him, though one night, watching him as he danced with Anne Randolph, she thought she knew why her circle had been won by him, and why Anne so ecstatically danced with him. There was no mistaking Anne's excitement. Twice thereafter Marie saw Stoddard coming toward her, and each time, dismayed by the knowledge that she wanted him to come for her, she evaded him by accepting another partner—once, when he was dangerously near, by whirling upon the dance floor with Estelle Buchanan. At last, however, as she was talking with Evan Weldon, she saw him coming once more. And this time there was no escape, for with an acquiescent bow, following Stoddard's formal request and Marie's equally formal acceptance, Weldon delivered her into his arms.

He danced well and would have danced better if she had permitted her body to harmonize with his. But the thought of surrendering to him, even while dancing, was intolerable, and she was like a wild creature, captive, struggling for freedom. Twice during the dance she looked into his eyes, to be startled by the knowledge in them, an awareness of the turbulence in her—a kindly and tolerant knowledge, with regret lurking in it. Her own were defiant, reflecting her resentment. Striving against the resentment was curiosity, which would not be denied. She knew so little about him, and at the end of the dance, when they went out upon the veranda for a breath of air and stood in the darkness near the railing, with the lights of the town below them, her mood was almost gay. But he was quietly thoughtful. He was watching the lights of a steamer traveling up-river, though his thoughts were of her, of her treatment of him. He had seen how she had evaded him tonight. And there was her resentment. The signs were unmistakable. He had been a fool for pursuing a romantic impulse, but he was not fool enough to believe that he could win the love of a girl who disliked him and who permitted him to dance with her only because he had performed a slight service.

"The river is beautiful at night," she said.

"Yes."

"You like it—don't you?"

"Yes."

"Because it is big or because it is beautiful—at night?" she said, studying his profile, for he was still watching the lights of the steamer.

He said laughingly: "Because it's wet. It's water. I've always liked to look at water. I even like the swamps."

"I remember. We spoke of this before. It was when you brought the news about Uncle Pierre. Do you remember?"

Yes, he remembered. He was certain he would never forget. He was still watching the steamer.

"Yes," he said.

"If you like water, why did you stay out there so long—where it is so very dry? Ten years," she added.

So she remembered. That made him wonder, and he looked at her, but the darkness was so dense that he could not see her face. She was a presence only. She could see him, though, outlined against the moonlight that flooded the river; a tall and vital figure; a man she did not yet understand, who stirred her, even while subtly offending her. He was so quiet, so positive and cold. Killing Calder had not bothered him. He had not even spoken of Calder. She doubted that he even thought of Calder. He was deliberate and merciless, and yet he had been romantic enough and impulsive enough to render her a service at the risk of his life, and to carry with him, next to his heart, the photograph of a girl he had never seen. Vaguely she now understood him and herself. Marching back through the years, her thoughts lingered upon the history of another Civil War, in England; upon the bloody fields of Naseby and Marston Moor, where the Stern and the Gay had slain each other because racial differences had been steeped in the chimera of superiority. Two centuries later the racial streams had flowed across the Atlantic; the Puritan reaching the cold climate of the North, the Cavalier sweeping into the savannas, to found his domain along the limpid rivers and in the fertile valleys of the Louisiana Purchase. Generations of racial instincts and the traditions of a people who had sought the warmth of a smiling climate were shaping Marie's thoughts as upon this veranda, overlooking the tawny waters of the great river, she watched the big man from the North who represented the ancient enemy. She should not have danced with him, but she had. She should not now linger here, hating him, yet she did so, wanting to, regretting that presently she would have to go. Traitor to her memories, disloyal to her people, she remained, fascinated, wanting to know more about him. While she had been thinking, he had answered her question, saying that he could give no reason for his stay in the dry country.

She said softly: "Were you born in the West?"

"No."

"In the North, I expect."

"No."

Ten years. "Weren't you homesick for your people?" she said.

"No."

Shocked, she stared at him. "Why?"

"There were no folks to go home to," he said. "There haven't been—for more than ten years." He laughed, but something in his voice made her think of how it had been with him through those empty years, and she was suddenly sorry for him.

"I think I know how you feel," she said. "The death of a loved one leaves us with a desolate sense of loss. A terrifying emptiness. I felt that way after Father was killed."

Here, after all, was a link between them. He had thought there could be none. A frail bond, but it had brought him a kind and understanding word, and a gentleness which seemed to envelope him, startling him because of its unexpectedness. A light from inside the house suddenly shone upon them, its soft radiance bathing her face. A thrill stirred him, sending a tingling tide of warmth through him—an exhilaration he had never known. He conquered it, but not until it had given him a flashing realization of the depth of his passion.

He was so close to her that he might have reached out and touched her, and almost he did so, so deep was his intoxication. But he resisted the impulse, remembering her hostility, her reluctance to dance with him. Fool, once more. Her present gentleness was natural human sympathy merely. He could not presume upon that. It was not the kind of thing he wanted.

He turned again to watch the lights of the steamer, now diminishing, blurred by distance. If he had not turned away from her at that instant he would have taken her into his arms. Not understanding her, knowing she did not like him, he had almost yielded to an overpowering impulse to take her against her will. His love for her was as resistless as the mighty waters of the big river on its slow journey to the sea, his passions as deep. The analogy furnished him with a flash of ironic amusement. Helplessly he had been caught by the irresistible charm of her; her vivid beauty, her quiet, cool voice, her eyes that sometimes danced as the river danced with the sun glinting upon it. He turned toward her and he was never certain afterward whether Marie moved ever so slightly closer or whether his arms reached out and drew her to him, but she was there, and the wonder of it brought a swift maddening intoxication upon him.

Holding her thus, passive in his arms, he looked down at her, losing himself in the clear, deep pools of her eyes, fighting against something he did not fully understand. It was as if he held within his arms a priceless treasure which could never belong to him.

He bent his head slowly. His lips met hers fiercely, hungrily. For a long moment he held her so, and then his head lifted, his big arms released her and fell to his sides. Marie did not move; she remained standing close to him, her eyes upon his, sobering him with the intensity of their contempt.

Words came to his lips and died there. He saw Marie step back a little, saw her lips part, heard the lashing scorn of her soft laughter. His face paled, and his lips drew into a straight line.

And her voice, low and guarded, as if she wished no one but him to hear, came to him from an incredible distance, full of derision and bitter mirth.

"Perfect, Mr Stoddard, perfect! Your darling of the swamp has taught you much. But she should have taught you that changing the garments of a plainsman does not make him a gentleman!"

He took a quick step forward; his big hands seized her arms, drew her roughly to him. His eyes flamed, and she saw the corded muscles flex along the hard line of his jaw. Her own eyes widened; wonder and a little fear crept into them.

"Allie Tuttle is honest," he said, shaking her a little as if to make her understand. "She expresses the things she feels. I do not love her, but I do admire her. She is brave. I love you, and I'm ashamed of it. But I can't help it. You've got yourself steeped in the damned foolish traditions of your beloved South until you can't realize that the rest of the world may have some virtue too. You're a narrow minded, bigoted little fool with an ingrained pride, and you will never be a real woman until you get the pride knocked out of you!"

He was gone, striding away across the moon-splashed veranda, a clenched fist swinging at his side.

CHAPTER TWENTY-THREE

Beyond Yancy's—where Clell and Dex had sought refuge from their terror—beyond the end of the gumbo road, deep into the far-spreading reaches of the giant alluvial valley of the Father of Waters—a mighty lowland watershed whose rivers roamed sluggishly out of their beds to seep and trickle into adjacent swales and valleys, submerging the land until they covered everything but the knobs of the hills, stagnating there to create miasmatic vapors and green slime and hoary moss and dank green vegetation—the wilderness realm extended. It went into forests, where the water lapped the exposed roots of giant cypress trees, their green fronds curtained by gray festoons of Spanish moss; it stretched into bog and bayou, into the dark gloom of unexplored recesses, where a threat, somewhere lurking, held a foreboding and brooding secret purposefulness.

Today the threat rode with Forbush, accompanying him, following him, closing in around him when, threading a precarious way through the sodden country, he halted for a moment at a swamp hovel and spoke to its occupants—a gaunt man whose wife and children watched him from a doorway and a window. Dozens of times in his two-day ride Forbush had talked with swamp men, riding far out of his way for that purpose, into settlements; once skirting the edge of a cotton plantation on higher ground—a lordly place boasting a giant cotton gin and a great white house which looked down in placid contempt upon the squalor and poverty of the swamp people. The house was so distant that it appeared merely as a vision, however, but even there the all-pervading threat lingered, becoming sentient and articulate when he talked with a group of swamp people who preyed upon the cotton fields.

"Thar's somethin'," said one man. "A ha'nt or a hex mebbe. Hit hain't nothin' we kin see. We don't know whut hit is or whar hit comes from."

"Hit kin write," whispered another. "And hit kin drive a knife powerful hard and shoot a gun. We find a dead man, knifed or shot, and thar's his boots, and a card with writin' on hit, tellin' his name."

"Hit hain't always boots," volunteered a third man. "Weems and Bixby weared moccasins. They was a card on them too. We're gittin' skeered. Yestiddy Mose Bolan loaded his traps on his mule and went north, sayin' he wasn't comin' back."

With unvarying uniformity the tale was repeated. Forbush's two-day journey extended to four, for everywhere it was the same—the swamp men terrorized, inactive, reluctant to leave their hovels, refusing, singly, to traverse the swamps. They were certain that the sinister enemy was a supernatural force. "Yo' cain't fight nothin' yo' cain't see," declared a hollow-eyed denizen. They shook their heads forlornly when Forbush assured them that the enemy was human. Panic had gripped them. There was talk of an exodus.

Leaving his horse upon an island in the swamp, Forbush pushed on, in a punt poled by a swamp man, to the edge of a black bayou perhaps a mile wide where two swamp men, in the gray of Confederate uniforms, barefooted, hair long, black and matted, bushy bearded, were perched upon the huge roots of a cypress tree, fishing, their lines dangling from crude poles. Behind them was the huge swamp through which Forbush had come, ahead of them was the black water, and then the opposite shore of the bayou, rank with swamp growth and deadfall. Over there, gleaming like an emerald set in debris, under high-towering trees and the inevitable moss veils, was a clearing and a cabin, the cabin to which Clara Burleigh had been taken following the burning of the Clara Belle.

Not since Stoddard had stared at Forbush's boots, after removing Calder's, had Forbush suffered a twinge of fear. Amazement, together with swift apprehension, had stirred him upon hearing the evidence of the Riders' swift attack, but fear, such as he had felt in Stoddard's presence, had not come to him from any other man. So now, feeling a certain way about Vauchain, whom he had always hated and never feared, despite the Leopard's merciless and brutish ferocity, his gaze was level with design and his lips tight with determination as, his punt floating toward the fishermen, he watched the emerald clearing.

The punt bumped soddenly against the cypress roots and moved lazily there as Forbush looked at the two fishermen, who greeted him with familiarity flavored with respect. Their faces, like those of the other swamp men Forbush had met, were long and solemn, their eyes furtive. Yes, the stories of the finding of boots on the Yallobush, at Yazoo Pass and at the Black Bayou were true.

"Back thar, under the willers," said one of the fishermen, shuddering. "Hit were Ed Vassey."

"What is Vauchain doing about these killings?" said Forbush.

The man grinned wryly, showing yellow teeth in an aperture of his heavy beard and mustache. "Him?" he answered. "Nawthin'. Nobody's seen him closet sence the Burleigh gal was brought hyar."

Forbush drew a deep, lung-swelling breath, which he seemed to hold, bated, while his face whitened.

"Where's he been?"

"In his shack with the gal. Thar's been high jinks over thar. Lights at night, and the Leopard singin'. The gal wailin' and cryin'."

"Damnation!" cursed Forbush, expelling the breath he held.

"Twice the gal tried to git away," continued the fisherman. "The fust time she got into the swamp 'fore he ketched her and brung her back a-clawin' at him. The next time she got as fer as the tother edge of the clearin' when he ketched her and toted her back. Thet time she was nakid. Sence thet happened nobody's seen her."

The punt rocked from the convulsive movement of Forbush's muscles. Then it floated motionless, as Forbush, rigid and pale, stared at the emerald clearing.

Under Forbush's orders the boatman swung the punt about and poled it along the shore of the bayou to the emerald clearing, where Forbush stepped out, telling the boatman to wait there for him. Then Forbush, with the boatman lounging in the punt, watching curiously, strode slowly toward the cabin, rounded a corner of it, where, unobserved by the boatman, he stood while he drew a heavy revolver from the waistband of his trousers, under his coat, and examined it, raising the hammer of the weapon to a full cock. One could never be certain about Vauchain's moods, and Forbush's hatred of his chief was deep and bitter.

He listened but heard no sounds except the gentle lapping of the water against the cypress roots and the soft rustling of the leaves in the slow breeze, the peculiar rasping and fluttering of the moss curtains glowing silver like in the sunlight, and from somewhere the song of the cardinal. The gloom of swamp and forest was heavy with the odor of decaying things, yet permeating the stench was a refreshing, lingering and permanent aroma, the pungent and pleasing scent of growing cypress.

Hoary moss grew in the chinks of the cypress logs that formed the walls of the cabin. Moss and logs were dripping with the dampness of the night mist which was now rising and disintegrating in the sunlight. The cypress slabs forming the roof were obscured by a fleecy white mist that writhed and undulated. Forbush's boots made no sound in the spongy soil as he moved to a heavy plank door in the front of the cabin and knocked upon it.

"Come in," growled a voice—Vauchain's.

In a massive chair, facing the door, which Forbush left open as he entered, was Vauchain. He was short, broad, heavy, powerful. His legs, extended as he reclined in the chair, were encased in knee-length black velvet breeches and silk stockings, tight fitting, revealing bulging muscles. He wore dark moccasins with broad laces. There were silver buckles at his knees, and at his waist a broad leather belt from which, upon the left side, its black stock protruding, was suspended a long-barreled pistol of ancient design. From a sheath in the velvet breeches on his right thigh extended the haft of a heavy knife. He wore no upper garments, and his naked torso, browned by wind and sun, was sheathed with great muscles which looked tough as leather. His round head, with black bristling hair and prominent ears, was set upon a bull-like neck, and his wild appearance was emphasized by flaring nostrils, small, round, glittering eyes and a wide loose-lipped mouth. Secret, mocking mirth was in the glance he gave Forbush, but guarded watchfulness was there, too, and suspicion.

"Avast there, mate," he said thickly. "So you've come snooping at last?"

Drunk and dangerous was Vauchain. Often drunk, always dangerous, with a violent temper, a beastly and inhuman disposition, and bloodthirsty impulses. Forbush knew these things, yet he did not fear Vauchain, and Vauchain knew that Forbush did not fear him. He knew, too, that Forbush hated him. Away back it had started, away back at the beginning of their acquaintance, in the Caribbean, around Jamaica, on the decks of pirate ships, spawned in jealousy, distrust and lust for power. Hatred, governed by respect. Forbush, too, was dangerous. A worthy enemy, not to be held lightly.

"Not snooping, Vauchain," said Forbush softly.

"Damme, no! Never that. But you're here, blast ye! And what for?"

"To inquire about the health of the lady I sent to you—to care for until I came."

Vauchain shook with laughter, uproarious and somehow obscene, his lips loose, his stomach heaving. Yet his eyes did not laugh or squint. They were bright and piercing and hooded with the guarded watchfulness of reptilian malignance.

"The lady?" he said. "Gadzooks, you did send her! A beauty too. A stubborn wench, though, sirrah."

"She seemed not so to me, Vauchain. Upon the wagon seat she snuggled up to me quite trustingly."

Vauchain chuckled. He was hugely amused, but not for an instant did he cease watching Forbush.

"You've treated her well, I hope," said Forbush, equally watchful, his voice low, his gaze level.

"Damme, yes! As well as you would treat her, if not better."

So now, knowing Vauchain, Forbush understood what his treatment of Clara Burleigh had been. But he smiled, not wanting Vauchain to know that he understood. It was not yet time. There was Vauchain's pistol, close to his hand, and the long knife, which Vauchain could throw with lightninglike swiftness.

The hatred between them, never fully betrayed, always glossed over with exterior politeness, which both knew as mocking pretense, would become open and deadly only when they knew there was no other way. There was no other way now. Vauchain knew it, and Forbush knew it. Forbush had sent Clara Burleigh to Vauchain, to shelter her until Forbush should come. He wanted her, and Vauchain had taken her. Atavistic impulses governed both men; primitive lusts beat in their brains and made of the girl a primal urge. Inflamed by desire, hating murderously, they, each with his own craft and cunning, sought to postpone the inevitable clash until one or the other, the fortunate one, could seize upon an advantageous moment.

The morning sunshine came through an open window and beat upon the earthen floor. Its light disclosed a litter of uncleanliness as it revealed the chinked walls, faintly green with moss; the cobwebbed rafters of the roof; a rusted stove in which there was no fire; a crude plank table, a cupboard, some cooking utensils and rickety chairs. There were two rooms in the cabin, as Forbush knew: the room now occupied by Vauchain and himself, and a bedroom reached by a flimsy door in a partition composed of cedar poles loosely constructed, the interstices plastered with gumbo mud which had hardened to a repulsive grayish black with scrofulous patches from which the mud had flaked and fallen to augment the litter upon the floor.

Beyond the flimsy door was Clara Burleigh. Forbush was wondering about her; and Vauchain, with his secret knowledge of what had happened to the girl, was enjoying Forbush's wondering, knowing that in the end he would go to her, for that was why he had come, and why, for an instant, his gaze had strayed to the door. Almost, in that instant, Vauchain had grasped the advantage he sought, and his hand had moved stealthily toward the stock of the ancient pistol. Slight as the movement had been, Forbush had detected it, and now the hand was motionless, and Vauchain glared his frustration.

"A door, Forbush. A door leading to my bedroom," he said, his manner smoothly unctuous. "She's in there. Go in and see her if you like."

Forbush laughed, with his lips making a straight line for the sound to come through.

"My impatience needs discipline," he said. "And my passion for her will be strengthened by delay." It was his way of telling Vauchain that he did not contemplate offering his back as a target.

Said Vauchain tauntingly: "So the lion's teeth have been drawn? Or perhaps the beast is toothless from age. How those despoiled husbands would enjoy you now, Forbush! And gloat over you, forsooth."

So Vauchain gloated, thought Forbush. He said steadily: "The lion is not judged by the jackal, Vauchain." He bowed from the hips and with the movement swept aside the coat that concealed the heavy revolver in the waistband of his trousers. His right hand gripped its stock and drew it suddenly backward so that it lay tight against his right hip, the long barrel horizontal, pointing at Vauchain's chest.

Startled, Vauchain thought there would still be time, for Forbush's gun would have to be lifted to the level of his eyes before he could take the necessary aim, and the ancient pistol was coming out when Forbush's weapon, still at the latter's hip and still horizontal, roared with reverberating thunder and belched its heavy bullet into Vauchain's naked chest. Stark incredulity stared from Vauchain's eyes, savage triumph glowed in Forbush's as, seeing how the ancient weapon in Vauchain's hand drooped floorward in his loosening fingers, he sent another bullet tearing into Vauchain's now quivering chest, and another and still another, until the mammoth body sagged inertly and the staring hooded eyes could see no more. And then, after calmly reloading the weapon and critically watching Vauchain, Forbush opened the flimsy door and peered into the bedroom.

Clara Burleigh was lying, rigid and still, in the bed, the pallor of death on her face. Forbush did not go into the room then, for he heard a whisper behind him and turned his head to see that Vauchain's lips were moving. "Swamp fever, it was," he was saying. "Swamp fever."

CHAPTER TWENTY-FOUR

Death had been the victor, leaving to Forbush the mystery of what had preceded it. Vauchain's last breath may have been given to the utterance of a mocking jibe, designed to stab Forbush with a jealous doubt or to express derision. The girl was dead though; there could be little doubt of that, for she was rigid and cold to Forbush's touch, even though, as he peered intently at her, she seemed merely to be sleeping. Her eyes were closed—Vauchain had probably done that—and there were no marks of violence, no marks at all.

Forbush turned away from the bed to see his boatman standing in the outside doorway—through which Forbush himself had entered—staring curiously at him. The boatman had seen Clara Burleigh, for his eyes were wide with a sort of horrified inquiry.

"Daid?" he whispered.

"Yes," answered Forbush.

"The Leopard too," said the boatman, staring at Vauchain. "Yo' shore busted him, didn't yo'? I heerd the shootin'."

There were now other sounds to hear, and Forbush heard them. Likewise the boatman. The splashing of water as of poles being furiously wielded, the bumping of boats against shore obstructions, and voices, chattering and shouting. The swamp men had heard the shooting and were coming to investigate. Presently there were several of them at the doorway, peering in, wide eyed, craning their necks as they sought to visualize the details of the tragedy.

Grimly standing there, confronting them, Forbush offered no explanation, though he implied dire consequences to all of them.

"Clara Burleigh's dead," he said. "We've got to get her out of here and bury her where she can't be found, or we'll all lose our boots. And keep your traps shut. Nobody knows anything. You've never seen the girl or heard of her. Understand that?" He broke in upon their chattering, telling them to scatter to their retreats. "Two of you get Vauchain out of here and bury him. You"—pointing to his boatman and another swamp man—"take the girl in your boat and hide her so deep in the swamp that nobody will ever find her. A day's travel. I'll go alone."

Except for the four designated to remain, the swamp men vanished, scampering hurriedly as if fearing the immediate vengeance of the mysterious Riders. Forbush stood in front of Vauchain, mocking him.

"Swamp fever, eh?" he said.

He strode to the door, paused there, looked back at the swamp men, who were already beginning their appointed tasks, stepped out and was gone. The clattering of a pole against a boat, and a swishing of water, told the men inside that Forbush was leaving them.

Forbush's boatman—a tall straight man with a short bushy beard, long hair, and black eyes of a peculiar piercing coldness—was wrapping Clara Burleigh's body in all the available bedclothing. He was doing this alone, having sent his companion to the shore of the bayou to prepare the craft in which the body was to be carried. Nor did he require any assistance from his companion after the body had been prepared. He lifted it, carried it through the partition doorway and thence through the outside doorway to the boat, into which he stepped carefully, finally to let himself sink slowly to the bottom of the boat near the bow, his burden in his arms. His companion—who was known as Snakehead, probably because of the peculiar shape of his brow and the grouping of his features, which caused one to think instantly of a pit viper—pushed off and began to pole the craft along the shore line of the bayou and finally into the slimy waterways of the swamp.

After the boat had penetrated into the swamp for a distance of a hundred yards it would be no longer visible to anyone who might have been watching it from the shores of the bayou. Snakehead plied the pole indolently but skillfully, occasionally darting glances at the boatman—whom he called Arkansaw—and at Arkansaw's burden. Snakehead's eyes were veiled with something he did not wish Arkansaw to see, for he never looked fully at the latter and seemed, as he poled the flat-bottomed craft farther and farther over the gloomy water aisles, to be enjoying an orgy of evil thought. Like the other swamp men, he was bearded and had scraggly uncut hair. He wore moccasins, flapping trousers and a tattered shirt, a belt, and a long-bladed, big-hafted knife in a sheath at his right thigh.

"Curious way to tote a corp'," he said after poling the craft for upwards of two hours.

"Yup," said Arkansaw. "I'm a-pityin' her sorta."

"The Leopard didn't pity her none," laughed Snakehead.

"I'm afeered not," said Arkansaw.

"Yo're afeered, air yo'?" Snakehead grimaced hideously. "Whut fer air yo' afeered about whut heppened to her? Nawthin' thet heppens to them air rich nabobs is wuth gabbin' about."

"Maybe she war'nt a rich nabob," said Arkansaw.

"War'nt, eh? Wal, she war. The Clara Belle was stinkin' with money. Silks and velvets and silver trimmin's and sech."

"Yo' didn't see hit," scoffed Arkansaw.

"I shore did. War'nt I thar, helpin' the boys to raid hit? And war'nt I one of them thet teched a fire to her? And now we're puttin' the gal whar nobody won't see her no more." He ceased poling. "We've come fer enough," he said. "Let's chuck her in thet bed of rushes over thar. Nobody won't know the difference. I got a flask of likker. We'll drink hit and loaf the rest of the day."

"I aim to do as I'm told," demurred Arkansaw.

Snakehead worked the punt to the edge of a small island which was carpeted with dead and rotted leaves through which grew etiolated swamp weeds, barren mulberry bushes and lacy ferns. Some deadfall was there, and a huge cypress log, polished by the elements until its surface was smooth as glass. Its roots, dragged out of the earth by the tree's fall, reared high, grotesque, bleached white, like the skeleton of some prehistoric, tentacle-appendaged monster. Spanish moss trailed down from the living trees.

The punt grounded at the edge of the island, and Snakehead rested and waited, looking at Arkansaw. "I don't aim to do no more polin'," he said. "Effen yo' don't hanker to put the corp' in them rushes, yo' kin dump her out on the island whilst we stretch our laigs and drink our likker. I'll hold the boat till yo' git out with the corp'."

Moving carefully with his burden, Arkansaw stepped from the punt to the low-lying land, carrying the blanketed body to the log, where between some upthrust roots he balanced it so that it would not fall off. When he turned, after completing this task, he saw Snakehead, standing at a little distance, drinking deeply from a heavy metal flask and peering curiously at him as he drank. Snakehead brushed his lips with the back of one hand as with the other he presented the flask to Arkansaw. "Hev a drink," he invited. "Hit's tol'able good likker."

Arkansaw drank, grimacing.

"Yo' ain't used to drinkin' likker," said Snakehead. There was the glimmer of incipient doubt in his eyes, and he stood there, hands at his sides, studying Arkansaw. "Don't they drink likker whar yo' come from?"

"Shore. Some do. I ain't got no stummick fer hit."

"Yo' got stummick to tote a corp' in yore arms," stated Snakehead. "Yo' wropped hit up with beddin'. Yo' bin nigh a-huggin' hit. Whut fer did yo' do them things?" Snakehead's doubt had become suspicion, and his right hand, which until now had been idly hanging at his side, crept up a little along his thigh, the fingers spreading, gliding to a point over the haft of the knife protruding from its sheath.

"I cain't tell yo' why I don't like likker," said Arkansaw, slowly backing away from Snakehead. "But I'll show yo' why I wropped the gal up and why I bin totin' her so keerful. Yo' stand thar a second." And Snakehead, his thoughts diverted from the knife through his suddenly aroused curiosity, permitted his gaze to rove from Arkansaw to the swathed bundle on the log.

Arkansaw continued to back away from Snakehead until at last he stood beside the body. There, still facing Snakehead, he ran a hand into the folds of the bedclothing. Then he stood motionless, his eyes gleaming with mocking coldness. Snakehead was watching for the withdrawal of the concealed arm and did not look at Arkansaw's eyes.

"Whut yo' gittin' at?" he whispered huskily, suspicious again.

"She's alive, Snakehead."

"Whut!"

"Yup," said Arkansaw. "I knowed hit when I was wroppin' her up, thar in Vauchain's shack. I leaned clost to her and felt her breath on my face."

"Why didn't yo' tell Forbush?" said Snakehead, his veiled eyes glittering with a new suspicion, half formed, wondering.

"Because I'm going to take her back to her folks, Snakehead."

"Yo're whut!" gasped Snakehead. He was seeing a new Arkansaw. Not a swamp man. He had heard a different voice. Not using the drawling idioms of the swamp, but the sharp, crisp, confident words of an outsider, an alien, a dreaded secret enemy of the swamp clan. His evil eyes bulged with sudden terror. He stared wildly, with dawning despair, with furtive hope, at the punt and into the gloomy and dismal water channels of the swamp.

"Look at me, Snakehead," said Arkansaw, and Snakehead saw a long-barreled pistol in Arkansaw's right hand, which he had drawn out of the bedclothing in which Clara Burleigh's body was wrapped and which he had placed there while Snakehead had been poling the punt to this point, having drawn the weapon from the folds of his shirt.

The big gun roared. A knife, weakly thrown, flashed past Arkansaw. The big gun roared once more.

In that heavy atmosphere, water-laden, with dripping mists of vapor swimming low, there was no echo, no reverberation, and silence instantly swept in heavily, as before. Arkansaw stood watching. A long time. Listening. When at length he restored the pistol to the folds of his shirt he turned and looked down at the bundle on the log, carefully pulling aside the bedclothing until Clara Burleigh's face was exposed. Bending over, he placed his face close to hers and listened. She was breathing. He smiled as he pressed her eyelids back and saw them close again. A faint pink tinge of color stained her cheeks, and he stooped and picked up Snakehead's flask, uncapping it and moistening the girl's lips. The swamp liquor, though vile, had a stimulating effect, and after an hour of continued effort he saw the pink in her cheeks deepening and spreading and her breathing becoming more regular. Another hour passed, and still another, while he spent part of his time forcing drops of the liquor into her mouth and the rest of it away from her. At last, on one of his trips, he stood back and surveyed his handiwork.

Upon two small parallel limbs of a dead tree he had placed two moccasins, which he had removed from Snakehead's feet, tying them to the limbs of the tree with pieces of wild grapevine. On the white polished bole of the tree itself he had written in black characters: "Snakehead. His moccasins. River pirates, get out or die. The Riders."

He heard a rustle and saw the bedclothing move as he leaped toward it. Clara Burleigh's eyelashes were fluttering, and her lips were working soundlessly. He got a few more drops of liquor into her mouth and smiled happily as her eyes opened and gazed into his with dull and puzzled incomprehension. As he watched he saw horror there, fading gradually as she continued to look at him.

"Oh," she whispered shudderingly, "you are not—not Vauchain! Who are you?"

"A friend, Miss Burleigh," said Arkansaw. "You're safe now. I've come to take you back to your father."

For another hour, hopefully, her eyes glowing as she watched Arkansaw's face as he whispered to her, comforting her, reassuring her, she rested there on the log. Then, feeling that she was strong enough to travel, Arkansaw took her into his arms, her body no longer rigid but limp with relaxation, and carried her to the punt, placed her in the bow with the bedclothing wrapped snugly around her, stepped into the stern, pushed the craft off and poled it swiftly away.

CHAPTER TWENTY-FIVE

The grounds surrounding the Villers' home were more calm than their owner when at dawn she awakened quickly, having slept very little, to gaze perplexedly out of the nearest open window of her bedroom, to wonder what had changed. Apparently—outside the window at least—the bright morning was the same as other bright mornings, full of aromas, sunshine, peace and the twittering of birds. Not until she remembered what had happened to her the night before, when Stoddard had kissed her, did she realize that the change was in herself. Anger perhaps. Something unusual and stirring. Gazing at her reflection in the big mirror of her dresser, she saw that her cheeks were flaming, and that the crimson stain deepened when she became conscious of it.

Frowning when she appeared in the breakfast room an hour later, in a white summery frock with a ruffled skirt, short puffy sleeves, tight bodice, and low square neckline, she was astonished to discover that the breakfast room looked different. Even Hester, her black servant, a former slave, now free and more devoted than ever, seemed different. She stood in the kitchen doorway grinning admiringly, her ample bosom swelling, her white teeth gleaming.

"Lawdy, Missy Marie, yo'-all looks go'gis dis mawnin'. What happened to yo'-all?"

"Nothing, Hester."

Hester shook her crinkly head in puzzled disbelief. "Somethin' shuah heppened," she muttered to herself over the stove in the kitchen.

Equally observant, but more discreet, was Anne Randolph, when she rode into the Villers' yard in the Randolph carriage later in the morning to greet Marie. Anne was a quiet girl, tanned, freckled, good looking, with a wholesome charm of manner that made you unaware that her nose might be a little too uptilted and her mouth a trifle large. Her eyes held you. Gray tranquil eyes, with depths unfathomable, flooded with lazy humor and knowledge.

The Randolph carriage contained many packages and parcels, and this store was augmented by other bundles and packages and parcels brought out by Hester and Marie. At least once a week, perhaps oftener, Marie and Anne made pilgrimages into the back country to visit the most helpless of the human wrecks spewed out of the carnage of war as so much debris.

"I'm taking Oran Stillwell that pipe he wanted," said Anne, studying Marie's eyes and deciding they veiled something. "And a pound of his favorite tobacco." . . . What had happened to Marie? . . . "I had to send to Vicksburg for the pipe," added Anne, and while the Negro coachman turned the horses, and Marie checked off the various articles piled about them in the carriage, Anne's quiet eyes were observing the queer tightness around Marie's mouth—an expression which always appeared there when Marie was provoked to indignation.

To reach the road that would take them into the back country they had to pass Judge Marston's house, and they saw the judge near the gateway of the drive, weeding a bed of roses. He came forward when the carriage stopped and eyed the ladies judicially—and approvingly.

"You'll spoil those boys yet," he declared. "At first it was only a few things, mostly necessities. Now I'll wager these packages contain luxuries."

"You don't spoil them, do you, Judge?" said Anne.

"Why, no. Of course not."

"Yet I've often heard that wine is a luxury."

"And a medicine too," defended the judge.

"True," said Anne softly. "The older the better. So you gave them your vintage of 1826, musty and cobwebby. Medicine of course."

The judge blushed.

The road they were to take led downward through the judge's plantation and beyond to a lowland country into which, far away, merged the slope of an upland where the road made a wide sweep around the base of a small hill. Marie detected movement there and looked inquiringly at the judge.

"Weldon and Stoddard," he said. "Back in there somewhere they are to meet Galt and some of his riders."

Marie's face paled, but instantly the color surged back into it, and Anne smiled as she pretended to be interested in some packages in her lap. She bent over them, feeling Marie grow rigid. So it was Stoddard who had brought the blushes and the provoked tightness of Marie's lips. What had Stoddard done?

Anne liked Stoddard and from the first had defended him against Marie's prejudices. In the early days—particularly when she had accompanied Marie to Vicksburg—she had wondered how Marie could so steadfastly dislike Stoddard. Stoddard could have captured Anne, and no prejudices or foolish sentiment about the war would have marred her surrender. But of course Anne did not want Stoddard if Marie wanted him. She knew Marie loved him. Moreover, she knew that Marie knew she loved him and that she was fighting valiantly against admitting it, even to herself, stubbornly calling upon her racial pride whenever there was a possibility that love might win. In Anne's mind there had never been any question that love would win. She knew that Marie would fight resolutely; that storms of emotion, tragic enough, would shake her, but that in the end she would surrender. Therefore, as the carriage went down the road toward the back country and Marie pretended a lack of interest in Stoddard and Weldon—although occasionally she glanced at them as they rode far ahead of the carriage— Anne was enjoying her friend's agitation.

"Evan likes Mr Stoddard," said Anne.

"Does he?" said Marie. She seemed to stiffen defensively. And Anne persisted.

"Haven't you noticed it? Evan is always with him. And Colonel Darcy likes him too. Do you know that after the party at Colonel Darcy's home last night the gentlemen demanded that Mr Stoddard appear before them all to respond to a toast, and that, when they searched for him, he was nowhere to be found. Colonel Darcy was greatly disappointed."

"Colonel Darcy is too effusive."

"Why, Marie! He's an old darling. And he isn't the only one who likes Mr Stoddard. He has become very popular. They all appreciate what he has done. Mary Littlefield is wild about him."

No answer from Marie. She had never liked Mary Littlefield.

"He dances beautifully," said Anne, adding: "Marie, you danced with him, though it seemed you didn't like to. Didn't you want to dance with him?"

"Certainly not."

"But you did."

"Because I couldn't help it. It was Evan's fault."

Marie glanced sharply at Anne. She was suspicious of Anne's persistence, but Anne calmly continued: "They are whispering that there is a mystery about him, Marie."

"Any stranger is mysterious, Anne," said Marie.

"I think I know what you mean. If a stranger doesn't talk very much people begin to wonder about him. That makes him interesting. Women want to know what he is thinking about. Well, he is mysterious in that way too. Nobody knows anything about him, except that he brought your uncle Pierre's belongings here and that he is a friend of Judge Marston and Evan Weldon. And people are talking about how, quietly, he has forced some of the most notorious waterfront criminals to leave town. They were afraid of him. Two or three times they have tried to kill him."

Marie caught her breath and sat very still. Apparently unaware of Marie's agitation, Anne continued.

"Evan has had two or three men follow him whenever he goes out on the streets after dark. But that isn't the mystery. Marie, Colonel Darcy is president of the Planters' National Bank, as you know. And Colonel Darcy says that Mr Stoddard is not a poor man, as all of us thought. He is something more than a mere cowboy or a peace officer. I can't give you any details, for Colonel Darcy didn't mention any, but his credit at the Planters' National is practically unlimited."

"The possession of money doesn't make up for his faults," Marie said.

"What faults?" asked Anne, pretending to inspect the string on a package.

"He isn't a gentleman," declared Marie.

Anne did not ask Marie to explain, for the tight lines were again around Marie's mouth. Stoddard's kiss had not offended her as much as she had led him to believe. It had thrilled her, and even now she could remember the turbulent deliciousness of it, her wild impulse to return it, and how hard it had been for her to pretend the scorn and contempt she had employed to save her pride, and to show him that his ruthlessness was objectionable to her. But his words, after kissing her, had rankled. "I love you, and I'm ashamed of it." The words, short, sharp, crisp; his voice, expressing contempt. She would never forgive him. And Anne, feeling there was something here that she did not understand, wisely became silent.

The carriage rolled on through the great lowland country, and several times Anne stole glances at Marie; wondering, curious glances. For a change had come in Marie, in her appearance and manner. The blushes no longer stained her cheeks. Her color was normal. The tightness around her mouth had disappeared, and a smile lurked there. And in her eyes was arrogance that Anne knew well.

It was something that could not be settled by evasion or equivocation. Diplomacy would not work, and procrastination would be futile. Sooner or later Marie would meet Stoddard—a meeting which now seemed unavoidable—and then, facing him, she would talk to him straightforwardly—as she should have talked after he had delivered himself of his opinion of her. She also had an opinion—of him. All night, sleeplessly, with his kiss on her lips, resisting all her efforts to erase its memory, she had formed opinions of him—all of them confusing, none of them complimentary. Vainly, though, she had tried to solve the mystery of her feelings toward him. And now, watching him as he rode a little distance ahead of the carriage, she was conscious of a breathless ecstasy; the emotion that all night and this morning had revealed itself in her blushes—which she knew Anne had seen and interpreted. But Anne, of course, could only interpret what she had seen. She could not possibly know that the stormy indignation Stoddard's words had aroused had become a cold, calm, though vindictive, determination to hurt him, and the change Anne had seen in her grew more noticeable until at last, reaching a place where another road angled off into the low country toward some timber miles away, where the edge of the great swamp lapped the higher land, Marie was almost sedate when she saw Stoddard and Weldon waiting there. But there was an ominous flash in her eyes which caused Anne to catch her breath with a sudden divination of what impended.

"Poor Stoddard!" thought Anne as, both riders facing the carriage, one on each side, she greeted them:

"How fortunate!" she cried. "Now we'll have company on our visit to the wounded veterans—and perhaps a party at Stillwells'."

Stern-faced Evan Weldon seemed distressed and shook his head negatively and somewhat grimly.

"It desolates us to decline, ladies, but it is impossible. We have work to do."

"With the swamp people," said Anne, her eyes suddenly solemn. "What a beautiful horse!" she exclaimed, looking at Weldon's mount. "Why, it's Polestar, isn't it?" There was a flutter of skirts and a slithering of parcels and packages, and then Anne was out of the carriage and at Polestar's head.

Stoddard had halted close to the carriage, quite by accident on Marie's side, and he was wishing he could change places with Weldon, for he found himself gazing into two pools of implacable wrath in which floated—or seemed to float—little flecks of contemplative derision. It came as something of a shock to him, to see her sitting there so quietly calm in spite of the wrath in her eyes, steadily watching him, seeming, as she looked him over from head to heels, to be seeing him for the first time and disapproving what she saw.

"It's Mr Stoddard in a new role," she said when Anne and Weldon had passed by and out of hearing distance. "Last night the sighing lover, today a bepistoled killer. One can not anticipate your moods, sir." Her rippling laugh and low voice were ineffably mocking.

"Or a lady's temper," he said, gravely bowing to her.

"We learn, it seems," she said dryly and looked him up and down once more, as if making mental note of the details of his garments. Her gaze lingered upon his boots, soft topped, high heeled, with small roweled spurs, noting that the straps were gray, with flat buckles. Also that a rowel on the right spur was broken.

"Vicious to horses," she said; and he, looking at the broken rowel, explained its absence.

"Misjudged again," he said, frowning a little, for he was a trifle uncomfortable under her scrutiny. "A bullet clipped it."

"So you are misjudged," she said. "Well, then, being misjudged, you should hesitate to judge others." She looked at Anne, who was up on Polestar with Evan Weldon, riding slowly away from the carriage, and then back at Stoddard, who was gravely watching her.

"Your wide experience has made you infallible, I suppose," she said with a sigh which almost convinced him that she regretted what she was doing, but which instead had its inception in a glance at his hair—boyishly tousled, for his hat was in his left hand and had been there from the instant of the arrival of the carriage—with a brown sheen in it which had attracted her the first time she had seen him in the daylight, on the porch of her home when he had stooped to pick up her photograph.

"Do you find many people who disagree with you, Mr Stoddard?"

"Certainly."

"And I suppose you shoot them."

She baffled him, but he faced her squarely, respectfully, patiently.

"Not always," he said.

"Ah!" she breathed, smiling faintly. "So some do escape your wrath?"

He was looking at her stubborn chin which, he decided, was only stubborn when its owner was angry. And she was angry now.

"And do you love *your* country, Mr Stoddard?"

"Of course."

"And do you honor its traditions?"

She had puzzled him, but now he understood her and knew the depth of the bitterness his condemnation of her had created. He had regretted his words and the impulse which had driven him to utter them. But the impulse had been provoked by her slighting references to Allie Tuttle, whom he knew to be honest, and who could not conceal her most human traits. A complex girl was Marie Villers, who had made it plain that she did not like him, that she tolerated him only because of Judge Marston and Evan Weldon, and treated him civilly because he had brought her uncle's belongings to her, yet had made an epithet of the term "Yankee" when applied to him. He loved her and would not defend himself.

"I do," he said, answering her question.

Confidently, perhaps hopefully—for she held her breath for an instant—she had expected that when he discovered her purpose he would make an attempt to apologize for his indiscretions. And then, having properly humbled him, she would ignore him until Anne returned to the carriage. But when he continued respectfully to sit there in the big saddle with its high pommel; his tousled hair waving in the slight breeze, his blue eyes perplexed but somehow smiling with patient resignation, she knew that he had not repented.

"Then of course, Mr Stoddard," she said, watching him, wondering when he would betray evidence of being hurt, "you must know that the traditions of your country are foolish—that you are steeped in them. And that, because you honor those traditions, you are narrow minded . . ."

He bowed.

". . . bigoted . . ."

His eyes were still steady, still patient.

". . . and forgetful of virtue. Furthermore, you are a fool with an ingrained pride——"

"I am a fool," he said.

"—and you will never be a real man until you get the pride knocked out of you! And I hope it is knocked out of you, because—because of what you have done to me."

His own words to her, almost. She did not look at him again but busied herself with the packages in the carriage, ignoring him, for he had not moved but sat there looking at her, now realizing how she must have felt when, after forcibly kissing her and telling her he was ashamed of his love for her, he had so ruthlessly accused her. Once again he had acted the fool, and once more his pride, which he had never lost and which, he thought wryly, she hoped would be knocked out of him, asserted itself, perhaps somewhat damaged, and he sat there, silent but strangely unrepentant.

And there Anne and Weldon, returning, found them—Marie busy with the packages and parcels; Stoddard looking at her.

"They've quarreled," whispered Anne to Weldon, who would not have noticed anything. Weldon helped her down from Polestar and stood beside the carriage after she had entered, lingering there. Then Stoddard, seeing Anne and Weldon watching him, bowed to them and smiled. Anne thought he waited somewhat expectantly to catch Marie's eye, but when she continued to sit there, engaged with the packages and parcels, ignoring him, he slowly restored his hat to his head, concealing the tousled hair, which Anne, too, was admiring, tightened the reins, balanced himself in the saddle and urged the horse to where Weldon stood beside Anne.

He regretted leaving them, he said, but certain affairs in town demanded his attention. Again he looked at Marie, but Marie had turned away. However, Anne, struck by a sudden queer pallor on Weldon's face, and a tightening of the muscles around his mouth, and a look of deep anxiety in his eyes—these changes from his steady, calm sternness making him seem years older—was alert. And seeing him draw Stoddard to him to whisper to him, she listened.

"Be careful from now on, Stoddard," said Weldon. "Do you hear, old man? They're moving. They're desperate. Be careful, won't you? And remember what I told you about the swamp sweetheart!"

Stoddard nodded, smiled and rode away toward Chandler. Startled, Anne stared hard at Weldon.

"Is he really in danger, Evan?" she asked.

"Yes, Anne," answered Weldon uneasily, his eyes troubled. "He's been in danger all the time. The waterfront criminals have threatened him. He laughs at them. Anne"—he looked at Marie—"he is the bravest man I ever knew!"

When Weldon rode away, down the lowland road toward the timber, and the carriage continued on its way, Marie sat very still, her face pale, staring after him, thinking of his ominous words, remembering her last words to Stoddard and wishing she had not uttered them.

CHAPTER TWENTY-SIX

In Anne Randolph's mind, back where she stored many fragments of thought which were kept there for her own purposes and never exhibited, were memory images of Marie Villers' character, implanted there during the years of her association with her friend, which now aided her in understanding Marie's attitude toward Stoddard. She remembered Marie's pride in the Southern regiments recruited from the countryside, and how Marie had anxiously sought news of them—to rejoice in their victories and grieve over their defeats—betraying flaming interest in everything that happened along the far-flung battle front; hating the Yankees; pridefully minimizing the South's defeats and magnifying its victories. Burning in Marie in those days was the sustaining fire of racial pride, which was not so strong in Anne, who felt that courage could not be fixed by boundaries or excluded by contempt, even though her prayers for the success of the Southern armies were as devout as Marie's. So Anne, more calm than her friend, was able to banish the deep prejudices which might have shortened her vision and her sense of values and to clearly see into the problem which had confused Marie—pride and prejudice, inextricably interwoven. A passionate belief in self, and a determination to make no effort to understand others.

At the McMillans', where Randy's empty sleeve was seen and the gifts thankfully received, Anne talked very little. Later, when they reached the Elliot place, Anne watched Marie as both girls listened to David Elliot talk about the war, his legless trousers emphasizing the part he had played in it.

"Grape and canister," said David, explaining the incident of the amputation.

"Do you hate the Yankees as much as ever?" asked Marie.

"Sort of gettin' over it, Miss Marie," he answered. "I've had a powerful lot of time to think about it. Them boys didn't aim at me perticler, I reckon, no more than we aimed at a perticler one of them. And it were a Yankee so'jer that found me and helped me. I was surprised somewhat, havin' heerd that the Yankees killed all the wounded."

At Abbots' place, where they talked with Keene Abbot and shuddered over the ghastly scars that disfigured his face, Marie seemed thoughtful and more gentle than usual. She had nothing to say when the carriage left the Seeger home, where Will and John, victims of lung trouble, attributable to the war, were visited. But between the Seeger home and Stillwells', where the road ran down once more to the lowland and drew nearer and nearer to a distant timber line where the girls knew the swamp swept in, Marie said:

"Anne, what did Evan mean when he warned Mr Stoddard?"

Anne's pretense of astonishment seemed genuine enough. Her voice even had a note of gentle mockery in it: "Why, Marie, you don't mean to tell me you were thinking about that Yankee?"

"Not thinking about him, Anne. Just wondering. I couldn't help hearing Evan talking to him. But I couldn't catch his words."

"My gracious, you *seemed* to be listening!"

"I wasn't."

Anne laughed. "What on earth did you do to Stoddard? He looked positively crushed. Tell me, please. I'm dying of curiosity!" Thus, lightly, Anne evaded.

"Anne, at Colonel Darcy's house last night Mr Stoddard did something to me for which I rebuked him, and——"

"He kissed you!" interrupted Anne quietly. "If he didn't he should have," she added instantly and leaned back among the cushions the better to see Marie's face, into which high color was sweeping.

"How did you know?" asked Marie, studying Anne.

"You've been blushing all morning, honey. And you liked it, but you didn't like the way he did it, and I don't blame you. I'd feel the same way myself, yet he's terribly handsome, and I wish he had kissed me instead of you."

"Anne!"

Anne smiled. "You've quarreled with him, Marie. And if you have really sent him away from you, I warn you that I shall throw myself at him."

Anne's devastating frankness was disturbing, somehow, and, at this moment, unwelcome. Deeply troubled by passions which after her quarrel with Stoddard had suddenly become tumultuous, Marie was amazed to find herself on the verge of tears, which, springing from a vague and indefinite apprehension of tragedy that had been coming all morning, was as mysterious as her own feelings and had been deepened by Evan Weldon's ominous warning to Stoddard, which she had heard. Suddenly she realized that words and actions were really not the important things in life; that what you said and did were the negligible expressions of surface impulses and had nothing whatever to do with your real feelings; that you sometimes said things you did not feel, and that regret over saying them could not be assuaged. So Anne's reckless declaration of interest in Stoddard was less disturbing than it might have been, and Marie sat there, her eyes clouded, moist, watching the timber line grow nearer, feeling the breath of the swamp drifting in to mingle its pungent cypress aroma with the clean and sweet-scented atmosphere of the higher country. The nearer they approached the Stillwell plantation the stronger grew her presentiment of the imminence of tragedy, the more disturbing her apprehensions.

"Anne," she said suddenly, repeating a question she had asked before and which Anne had evaded, "what did Evan mean when he warned Mr Stoddard?"

"He warned him about the waterfront criminals and about the swamp people. They've threatened Mr Stoddard."

"Did you notice Evan's face, Anne? He seemed frightened."

"Yes. Marie, he loves Stoddard."

"Yes," agreed Marie. "And he said something about a swamp sweetheart, didn't he? What did he mean?"

"I don't exactly know, honey," said Anne, avoiding Marie's eyes.

"Not Allie Tuttle?"

"Of course not, honey. Why should Evan warn Mr Stoddard about Allie Tuttle?"

"I don't know. It just occurred to me." And in Marie's memory at this instant was the vivid scene of Allie Tuttle caressing Stoddard there on the dock, the day the swamp girl had brought Colonel Burleigh to Chandler. That scene, always present in Marie's consciousness, had troubled her during the night, after Stoddard had kissed her, and it troubled her now persistently. And in spite of Anne's denial she felt Allie was the swamp sweetheart Evan had referred to.

"I do believe you are jealous of that girl, Marie," said Anne, keenly but laughingly watching her friend.

Marie blushed, and Anne felt her suspicion turn to conviction.

"You are," she charged. "You do love Mr Stoddard. And you quarreled with him and sent him away from you."

But Marie was still seeing Evan Weldon's face as he had warned Stoddard, and she was not so much concerned about what Anne thought she had done to Stoddard as she was concerned about what the swamp people would do to him—something they had threatened to do, which Evan knew about, and which was troubling Anne, who would not talk about it.

"Anne, you know who the swamp sweetheart is and you won't tell me," charged Marie.

Anne shook her head.

"It *is* Allie Tuttle," insisted Marie. "And Evan warned Mr Stoddard to be careful of her."

"They won't do anything to Mr Stoddard," smiled Anne. "And perhaps Evan did refer to Allie Tuttle. What of it? Allie can't run away with Mr Stoddard unless he wants her to. And the swamp people wouldn't dare attack Mr Stoddard."

But the swamp people had dared to do other things, Marie knew; things like the burning of the Clara Belle, the abduction of Clara Burleigh and the murder of the Clara Belle's crew. They had dared to do those things, and they had dared to commit other acts of violence, the details of which, now only half remembered, recurred to her.

The carriage now rolled through a stretch of timber close to the swamp, and ahead of them they could see the white walls of the Stillwell home, and at their right the waters of the swamp, glittering wherever the sunlight stabbed through the trees, black in the lurking shadows, somber, foreboding, mysterious, heavy with its horrible secrets.

And now both girls, silent, were staring into the swamp, thinking of Clara Burleigh; and when at last they reached the Stillwell house to be greeted by Hatfield Stillwell, Oran's father, their faces were solemn with the thoughts which the swamp had brought to them.

At every point where the swamp came in it dominated. Monstrous, moist, vapor laden, filled with its ghastly lacing of moss and spreading its interior gloom, it seized upon the smiling lands it touched and built there its bogs, its vile green pools; encroaching upon the lowlands with its protoplasmatic verdure, its slime and its loathsome reptiles. It could not reach the Stillwell house, which was upon an upland in a grove of sturdy walnuts and oaks and hickorys which towered above the native bottom growth and spread a cool shade, which was welcome to Marie and Anne as they sat in easy chairs, brought out to them by Oran's father, and talked with Oran, in his big reclining chair, almost horizontal, which he never left, and watched his face as the gifts they had brought were unwrapped and displayed.

Oran Stillwell had participated in many battles, and he liked to talk about them, which he always did at some length, supplying many gruesome details, his hollow eyes flashing, his voice, during the years gradually diminishing in volume, extolling the heroism and the sacrifices of the Southern armies; Marie listening, responding to the veteran's moods, her color coming and going, her gaze far away, envisaging the distant battlefields. But Anne, not less patriotic, had found Oran's repetitious descriptions somewhat monotonous, and latterly she spent a great deal of her time with Mrs Stillwell—Oran's mother—in the spacious kitchen of the Stillwell house, talking about recipes and needlework, and indulging in trivial countryside gossip.

Now Marie was alone with Oran, and the veteran was at Missionary Ridge, where in his recital the Union and Confederate forces were locked in a bloody, stubborn struggle. The battlefield was a mental one upon which Oran, with the precision and accuracy of memory, moved his regiments and his artillery units with chessboard strategy. Clearly he remembered the regiments, and named them, and the artillery units and the cavalry. As the battle continued to rage, Oran, glancing at Marie, saw the faraway look in her eyes and thought she was seeing his troops and hearing the thunder of his guns. He marked the pallor of her face, though, replacing the flush that had always been there during previous recitals, but he could not know that Marie was not thinking of the battle at all but was staring into the swamp, thinking of Stoddard and of Evan Weldon's warning, and fighting the subtle terror which had been stealing over her all morning and which sight of the swamp had somehow accentuated. She had never liked the swamp. A few times, only, had she been in it, to return solemnly afraid. Huge, silent, mysterious, the swamp had been to her a fixture, a place; visible; its vast reaches to be imagined. Lecherous, its slime and its poisonous vapors, its rotted verdure, its deadfall and its mephitic gloom were things which, once seen and felt, were not to be forgotten. Like the lowlands of the plantations, the forests in the distance, the low hills dotting the countryside, and the Mississippi itself, she looked upon the swamp as being merely a part of the country, and like the rest of it, inevitable and ever present.

Today though, looking at the swamp, she was conscious of a dread fascination; of awe for its magnitude; of a stealthy terror for what it concealed, for the unknown menace it held.

CHAPTER TWENTY-SEVEN

Among the other unpleasant impressions the day had made upon Marie was the distinct shock she had received when Oran Stillwell, finishing his battle stories, had told her that, so far as he could understand the war, the Northern soldiers had exhibited no personal bitterness toward their Southern adversaries, but that they had fought because their government at Washington had decided that only war would settle the controversy about slavery. The Northern white boys were not eager to sacrifice their lives for the black men. Only a sense of duty, and the power of the government, forced them into the slaughter. Underneath, perhaps, lurked national pride and a conviction that the Union should not be dismembered.

"Yes, of course, Marie," said Anne as, riding homeward in the early evening, she and Marie talked. "Oran is right. The Northern boys hated war as much as our boys hated it—as much as we hated it. I'm certain that there never was a war in which the common soldiers fought merely for love of fighting. Many of the soldiers on both sides were forced into war by their governments. Now don't look so outraged, Marie"—as Marie's eyes flashed with sudden indignation and denial. "You know it's true that the South had its laggards, and I'm certain that not all of our boys who faced the Yankee guns did so because they wanted to. There was a great deal of stubborn pride on both sides, Marie."

If Marie thought Anne was being disloyal to the South she did not say so. Indeed, she said very little through the rest of the ride, for the shadow which had run through the day's events seemed to deepen as the day grew to its end. It had started—as all unpleasant mental adventures start—with herself, in her determination to hurt Stoddard. The shadow had been deepened by Evan Weldon's warning to Stoddard and darkened still further by the dismal appearance of the swamp and by her thoughts of Clara Burleigh. If she had succeeded in hurting Stoddard the day would have been pleasant. But she had not hurt him. And now, as she thought of his quiet patience, of the way he had looked at her—his eyes filled with mild wonder and calm resignation—she was almost ready to admit that what he had told her about herself was true. And if he had not told her that he was ashamed of his love for her she might have felt that she had been altogether foolish. All day that one thing had kept her from taking Anne entirely into her confidence.

Dusk was hovering over the country when the Randolph carriage, bearing Anne and Marie, passed Judge Marston's house, and the girls saw the judge standing well back in the grounds in front of the house talking with a grotesque-looking, ragged, bearded, long-haired man. The judge saw them and waved to them, and Anne ordered the carriage stopped, smilingly returning the judge's greeting. Marie, silent and still, did not share Anne's exuberance of spirit, for, with the night coming on, the strange uneasiness that had oppressed her all day was increasing, so that her senses, alert to lurking danger, were acutely conscious of everything that seemed unusual. Sight of the tattered man talking with Judge Marston had startled her; and when, in turning away from the man to approach the carriage, the judge swiftly placed a finger to his lips, as if to enjoin the man to silence, she was certain the man was the bearer of news—bad news perhaps—which the judge would not divulge.

But the judge was smiling as he greeted them, and Marie could see no sign of agitation in his wise, kindly eyes.

"How did you find our friends?" he inquired.

Anne replied that the veterans were doing well.

"And still fighting the war, I reckon."

"They'll never forget it," said Marie.

"That's the trouble with all of us, my dears," said the judge. "We insist upon remembering things we ought to forget. We never forget our tragedies or—our prejudices. But those men, whose bodies were wounded, have some excuse. Perhaps killing the Yankees over again helps to relieve their bitterness. If they get any satisfaction out of it, all well and good. And I sometimes think that the boys—particularly Oran Stillwell—make some concessions to their imaginations."

"David Elliot confesses he is getting over *his* bitterness," said Anne. "And even Oran Stillwell says that there was no personal animosity in the fighting."

"That is promising, coming from Stillwell," said the judge. "Poor fellow! If men like Stillwell—who bear the physical scars—can forget, it rather makes the rest of us—who suffered injuries only to our pride and pocketbooks—seem stubborn, leaving us with only our pride. We must all forget the war, my dears, for we can't fight it over again; and it is foolish to hold resentment. The Lord sent a rainbow to remind us that he held no resentment against us poor sinners, and the South ought to build another— out of forgetfulness."

The judge's philosophy, or something like it, Marie had heard before, but now, somehow, it struck deep and set her to wondering if the judge was right. Looking back, she could see that he had been right many times. But the tattered man disturbed her, causing her to forget the judge's philosophy in a more immediate concern.

"That man, Judge Marston," she said, pointing. "He is a swamp man, isn't he?"

"Yes, my dear."

"Has he brought news of Clara Burleigh?"

"Unfortunately not," the judge said regretfully. He leaned closer to the girls, as if to make certain the coachman did not hear, and whispered to them. His eyes were serious, anxious. "The man in the yard is Crosby Gillis, one of Galt's men. Remember that if his identity is discovered his life won't be worth a picayune. Some news that Evan Weldon must know immediately is being carried by Gillis. Did you see Weldon today, and did he tell you where he was going?"

"We saw both Mr Weldon and Mr Stoddard," said Anne. "Mr Stoddard rode back toward Chandler, and Evan rode down the old Sycamore Road. He didn't say where he was going, but I got the impression that he expected to meet someone at the edge of the swamp."

"Good!" said the judge. "He told me this morning that he was to meet Galt there, but now Galt can't meet him, and I want to be sure."

"What has happened, Judge Marston?" asked Anne.

"The swamp people are concentrating—those who are determined to fight it out with the Riders. Some have been killed; others have fled North. The most desperate of them are staying. Nobody knows what is in their lurid minds. But there isn't any danger, after all, to people who stay away from the swamps. The Riders will attend to those fellows."

"Where is Mr Stoddard?" inquired Marie in a voice which held a suggestion of the tenseness that had whitened her face.

The judge laughed, answering that during the morning Stoddard had ridden past on his way to town. "I talked with him," he added. "But I recollect he didn't have much to say. He never does talk a great deal, does he?" He looked at Marie quizzically.

The Randolph carriage returned empty to the Randolph home, for Anne spent the night with Marie, for the purpose, which she kept to herself, of attempting to keep Marie's mind off her quarrel with Stoddard and to convince her—if possible—that Stoddard did not deserve the treatment she had given him. Anne found her self-imposed task difficult, for Marie was silent and uncommunicative and would not talk about Stoddard. It was not customary for Marie to be so preoccupied, and Anne for once was baffled, but wise, for she did not mention Stoddard, leaving Marie to her thoughts, which were of the day's events, of her presentiment of something sinister hovering near, of her own emotions, which were so turbulently contradictory that they frightened her, and of the quiet patience in Stoddard's eyes which she would never forget.

CHAPTER TWENTY-EIGHT

While Marie and Anne were visiting the wounded veterans, and Marie was striving with emotions and passions deeper than any she had ever known; while Stoddard had been riding back to town after enduring Marie's careful and complete indictment—which had astonished him, even though he deserved it; and while over swamp and town and countryside hovered a voiceless and lingering threat of something portentous about to happen—an atmosphere of guarded silence, all pervading, which swept over the swamplands, through the shacks of the water front, into the stores and business offices and even into the residences on the heights above town—a knowledge that the crisis was at hand; that the mysterious Riders were somewhere massing for a final blow at the river pirates and the criminal element of the water front, and that these desperadoes, sensing the clash, frightened, desperate, were preparing, scheming and planning to resist—while all these things were happening, even while Slade Forbush was striding through a heavy moist darkness toward the Planters' House, James Craftkin was lying drunk in his room at the ancient hotel. Craftkin, a tall man, seen only once by Stoddard as one day he had been helped to his room by Slade Forbush and a Negro porter, was finishing an extended alcoholic drinking bout and was now awakening to a sober minded, though vicious, realization of the impending crisis, which his whisky-sodden senses had only vaguely comprehended during his semisober moments of the past several weeks. Nominally Vauchain had been the head of the swamp clan, but the real force, the malign genius of the pirate organization, was Craftkin. And now, his thirst gone, he sat in a big chair in his room at the Planters' House—a rear room—in the dark and gathered together his hazy recollections of recent events. He was tall and powerful, with a pronounced stoop to his shoulders. This physical fault, together with his long scrawny neck, which was spotted like a vulture's; and heavy, shaggy brows under which projected a long curved nose, beaklike, which twitched continually as if testing various scents; a wide thin-lipped mouth, always drooping at the corners; and deep-set eyes of a brilliant black, caused him to look like a human replica of a giant bird of prey. With Vauchain and Forbush, and several others of the present swamp clan, he had sailed in pirate ships which had terrorized the Gulf and the Caribbean, and had there acquired the mannerisms of his type. Originally from the slums of London, his Cockney speech was flavored with the salty tang of the sea.

When, perhaps an hour after awakening, he heard a step in the carpeted hall and a light tapping at the door of his room, a paroxysm of rage racked him out of his chair and sent him to answer the summons.

"Ow!" he ejaculated upon seeing Forbush in the lighted hallway. "It's you, eh? It's aboht time ye hove to. Where in 'ell ye bin?"

Forbush was arrayed in the garments of a gentleman, playing a role he always assumed in the town and its environs. He did not answer Craftkin but strode into the darkened room, found a lamp on a table and lighted it, adjusted the wick, and stood, handsome and picturesque in the lamplight, looking at Craftkin, who was again in the big chair, pale, his bright eyes glowing with amused malice. He had always disliked Forbush's sartorial splendor—and Forbush himself upon occasions.

"Wot's all this 'ere aboht boots asproutin' in the swamp?" he growled. "An' aboht some of our men skeedadlin' North like the devil was after 'em?"

"All true," answered Forbush.

"An' who's bin doin' it?"

"The Riders."

"The Riders, eh? An' who in 'ell is the Riders? Tom Bowlin' 'as bin tryin' to tell me right along but, blast 'is 'ide, hi 'aven't believed 'im. Tom Bowlin's a liar an' the truth eyen't in 'im."

"You've been too drunk to understand," said Forbush. "I've told you about what's been happening, but you've looked at me like a damned owl. And laughed at me to boot."

" 'Ell!" said Craftkin, glaring. "Who's leadin' the Riders?"

"Weldon and Galt and this new man, Stoddard."

" 'Im, eh? What's Vauchain doin'?"

"Vauchain is dead—killed."

Craftkin's body stiffened. His eyes glittered. "Who killed 'im?" he almost whispered.

"The Riders," lied Forbush.

"Where's the Burleigh girl?"

"Dead."

"Who killed 'er?"

"Vauchain."

"Blast my 'ide!"

Craftkin sat, hands on knees, facing Forbush, looking up at him, his bright eyes thoughtful with wickedness, with gathering malice and speculation. "Vauchain's dead, eh?" he said, his long upper lip, slightly prehensile, twitching into a derisive half-smile. "Serves 'im bloody well right. 'E was too damned greedy. An' a fool aboht women. So 'e's got hisself killed. And the Riders done it. Now, them Riders, Forbush. Hi've bin 'earin' aboht 'em, off an' on, seems like. 'Ow many Riders?"

"I don't know. Nobody knows. And they are not really *riders*."

" 'Ow, they're Riders, yet they eyen't riders. Wot in 'ell you givin' me?"

"They don't ride. They roam the swamps and get friendly with our men. They get a man alone, kill him and hang his boots up, with a card on them."

"I've 'eard that. Wot I'm askin' is, 'ow many of our men 'as bin killed?"

"Twenty or thirty so far. That many more have been scared out and have gone North."

" 'Ow many riders 'as bin killed?"

"None."

"None!" glared Craftkin disgustedly. "Eyen't we got no fightin' men in our crew? Damned sissies, I calls 'em!"

"The men can't find them," said Forbush.

"Can't, eh? 'Ell, so they can't find 'em? They gets their throats cut, and they can't find 'em! They don't know 'em, eh? They can't find Galt, and Weldon, and this 'ere new man, Stoddard, eh? They're the 'eads of the Riders, and nobody kin find 'em. And Weldon and Galt aridin' around town 'ere. I've seen 'em. And nobody kin find 'em. And this 'ere Stoddard—in the same 'otel with us. 'Is room right across the 'all."

Forbush stood staring into his chief's evil eyes, which were now regarding him steadily with a meaning that Forbush could not mistake. Craftkin leaned back in his chair, smirking as he saw that Forbush understood.

" 'Ang the capting and the mates to the yardarm, and the crew sails the ship on the rocks, 'avin' no navigator. Eh, mate? You didn't think of that? Blimme, that's wot makes a capting a capting!"

Forbush's face was now pale as he listened further to Craftkin, who, whispering softly, asked numerous questions about Stoddard and Galt and Weldon, and about the swamp men—where they could be found; naming them; inquiring about boats and crews and referring particularly to a certain island in the swamp, which he called the "Willows." He wanted to know how many of the swamp men were there, again naming them, finding there were three.

"Four, with the sweetheart," he laughed and noted how Forbush's eyes glittered darkly with cruel anticipation. Forbush, considering the possibility of disposing—with no danger to himself—of the man he feared, followed Craftkin's plan with burning interest, with long sighs provoked by imagination and by his knowledge of Craftkin's cruelty. A point of land extending into the swamp in some timber east of town—the point known as the "Needle"—was discussed; and a cart and a horse and a driver were mentioned. Then, after a time, Forbush softly opened the door of the room and peered out into the hall, having extinguished the light in Craftkin's room. The door of Stoddard's room, directly across the hall from Craftkin's, was closed, and no light showed between the bottom of the door and the carpet that ran under it. Forbush stepped out into the hall and made his way stealthily to the rear, where a door opened upon a wooden stairway leading down into the grounds and the garden. As he descended he carefully felt his way in the moist darkness, and at the bottom he explored the grounds and the garden and finally vanished into the surrounding shadows.

Out of the same shadows about two hours later appeared Forbush. He again explored the grounds and the garden in the vicinity of the rear of the hotel, pausing every few steps to listen and to peer about as if to make certain no one watched him. Ascending the rear stairway as slowly and as carefully as he had descended, he stood for a time on the upper platform, listening. Satisfied that the hallway was clear, he opened the hall door, softly closed it, leaving it unlatched, and moved to the doorway of Craftkin's room, which he entered without knocking, finding the door unlocked, as he had left it. Closing it behind him, he stood waiting. A match flared with a greenish-yellow flame, and its light showed him Craftkin, a giant and satanic figure with gorillalike arms, bending over the lamp on the table, lighting it.

"Fixed?" asked Craftkin, peering at him.

"Everything."

"Where's 'e?"

"Riding somewhere. Visiting. He told the livery-stable man he'd be back before midnight."

"Rode 'is 'orse, eh? 'Is 'orse in the livery stable?"

"No."

Craftkin sank into the big chair he had previously occupied, stretched his legs and relaxed his misshapen body, smirking evilly, his long arms dangling over the sides of the chair.

"Captings," he said reflectively. "A capting is a bloke as does things an' 'as things done." He reached over, blew out the light and again relaxed in his chair. Forbush also found a chair. Both men sat there in the pitch-darkness, whispering, listening.

Voices floated up the great front stairway and died in the silence of the rear hall. Several times footsteps sounded on the soft carpet of the great stairway, but none came as far as the doorway of Craftkin's room, and the dim hall light, midway between the front and the rear of the hall, threw no shadows visible to Forbush and Craftkin after, acting upon Craftkin's orders, Forbush opened the door and swung it wide so that both men could see the door of Stoddard's room.

Shortly before midnight there came another step on the front stairway and a voice—Stoddard's—speaking to someone below.

"Stoddard!" whispered Forbush.

Swiftly, in spite of his ungainly figure and misshapen shoulders, Craftkin got out of his chair and moved toward the doorway, feigning drunkenness, his long legs wobbling uncertainly, bending at the knees, his long arms dangling at his sides like the wings of some monstrous bird flapping.

This was the apparition which confronted Stoddard as, dressed as when he had sat in the saddle talking with Marie, he stood before the door of his room, key in hand. He turned to face the man and smiled as the latter, his head drooping, his great body swaying, lurched against him, mumbling something which sounded like an apology, and grasped Stoddard's arms as if to keep himself from falling. He seemed to be very drunk, for, instead of straightening, he lurched against Stoddard again, turning him around so that his back was toward the rectangular darkness of Craftkin's room. Then out of that darkness stepped Forbush. Swiftly, viciously, he struck Stoddard's head with something heavy and blunt and pliable, and Stoddard swayed and would have fallen if Craftkin's long arms had not suddenly gone around him with a powerful and purposeful grip. There had been no sound except the muffled thud of the blow. There was still none as Forbush and Craftkin carried Stoddard into Craftkin's room, placed him upon the bed; and Craftkin darted back to close and lock the door and to pick up Stoddard's hat, which had fallen, while Forbush, working in the dark, lashed Stoddard's wrists together with ropes that seemed to have been placed conveniently near; and his ankles, so that he lay there, bound and unconscious, while Craftkin again lighted the lamp and both culprits stood there, grinning and satisfied. Craftkin then forced a gag into Stoddard's mouth and secured it with a long neckerchief, which he tied tightly.

Later, with the sound of laughter and a humming of voices coming from the barroom, Forbush again opened the door and looked into the hall, listening. Swinging the door wide, he waited there until Craftkin emerged, carrying Stoddard's limp figure over his shoulder; then closed the door and preceded Craftkin to the rear door, which he opened and closed again after Craftkin went out, carrying his burden. Silently, slowly, Craftkin descended the stairs and, directed by Forbush, carried Stoddard through the grounds to a dark and deserted side alley, where they roughly tossed him into a waiting cart and covered him with a blanket.

The cart, a bearded man driving, rattled down the alley to the street, over the cobblestones of the water front and out of town, eastward over the dirt road that wound over a level into the wilderness, where after a time it entered a stretch of timber and finally came to a halt at the edge of the swamp, where a point of land extended into the water. There waited two men in a flat-bottomed boat, into which they carried Stoddard, dumping him unceremoniously into the bottom of the craft. There for a time they waited, doing something to Stoddard. And Forbush, watching the spectacle in the light of a sulphur match held by one of the swamp men, laughed with triumphant and mocking mirth.

"Damme," he said between laughs, "an inspiration, Craftkin! That will give them something to think about."

"A capting is a capting, Forbush," said Craftkin. Their laughter mingled. " 'E'll need nawthin' after we get through with 'im—damn 'is 'ide!"

Then the boat was poled away into the pitch-blackness of the swamp; Craftkin in the boat with Stoddard; Forbush standing on the point of the land. After a while, working with something, laughing, gloating, Forbush walked back to town.

CHAPTER TWENTY-NINE

The strategy of Evan Weldon's campaign against the swamp pirates was to instill terror into them, so that, yielding to panic, they would leave the country. So far, he had attained his objective. Drifting in to him by various messengers came word that some of the swamp people, stirred by the mysterious deaths among them in widely separated sections of the swamp, had ceased pillaging the country, and that those who were not staying close to their hovels were moving out. However, the exodus was confined only to the more timorous. The vicious, hardened criminal element remained, gathering here and there into sullen groups, alert, watchful and suspicious. They would have to be driven out by massed forces of Riders, their hovels burned, their strength destroyed in open warfare. So Weldon, having decided to change his tactics, had conferred with his lieutenants last night at the edge of the swamp at the end of Sycamore Road and had talked with Crosby Gillis—the tattered man seen by Marie and Anne—and had sent Gillis back to Galt with new orders for the latter.

At least one day would elapse before he could expect the Riders to reassemble for the new movement, and, forced to comparative inactivity in the interim—a period he had anticipated—yesterday he had arranged for Stoddard to accompany him this morning on a ride down-river. He was late for the appointment and rode directly to the livery stable, expecting to find Stoddard there, waiting for him. Stoddard's horse, saddled and bridled, was hitched to a rack just inside the doors of the stable, and the liveryman nodded understandingly to Weldon's question.

"Yes suh. He told me last night to have the hoss ready at nine. Thet hour is late fer him, Mistah Weldon. Neahly every mawnin' he's down heah directly aftah daylight, sometimes befoh—settin' on that bench just outside the doah, lookin' at the rivah. Seems he cain't look at it enough. He likes the watah. He's mighty neah all man, Mistah Weldon."

"He is, sir."

Weldon waited half an hour. Then he remounted and rode down the cobblestone street of the water front and up a slope to the Planters' House, where he dismounted, tossed the reins to a Negro groom who came to meet him, and entered the hotel, where the clerk, glancing at the keyboard, told him that Mr Stoddard was still in his room. The clerk looked at the clock, adding: "He's usually up and around before this, Mr Weldon. Shall I disturb him, sir?"

"Don't bother. I'll just run up myself. I know the room."

He was back in five minutes, puzzled.

"He doesn't answer. Are you sure he's in his room?"

"Positive." The clerk procured a duplicate key and, followed by Weldon, went up the stairs and along the hall to Stoddard's room, inserting the key and cautiously opening the door a little. Instantly he pushed it all the way open and uttered a startled word: "Egad!"

Stoddard's bed had not been slept in. The window shades were up, as the maid had left them; the water bowl and pitcher were undisturbed; the soap was in its receptacle, the towels neatly folded, unused.

The clerk stared at Weldon perplexedly.

"I don't understand it," he said. "He came in last night before midnight. He certainly did. I talked to him."

No, Stoddard had not gone downstairs again. The clerk was positive of that. But it was apparent that Stoddard *had* gone down, because he wasn't in his room, Weldon insisted. Apprehension swelled his lungs, drew the blood from his face and lurked deep in his eyes. Last night, violating a pledge he had made to himself when Stoddard had decided to stay in Chandler, he had withdrawn the bodyguard he had set over Stoddard—two men who had followed Stoddard everywhere at night. He had used the men as messengers to acquaint his lieutenants with his newest strategy.

While he stood staring at the bed, fighting off a creeping, panicky fear such as sometimes had seized him during the war, he heard the clerk calling to him, and he went out into the hall, to find the clerk opening the rear door, which led to the outside stairway.

"This door was unlocked," said the clerk. "It's never used except by the maids and the porters. If Stoddard went down at all it's likely he went down this way. The door being unlocked seems to prove it."

Weldon followed him out to the stair platform, and both men stood there for a moment, silent, anxious, looking down into the grounds. Moving so suddenly that he startled the clerk, Weldon went down the stairs, leaped the balustrade of a platform at the bottom and pounced upon an object lying in a flower bed near a clump of rhododendrons. The object was Stoddard's broad-brimmed felt hat. Both men recognized it instantly—the clerk with a gasp, Weldon with a tenseness that seemed to steal all over him.

"I was right," declared the clerk. "He came down this way."

"Carried down," said Weldon. He pointed to footprints in the damp soil of the garden, three sets leading away from the hotel, one coming toward it. Weldon examined them, following them until they were lost in the deep grass beyond the edge of the garden.

"I don't know what that set means," he said, pointing to the footprints leading toward the hotel, "but the man who wore those boots went away from the hotel, came back, and went away again. The footprints are different, so there were two men. One man was very heavy, or he was carrying something. I think he was carrying Stoddard. The footprints are twice as deep as the others. Stoddard's hat at the bottom of the stairs shows that he came down this way, but there are no prints left by Stoddard's boots. They have extra-high heels, and all these are flat."

"Egad, you're right!" agreed the clerk, staring at the footprints.

There was no panic in Weldon now. His face long, his eyes suddenly haggard, worried, a cold fire smoldering in them, he gripped the clerk by the shoulders and forced the man to meet his gaze.

"Think fast and straight," he said. "Did anyone other than a guest go up the main stairway last night?"

"No. Yes—somebody—let me think . . . Slade Forbush! He went up to Mr Craftkin's room."

Weldon took the rear steps two at a time, darted into the hallway and gripped the knob of the door of Craftkin's room, the clerk behind him, directing him. The door was unlocked; the bed had not been slept in, but on the white counterpane was the imprint of a man's body and upon the floor two short lengths of rope—which Forbush had not used and had neglected to take with him—which Weldon inspected.

The clerk stared.

"It looks like Craftkin and Forbush . . ."

"Exactly!" said Weldon, his voice smothered.

He went down the front stairway and out into the grounds, where for a time he stood beside his horse, his arms crossed on the saddle seat, his head resting upon them, as he tried to think clearly through a fog of futile rage and dismayed helplessness.

Finally mounting, Weldon rode slowly through the streets, trying hard to regain control of himself; fighting an impulse to race wildly from place to place, to search for Stoddard; reluctantly deciding that haste and fury would bring only confusion and no success. Craftkin and Forbush were men of wide experience in villainy; they were cunning and merciless; he knew they hated Stoddard, and that swiftly and surely they would do away with him. They had not killed him in the hotel or in the grounds in the rear of the building, for there were no signs of a struggle. The footprints in the garden seemed to be evidence that they had carried him away. Where? Not to the water front, he decided, for though in the shacks of the water front were places where a murder might be committed, it was also a place where the victim's body could not be readily disposed of, unless it should be carried away in one of the small boats that were always there, or secretly put aboard a night steamer, later to be dropped overboard. And when Weldon thought of such a thing happening to Stoddard the mental fog closed in on him again. It drove him to the water front, where he dismounted and walked along the edge of a wharf, peering into the small craft floating idly there; into warehouses and storage sheds; and into disreputable dives where the habitués stared at him curiously and shrank from the cold, questing, high intensity of his searching glances, noting his pallor and the grim lines around his mouth.

Until noon he prowled through town, frequenting places where, he had been informed, Craftkin and Forbush might sometimes be found. He could not find them. They were hiding, or they had fled to escape the wrath of the Riders.

Shortly after noon he rode into the high country back of town, past the Villers' home, to see Marie and Anne on the veranda. They waved at him and he replied, wondering about them—what they would say if they knew what had happened. No one was in sight at Judge Marston's place, and when he turned into the lowland road upon which, the day before, he and Stoddard had met Marie and Anne, a wave of emotion swept over him and all the morning's repression went out of him. At the end of the Sycamore Road, at the edge of the swamp, he met Galt and several of the Riders, camping there.

"They've got Stoddard," he said and saw Galt's face whiten.

The men wanted details, which he gave them and noted how their eyes burned into his, and how passion had its way with them.

He told them to begin a search for Stoddard and to spread the news of his disappearance to all the other units of the Riders as swiftly as possible. The new strategy, which was to kill the swamp pirates and burn their habitations wherever found, sparing only women and children, was to begin immediately. However, the Riders were to be tight lipped against divulging news of the tragedy to anyone in town. Weldon was thinking of Marie particularly, hoping he might soften the force of the blow to her, or that some miracle—it would have to be nothing less than that—would save Stoddard. He rode back to town and saw Judge Marston on the big veranda of his home, reading. He rode up, dismounted heavily and joined the judge on the veranda. The judge smiled at him, apparently observing no sign of his guest's agitation. Weldon's face was usually stern. Today the sternness had deepened, that was all. However, the judge himself was mildly excited, and as Weldon seated himself, the wise old eyes were glowing with inquiry.

"What is this rumor I hear about Stoddard?" he said. "A rumor that he has left town. Is it true?"

"Yes. Stoddard has gone away. Temporarily, we hope." Weldon could not meet the judge's eyes.

"I hope so too," smiled the judge. "Do you know, Evan, I have become quite attached to that young man."

Not again during his visit did Weldon mention Stoddard's name.

CHAPTER THIRTY

Sitting on the veranda, reading, after Evan Weldon left him, Judge Marston began to lose interest in the article he had been perusing—a section of the Revised Statutes of Mississippi, defining the jurisdiction of the courts. The judge found that his mind wandered from the stiff and formal phrases of the law to matters more intimate and personal; and finally, closing the book but carefully marking the page for further perusal, he leaned back in his chair, disturbed by a feeling that during the day something had happened—something illogical, which had vaguely worried him. Now, reviewing the day's events, he remembered. The rumor about Stoddard's leaving town. A court attaché had whispered to him and, oddly enough, he had wondered over the expression of concern upon the attaché's face. Not at the time, however. Later. Of course Stoddard was at liberty to leave town whenever he wanted to. But Stoddard had made many friends here, and the judge himself was one of them, and Evan Weldon another, and it was strange that he should leave without saying anything. He had not given Weldon any details, or Weldon would have mentioned them. He thought of Weldon's unusual sternness, of the way Weldon had said, "temporarily, we hope," in referring to Stoddard's departure, and decided Weldon had not told him everything he knew. He was uneasy and oppressed with an indefinable sense of loss.

The Randolph carriage stopped at the entrance of his drive, and Marie got out, to come toward him across the lawn, while Anne Randolph was borne away, waving at him.

When Marie visited his house she took possession of it, and the judge, as well as the servants, took orders from her and secretly exulted because she was so deeply interested in their welfare. She always brought with her an atmosphere which had been missing since the death of the judge's wife—the spirit of youth and vitality, which banished the oppressive emptiness, and a vibrant hominess which gave animation to rooms that had long been silent. There were no reticences between the judge and Marie, no reservations to create formality, and when Marie came out upon the veranda to find the judge absorbed in his thoughts, she laughingly charged that it was too nice a day for him to sit moping there.

"Not moping," he denied, "thinking."

"Of something serious, I warrant."

He pointed to the Revised Statutes, and she grimaced wryly and shuddered mockingly.

"I might have known it," she said. "You read law, and think law and apply the law, and I fear you'd eat law if I didn't come over occasionally and see to your diet."

"And spur my appetite with new dishes," he charged.

"Which you don't half appreciate, I fear."

"Even though I devour them."

"And look for more."

"I am becoming awkwardly heavy. Overfed——"

"And strangely solemn," she laughed. "You don't grow solemn over your lawbooks, though you are often sarcastic, and sometimes disgusted, but never solemn. What were you thinking of?"

"Of Stoddard," he said and saw a patch of color steal upward and stain her cheeks.

Conscious of the blush, and not wanting to let the judge know that mention of Stoddard had brought it, she pretended a lack of interest.

"Oh—Mr Stoddard," she said quietly and looked past the judge. "So Mr Stoddard makes you solemn." Her own thoughts of Stoddard had been solemn, too, and were solemn now, and during the night, stirred to unimagined depths, her prejudices had been assailed by a growing doubt.

"Yes," said the judge. "It's a very solemn thing to lose a friend. There is a quite dismal realization of loss."

Marie's heart seemed to stop. She said breathlessly: "Is Mr Stoddard lost?"

"Not lost. He has left Chandler."

Suddenly Marie knew why the judge was solemn. Her breath had come back, and with it a dull emptiness. "To go back to the Neutral Strip, I suppose," she said.

"Evan didn't say. I think he left without saying anything."

"That is like him," she said. "He has strange moods." She was thinking of the contrast between his passionate impulsiveness at Colonel Darcy's and the quiet patience he had exhibited under the lashing scorn of her words when he had faced her on the lowland road. She asked, almost breathless again: "Of course Evan wasn't worried about him?"

"No. I should think not. He spoke of Mr Stoddard's absence as probably temporary."

Once more color was back in Marie's cheeks, and once more she could return to her consideration of her prejudices against the Yankees, which she had always accepted as being definitely fixed, but which during the night, and at this moment, were not as formidable as they had been and, strangely, not even as persistent. For there were times, even as now, when she was not quite certain she still entertained them. Perhaps, after all, her stubborn pride in the invincibility and superiority of the Southern troops had been to blame. There was in her today a strange and dreamy tolerance, and her bitterness toward the North had been subdued by certain thoughts which had come to her during the night, thoughts which were really interrogations, to be answered in calm meditation—which was not in her now—and in impartiality and clear vision, which had always governed Judge Marston's decisions and judgments. Now, thinking of Stoddard, she said:

"You like Mr Stoddard, don't you?"

"Of course I do. I think you know that, honey."

"His being a Yankee makes no difference to you?"

"Not the least difference. I don't permit myself to be governed by prejudice, my dear. Mr Stoddard has many admirable qualities. Some faults, too, I suppose. Oh, just slight ones"—looking down his nose at Marie with judicial gravity. "And I suppose you have observed some of them."

"I have not observed him at all, sir!"

"Hmmm. Quite so. You have not observed him. You don't like Yankees and so you do not look at them. I will wager Mr Stoddard looks at you. He couldn't help it, my dear; and I wouldn't think much of him if he didn't look at you and admire you." He smiled at her. "I've heard that Yankees even fall in love. In fact, I believe love has no national boundaries. Someday, when the South's prejudices die out, Stoddard may even marry a Southern girl. Prejudice is nothing more than injured pride."

"The South's pride will not die," she declared.

"No. But it will cease to be injured. The wounds will heal and be forgotten. When that day comes we shall all see more clearly. Many of the legends built up by the war will be revealed as fabrications, some of them malicious. We shall discover that the people of the North were, and are, as human as we are, and subject to identical passions and emotions. We ought to know that now, but some of us don't and perhaps never will. You see, honey, the passions of war sometimes blind us to our faults while magnifying the faults of our enemies."

"I think that is the truth," she said, and the judge, astonished, wondered what had happened to her.

"And it doesn't hurt to admit it, honey?"

"No."

"Hmmm. Well, I reckon you're safe. If telling the truth doesn't hurt you, it shows you are getting to the bottom of things. Truths are always at the bottom, and they've got to be dug out. I've found it so in the many cases I have heard. Honey," he added gently, "you never talked like this before. What has come over you?"

"I think it was Oran Stillwell," she explained, blushing furiously. "He has suffered so much, and yet he forgives the Yankees. He made me think."

"Hmmm," said the judge. "Made you think, eh? Well, if more of us would think, there would be less fighting."

"You fought," she reminded him softly.

"And hated it. Marie, I've heard statesmen attempt to glorify war, but what they said didn't ring true and isn't true. Nobody ever wins a war. Both sides lose something they never regain. For every Southern boy who died, a Northern boy also died; and for every bitterness the South endured, the North suffered another. Northern girls waited for sweethearts who would never come back, and Northern mothers wept over the graves of their sons the same as mothers wept here."

How tragically true it all was, and how narrow her own views, now that the judge's broader ones had been presented. Yes, she was thinking now, really thinking, when for quite a few years she had been merely feeling. Her changing philosophy appalled her, for somehow it seemed to her that one's sympathies could not be broad enough to include both the North and the South. Perhaps, as Judge Marston had said only yesterday, "The South ought to build a rainbow—out of forgetfulness."

The South would forget, and the North. The storm had passed; the penalty of stubborn pride and vengeful rage—on both sides—had been paid in bloodshed and suffering, in ruin and desolation and heartbreaking grief; and no resentment, however deep, could ever heal the wounds. The wounds could be forgotten, just as Oran Stillwell was forgetting them and forgiving them. Succeeding generations, their faces turned to the future, would forget the past. They would build the rainbow.

CHAPTER THIRTY-ONE

"Bonnets shinin' in the sun,
Coots a-making' love,
Water like a lookin' glass,
Shows the clouds above.

"Shiners fer the takin',
Moss on every tree,
Toil and trouble plumb forgot,
That's the place fer me,"

sang the livery-stable man, sitting on the bench in front of his stable, where many times he had sat with Stoddard. He had wondered about Weldon's agitation over Stoddard not keeping his appointment. He had wondered why Stoddard had not kept it, and why, not finding Stoddard at the Planters' House, Weldon had ridden back and forth along the water front as if searching for him, peering into boats and warehouses and other buildings on the wharf, and stalking in and out of dives and brothels—and at last riding away unsuccessful. To several customers the livery-stable man had mentioned the incident, and late in the afternoon, when he had delivered two riding horses to the Planters' House, he had questioned the Negro groom.

"Somethin' powahful cur'os gwine on aroun' hyah," said the darky. "Mistah Weldon mighty distuhbed, somehow, ovah findin' Mistah Stoddard's hat in de gardin and a mess o' footprints theah too. I done ast de clerk wha'fer them things mean, an' he tol' me to shut mah dam fool mouf. 'Peahs like Mistah Stoddard left de hotel duhin' de night."

"Maybe he took the night packet to Vicksburg," speculated the stable man.

"Mebbe so—mebbe so."

The liveryman returned to his stable, and the groom sauntered around to the rear of the hotel, where he met and talked with the chambermaid, a vivacious black girl who occasionally took time from her duties to descend the rear stairway to the garden, there to exchange pleasantries with the groom.

As dusk came on, groom and chambermaid lingered long in the garden—so long that Colonel Burleigh, rapidly convalescing, grew impatient because some cigars he had sent the maid for had not been brought.

"These Southern hotels are fine," he told Allie Tuttle, who—in flowered dimity and white apron, making a picture upon which the colonel gazed reflectively and admiringly—was leading him to a big chair at a front window, where he could look out at the water front and the river and the swamp beyond. Day after day he sat there, staring, sighing, the anxiety in his eyes steadily deepening. How many times in his imagination Colonel Burleigh had searched the swamp only Allie Tuttle knew, and she knew only because she had learned to read and interpret the troubled cloudiness of his eyes; and many times, weary of staring and thinking, he leaned back in his chair and dozed, to feel Allie's hands upon his forehead. He began to await that soothing touch, and day by day his admiration for her increased, as did his satisfaction over her nearness to him.

"You remind me of Clara," he told her once. "She was always fooling around me too."

Many times he had questioned her about her family, her life in the swamp, and about her future. He found she had great natural intelligence, and that, in one way or another, she had informed herself upon a variety of subjects. She could read rather well, he thought, considering her lack of advantages. She was scrupulously clean and neat, and what he liked most about her was her startling frankness, which he enjoyed and encouraged.

Now, setting his chair at the proper angle at the window, he spoke of the cigars.

"I'll run down and git 'em fer yo'," Allie promised. "Melissy is allus traipsin' down into the garden to giggle love with thet nigger."

"A romance, eh?"

"Gigglin' ain't romance."

"Oh, it isn't? You think romance is too serious to giggle about?"

"Romance is love, an' love is somethin' thet hurts yo'."

"Oh, so you know all about it, Allie? Do you love somebody?"

"I love yo'. But hit ain't hurtin' love. I reckon hit's 'cause yo' been so helpless. And yo've been kind to me."

"I love you, too, Allie, as I would love you if you were my daughter. That is partly because I am grateful to you, and partly because you have a wonderful personality. Do you know that you are a very brave girl, my dear?"

"I'm always skeered," she declared. "I've even been skeered yo' don't like me."

The colonel laughed gently.

"Well, that's exactly the way I feel about you, Allie. I love you as I've always loved Clara. And if . . ." he paused, trying to overcome a sudden huskiness in his voice. "If Clara doesn't come back, I've been wondering if you wouldn't like to be my daughter, actually. I could adopt you—if your father and mother would consent—and take you back to Cincinnati with me, where you could go to school and become a lady."

"A lady like Marie Villers?" She was trying to repress her excitement, but her eyes were joyously shining and her cheeks were tinged with a newer and deeper color, and she suddenly swooped down upon the colonel, hugged him tightly and instantly retreated, to stand before him glowing with happiness.

"An' if Clara does come back? I'm sartin she will, Mr Burleigh. Then yo' won't want me?"

"I want you, and I'm sure Clara will want you—to repay you for what you've done for us. If Clara comes back she will love you as much as I love you."

Radiant, Allie went downstairs and got the colonel's cigars and gave him one, got matches for him, and hovered over him, and finally settled herself into a chair near him and sat there suddenly and strangely silent. And the colonel, whose senses and perceptions—like any invalid's—were keen and clear, smoked his cigar, and studied Allie's face, and smiled. For though Allie was happy over the prospect of becoming his daughter, something was troubling her, and the colonel thought he knew what it was. For during the weeks he had spent in this room, watching Allie and Stoddard together, listening to their voices, weighing their words and their expressions, observing Stoddard's indifference and Allie's palpitant eagerness, how her color rose when Stoddard came and how it faded when he went, and how she would sit for long intervals, as she was now sitting, brooding, wistfully introspective, he knew she loved Stoddard, and that, though she might never get over it, the time would come when she would cease hoping that Stoddard would return her love. She would have to think it out, of course, for she was sensible and honest—with herself as well as with others—and though renunciation would be hard, she had the courage to face facts, unafraid and uncomplainingly. That was why the colonel's affection for her was so deep.

"You'll find life in Cincinnati will be different, Allie," he said. "In the first place, there will be more people, more boys and girls of your own age. There will be parties and theaters, and dances, and new gowns and dresses."

Her eyes lighted, but there was still a shadow of sadness in them. "Will there be folks in Cincinnati thet want things they can't hev?" she asked.

The colonel did not smile, though he wished to. "Of course, Allie. The world is full of them. Even here in Chandler there are people who can't have things they want, and very often it is best that they don't get them."

"Why?"

The colonel, who knew what she was thinking, said gently: "Because things people want most sometimes bring them unhappiness. Unfortunately, the deepest unhappiness comes where a man and a woman marry without love, on one side or the other."

"I reckon yo're right. The one thet was doin' the lovin' would be unhappy. Thet would be a hurtin' love, wouldn't hit? But the other? Would he be unhappy too?"

"Undoubtedly. It would be torture for him."

For a moment she was silent, thinking. Then she said, "The one with the hurtin' love would be selfish. She'd hev got what *she* wanted. But she'd hev kept him from marryin' somebody *he* loved. And that wouldn't be fair, would hit?"

"Certainly not. Much as she loved him, he would grow to hate her."

She was thinking again. She sighed deeply. "I wouldn't want to make nobody unhappy," she said. "Not even to make myself happy." And now she smiled, and the sadness was gone from her eyes. "I hev been laffin' at Melissy," she added, "but I reckon gigglin' love is the safest."

At dusk there was a gentle tapping upon the door leading into the hall, and Allie opened it to admit the recreant Melissa, with the cigars she had been sent for. She curtsied to the colonel, apologizing for her tardiness. "I done met dat black rascal Clem down at de foot ob de stairs in de gardin," she said. "He was down dere, lookin' at de place whar dey found Missa Stoddard's hat and de footprints ob de men dat carried him away."

Startled, the colonel tried to rise from his chair, but Allie cried out sharply and forced Melissa to repeat what she had said.

"Las' night Clem saw dem carryin' Missa Stoddard down de stairs. He was in de gardin house and he saw Missa Craftkin and Missa Forbush in de hall light when dey opened de doh to carry Missa Stoddard out. Clem was skeered mos' to deaf and afeered to say anythin' about hit, 'cause he knows Missa Craftkin and Missa Forbush is bad folks. Missa Weldon was hyah dis mawnin', and he know Missa Stoddard was carried away. But he don' know dat Missa Craftkin and Missa Forbush put Missa Stoddard into a cart and druv' off wiff him."

Allie was taking off her apron, and the colonel saw her clasp both hands to her forehead. Then she took them away, and the terror in her eyes was understood by Burleigh. She was willing to give Stoddard up, but not that way. For an instant it seemed she was on the point of screaming, but the colonel's voice steadied her.

"Go and see Captain Weldon, Allie," he said. "Tell him what Clem saw. He'll know what to do. Take the hotel carriage. Go to Judge Marston's house if you can't find Weldon. Hurry, my dear. Every minute may count."

After Allie left, and while Melissa stood there staring, the colonel buried his face in his hands, knowing that with such sinister forces at work there would be little hope for the safe return of his daughter.

CHAPTER THIRTY-TWO

At the supper table Judge Marston had been preoccupied and absent minded, for several times Marie had been forced to address him a second time when she wanted to talk to him, and had smiled understandingly at his blank expression when she took him to task for not listening to her. He was in one of his moods—the sort of mood that came upon him when he was striving to interpret a point of law upon which the Statutes were not quite clear, or ambiguous. His boasted appetite had suddenly failed him, and he accepted Marie's gentle chiding patiently, without indulging in the airy persiflage which usually made their meals together so enjoyable. When, after supper, the judge went again to the front veranda, he carried with him a disturbing recollection of the day's occurrences and of the impressions these occurrences had made upon him. They were distinctly depressing, beginning with the rumor about Stoddard's leaving town—which was subsequently confirmed by Evan Weldon—his seeing several groups of Weldon's Riders racing toward the swamp, and by seeing Weldon himself thundering past, riding recklessly down the lowland road.

The day had been bright and clear, but with the dusk a hazy blanket of clouds had formed, suddenly deepening it, creating a humid and oppressive gloom which increased the judge's uneasiness. The depressing atmosphere was lightened by Anne Randolph, who arrived in the Randolph carriage and came tripping up the great stone steps to be greeted by the judge in the light of the porch lamps, which burned every evening, the weather permitting. Anne's smile was not as spontaneous as usual, the judge thought, and he gazed wonderingly after her as she went into the house to see Marie. Anne came out again after a little, without the smile. She seemed troubled and anxious.

"Judge Marston," she said, "is it true that Mr Stoddard has left Chandler?"

"I have Evan Weldon's word for it."

"Oh—then it's all right, I suppose. It must be all right, if Evan said so. I was frightened. I asked Marie about it, and she said she thought Mr Stoddard had gone back to the Neutral Strip. Then it isn't true?"

"What isn't true, my dear?"

"Why, the rumor—the talk in town about their finding Mr Stoddard's hat in the garden behind the hotel, and about Mr Stoddard having been carried away during the night by Craftkin and Forbush."

"That is ridiculous, my dear!" But the judge was startled, and he thought of the Riders passing the house, of Weldon riding down the lowland road toward the swamp, and of his vague and illogical impressions of something ominous impending. "There is nothing wrong, of course," he gently assured Anne, with a feeling that somehow he was attempting to reassure himself. "Idle talk, I presume. People like to exaggerate. They feel it makes them seem important."

"But Colonel Darcy was in the Planters' House just before dusk, and he said the clerk showed him Mr Stoddard's hat. They had found it in the garden, just at the bottom of the rear stairway. I came over as soon as I heard of it."

"Stuff and nonsense!" laughed the judge.

He did not feel like laughing as Anne went back into the house, and he walked to a far corner of the veranda, where in the darkness he stood for a time in a listening attitude, looking toward the swamp, without knowing what he expected to hear or see. He was staring into a wall of blackness which his eyes could not penetrate, yet because he had seen this section of the country nearly every day for more than half a century, he could visualize every foot of it from his own plantation to the Villers' plantation on the high level ground adjoining his; the fertile acres eastward, the lowlands beyond; the slope north of the Villers' house—half a mile of it, never cultivated, always overrun with gnarled brush and dotted with scraggly locusts and slender sycamores—to a stretch of wild bottom land, inundated in flood time, which was covered with swamp vegetation and through which ran a gumbo road, passable only in dry weather. Then the swamp, reaching west almost to Chandler and eastward for many miles.

On a night like this the slightest sound was magnified, and very clearly, from somewhere, the judge heard voices—the voices of men. They seemed to come from a distance, and he thought he could trace them to the lowlands beyond the slope near the swamp. But of course that was his imagination, for voices could not possibly carry that far, even tonight. A strange night, with a strange atmosphere. The judge missed a certain slumberous calmness which always hovered over the country. Without being able to understand what it was the judge became aware that something was disturbing the night's serenity. He sensed movement in the darkness, and he did not remember ever having seen that reddish glow in the sky above and beyond the timber line far away. The sun could not be doing that, because the sun had gone down hours before, and the glowing light was not steady, like a sunset, and it seemed to waver. When he finally realized that he was looking at flames his face blanched, and he was startled to observe that a rider had come down the drive toward him and was sitting motionless in the saddle, looking at him. There was light enough for him to see that the rider was Evan Weldon, and he said nothing as Weldon dismounted, hitched his horse to a post alongside the drive and climbed over the veranda railing. Still the judge did not speak. Something in him told him that words were unnecessary and futile. For the light from the nearest porch lamp, filtering through the darkness upon Weldon, showed that the man was spent, beaten. He leaned against the veranda railing and sighed deeply with weariness. He wore no hat; he was hollow eyed, his face was deeply lined and his chin was on his chest. Even before he spoke, the judge knew what he would say. He whispered it huskily.

"Stoddard's gone. Disappeared. We can't find him."

Even though the judge had suspected this, the bald statement shocked him, and for a time, though he sought to speak, his voice would not come. Finally he said: "You knew that this noon, Evan."

"Yes," bitterly: "I didn't want the girls to know until—until I was certain."

"Are you certain now, Evan?"

"Forbush and Craftkin carried him away. You know how Forbush hated him. I fear they've killed him, Judge."

Somehow, it seemed to the judge that the great, vital Stoddard would not meet death in that manner. This was hope. "Nonsense, Evan. Stoddard isn't destined to die that way. Even if they took him into the swamp, he'd manage to escape them. Many of them would die with him."

Weldon shook his head.

The judge turned to the railing at the end of the veranda and stood there, silent, his back to Weldon. Weldon, leaning against the front railing, stared at the floor. At last Weldon joined the judge and they both stood there watching the banked darkness beyond the Villers' home—a black wall which was now dotted with tiny points of light that flickered and glowed and wavered—and listened to faint popping reports, distantly reverberating.

"Shooting," said the judge.

"Yes. And fire. The scoundrels will never forget this night!"

Now both men stood silent again, and both, perhaps with the same vindictive thoughts, were imagining the scene that must be taking place in the swamp.

"Listen," said the judge. "Do you hear? Voices. Men talking. I heard them just before you came. They seem to be nearer now."

Some excitement jerked Weldon erect. "That's a party of Riders I left at the edge of the swamp east of town," he said. "I told them I'd be here. If they found any trace of Stoddard they were to let me know."

The voices, coming out of the darkness, could not be definitely located, for they seemed to float first from one direction and then from another. And when at last it seemed certain they came from the grounds in front of the house the judge and Weldon went to the center of the veranda, and Weldon went down the great stone steps to meet the men. Weldon was poised to run out into the grounds, hoping to keep the girls from hearing the message the men would be bringing, but before he could take one step a dozen grim-visaged men appeared in the light from the veranda and silently crowded around him. Their grim faces were as white as Weldon's when he saw what one of them carried; and the judge, standing on the edge of the veranda, not being able to see what Weldon saw, exclaimed sharply, his voice trembling with excitement:

"What is it, Evan?"

One of the men stepped forward uncertainly, reluctantly. Evan Weldon had sunk to one of the stone steps and sat there, his shoulders drooping, his face haggard, staring with horrified eyes at the objects the riders placed upon the edge of the veranda—two soft-topped boots, with high heels and spurs with small rowels. The tops of the boots, made of pliable leather, would not support their own weight, and they drooped downward to the floor, and the rider who had placed them there now drew a piece of card-board from inside his shirt and stood it against the drooping top of one of the boots. On the card, printed in black, were the words: "Stoddard. His boots."

The Riders, weary from their day's work in the swamp, stood there, their heads bowed. Weldon sat, grim, gaunt, his teeth clenched. The judge backed slowly away from the boots until he came into contact with a chair, into which he dropped suddenly, as if all the strength had gone out of him, and sat there staring, his face ashen, sagging. He seemed, sitting there, to have become very, very old.

They knew—all of them—the dread significance of the empty, plac-arded boots, wherever found; and they knew, too, that Stoddard, using Asa Calder's boots, had been the first to utilize them as a symbol. And perhaps into the minds of all of them—the Riders, Weldon and the judge—came thoughts of the tragic irony of this situation. But Marie, hearing the voices and suddenly appearing in the doorway, with Anne beside her, stood very still when she saw the boots and the placard, and only Anne, standing close to her, heard her gasp. And then she was still again and rigid.

Perhaps only Anne knew how deeply Marie had been shocked, for Anne, alone of all who watched her, knew she loved Stoddard. Weldon, who knew something about her many whims and her contradictions of conduct, which he could never anticipate, would not have been surprised to hear her calmly ask questions about the boots, for he was certain she had told him the truth when she had said she disliked Stoddard. The judge did not think at all; he merely stared at her as she left the doorway, crossed the veranda and stood near the boots and the placard, looking at them.

She had to be sure. And when she saw that the boots were really Stoddard's, that the spur straps were gray, with flat buckles, and that a rowel on the right spur was missing—shot off, he had said—she found herself seeing him as she had seen him yesterday, wearing the boots, looking so very handsome and boyish in his picturesque garments, with his tousled hair making him seem reckless and impulsive, and she did what she had wanted to do while she had been humiliating him—what she had wanted to do all night long, thinking of him. She smiled at the vision she had of him, as she had seen him yesterday; then, kneeling on the porch floor, she took the soft top of the right boot in her hands and pressed it tightly against her cheek. She swayed a little as she went into the house, while out on the porch the judge gulped; on the step Weldon fought hard for his composure; and the Riders scuffed their feet, moved uneasily and turned their faces away.

CHAPTER THIRTY-THREE

To the judge, sitting there in his chair on the veranda, staring at Stoddard's boots, came torturing thoughts. To Evan Weldon, on the steps, came the helpless and maddening rage of a courageous man, wearied to exhaustion, beaten—who knows not which way to turn. The Riders, standing there, muttering, their faces grim and white, watched Weldon when at last he strode among them. He spoke to one of them, a man he called "Jeff", asking him where Stoddard's boots and the placard had been found.

"Just east of the Needle," answered the man, a tall, strong-looking and intelligent rider. "There's always a pile of driftwood there, eddied in by the current. Right close to the road the boots were, hanging on two sticks of driftwood which had been stuck into the clay. The card was between the boots, stuck in another piece of driftwood which had been slit with a knife to hold it. We went out to the point of the Needle. There had been a boat there recently; and there was a lot of bootprints all around, leading back to the road, to some wheel tracks. A cart, we reckoned. It turned there and went back to town, where it had come from."

It was clear to Weldon now. Stoddard had been carried to the Needle in a cart and there taken away in a boat. What had happened then, and afterward, was the torturing question. Stoddard would not fare well at the hands of men who hated him.

It was Judge Marston who first heard the Planters' House carriage rolling down the drive, the horses racing, but all of them saw Allie Tuttle running toward them across the lawn, and watched her as she came into the light, to pause there and stare inquiringly at them, as if wondering why they had congregated there. Her face was as white as the judge's and Weldon's; but when she saw the boots on the edge of the veranda, and the placard, the question in her eyes was answered; and with dragging steps she swayed forward, closer to the boots, staring wildly, holding both hands over her mouth as if to stifle a scream which sought to come; the men watching her, pitying her because they knew what Stoddard had done for her.

The scream did not come, but her wild sobs shattered the funereal silence, as, throwing herself upon the veranda floor close to the boots, she yielded to the primitive urge in her and called upon Weldon and the Riders to avenge Stoddard's death. And when Weldon told her what was being done in the swamp by the Riders, she applauded him, springing to her feet to face the men, a vindictive fury raging through her. Then, to the amazement of them all, she laughed mockingly, though in the laugh was a note of wild hysteria.

"Craftkin and Forbush wouldn't kill Stoddard right off," she said. "They hate him too much for that. They'd take him somewhere in the swamp and torture him. They'd whip him. They'd give him to the swamp sweetheart!"

Weldon's face took on a grayer hue. His jaws were clamped together; his eyes were burning. The Riders stirred, muttering.

"I've heard of the swamp sweetheart," said Weldon, "but I've never seen it, and I don't know where it is."

Allie was suddenly among them, her words instilling a new hope into them.

"Thet's whut I come here fer," she said. "Soon as I heerd they'd took Stoddard I knowed whut they'd do to him. The sweetheart is on an island known to the swamp folks as 'Willows.' Hit air where Craftkin stays most of the time he's in the swamp. I don't know where hit is, but my pap does. He's been there and knows how to git there. Pap and Maw is livin' over at Green Bayou, in thet wild bresh back of the big mud bar. They're hidin' from Forbush, waitin' to go back home."

"I know where it is," said Jeff.

"We'll go find Pap and hev him show us where the Willows is. Maybe they ain't kilt him yet. Ef they hev . . ." She suddenly sank to the ground at the feet of the men standing around her, lifted her hands to the dark sky and cried beseechingly: "Stop 'em, Lord! Please stop 'em! The damned ornery devils!"

When, rising, after the emotional storm, she saw that the Riders were gone and heard the sounds of their going, she saw only Weldon standing there, looking at her. She would have followed the men; she fought Weldon because he would not permit her to go, and in the end stood there, having yielded to his persuasion.

He told her that the swamp was a shambles; that tonight it was no place for a woman, and that he and the Riders would find her father and have him lead them to the Willows. Then he followed his men, running across the grounds toward the swamp, while Allie went back to the veranda and sank down upon one of the steps and sat there crying.

The judge got up, crossed the veranda, went into the house, entered his den, sank into his favorite chair and sat there, crushed by the appalling weight of the tragedy. Upstairs in the dark, in the bedroom Marie always used when she visited the Marston home, she sat in a chair by an open window overlooking the swamp, Anne kneeling on the floor beside her, and there came no words or thoughts to lessen the desolation that had fallen upon them. Silence only, the emptiness of bereavement, of something gone out of life; the heaviness of regret for something said and done. Outside the window, in the banked shadows hovering over the swamp, were splashes of flame and the faint popping of guns.

Time, the thief of life, moved slowly, as if to impress this moment. It gave Marie a space in which to reflect how much Stoddard had meant to her; it wrecked her prejudices, shattering them into fragments that would never again be reassembled; it brought her a strange new humility.

"Oh, Marie, did you see Weldon's face?" sobbed Anne. "I felt so sorry for him. And Judge Marston, the poor dear! They both loved him, Marie."

"Yes-s," in a stifled voice.

"Don't you think there might be a mistake?" suggested Anne. "Stoddard may be alive, even if they did find his boots."

"No. He is too proud. He wouldn't let them take his boots off—if he were alive."

The judge, slumped down in his chair in his den, was charging himself with responsibility for Stoddard's death. He had influenced him. It made no difference that, later, he had warned Stoddard, had advised him to leave Chandler. He might have known the swamp people would do it, and he now knew he had expected it. There was no end to man's selfishness and stupidity. He thought of all of them on the veranda tonight, of their faces. Of Allie Tuttle—how in the wild abandon of her shock and grief she had thrown herself upon the floor near Stoddard's boots, calling upon Weldon and the Riders for vengeance. She loved Stoddard too. Marie loved him. But the swamp girl's spirit was the more militant.

Yet when Allie Tuttle rose from the step upon which she had been sitting, following the departure of Weldon and his group of Riders, she had no desire to fight anybody. She had no hope that Stoddard was alive. She had cried herself out, and she was now calm but hungry for companionship. She did not want to go back to the hotel. The Planters' House carriage still waited for her in the drive, but she mounted the steps and walked to the far end of the veranda, where she stood staring into the blackness, watching the dots of flame here and there, hearing an occasional shot. She knew what was happening.

"Give it to 'em, damn 'em!" she whispered.

A strange mood came upon her. Malicious perhaps; though the malice was tempered with pity now that she no longer looked upon Marie as a rival who would one day carry away the man she had wanted. She was curious. She had never seen Marie except at a distance and she wanted to get close to her, to see what had made Stoddard fall in love with her.

She stepped tentatively through the great front door, pausing in the big hall to stare at the richness and to absorb the dignity of it all, feeling a little timid now, which did not affect her determination to do what she had decided upon. Her steps made no sound upon the soft carpets of the hall or the stairs, and when she had passed the open doorway of the judge's room, to see him huddled in his chair, she paused only momentarily, pitying him. At the top of the stairs, in the upper hallway, she listened and heard Anne and Marie talking. Following the sound of their voices, she reached the doorway of Marie's room and stood there. Now she was no longer timid or embarrassed. The tragedy had emboldened her; her renunciation had quieted her jealousy and her envy, as it had also, somehow, taken away her awe of the "quality folks."

It was Anne who first became aware of her and called sharply:

"Who is it, please?"

"It's me—Allie Tuttle."

"Oh," said Anne and felt Marie turn in her chair to face the door, to see only the swamp girl's shadowy outline.

"What is it? Has something happened?" asked Marie.

Allie knew why the girls were sitting there in the dark.

"Yo've seen his boots?" she said.

"Yes. Oh, Allie, do you think they've killed him?" asked Marie, quaveringly.

"They wouldn't kill him right off," said Allie. "And they wouldn't leave him live too long, neither. They hate him. Afore they'd kill him they'd whip him—like they've done to some—and give him to the swamp sweetheart."

Allie Tuttle was not the sweetheart of Marie's suspicions. The sweetheart was something ghastly, horrible. "What is it, Allie?" Marie implored, dreading Allie's answer.

"It's a torture machine. Vauchain brought it hyah. Hit's iron. They put a man in hit and hit hugs him to death. Hit's on an island they call the Willows. My pap knows whar it is, and Mr Weldon and his Riders hev gone to try to find my pap, to show 'em. But I reckon Mr Stoddard is dead."

"Oh, Allie," sobbed Marie.

Allie was silent, listening. She was cold, calm, almost indifferent to feeling. The difference between herself and the quality folks was not so vast after all. Common disaster disclosed a common susceptibility to grief. Marie was frankly crying.

"So yo' loved him," said Allie.

"Yes."

"An' wouldn't let him know hit. An' he loved yo'."

"How—how do you know that?"

"He told me. He said yo' wouldn't hev him 'cause he was a Yankee. Things hev got a hell of a way of gittin' messed up. Hit's 'cause we ain't brave enough to do what we orter do. Efter he pulled me out of the water when I was goin' to drowned myself—bein' skairt of what Forbush wanted to do to me—I told Mr Stoddard he could hev me as his woman. He wouldn't hev me. Said he loved another girl. The other girl was yo'. He hadn't seen yo' yit. He'd fell in love with yo'r picher. I seen hit in his pocket efter he took me to the Planters' House to nurse Colonel Burleigh. He told me he had to be 'loyal'—thet all of us had to be loyal. I wanted him, but he didn't want me, and so I give him up. He wanted yo', and yo' didn't want him, and now nobody kin git him."

As silently as she had come, Allie went down the hall to the stairs.

CHAPTER THIRTY-FOUR

Poling the flat-bottomed, blunt-nosed boat through the swamp, with Clara Burleigh comfortably resting in the bow, Arkansaw knew he had many problems to solve before he could place the girl safely in her father's arms, as he had promised. First, there were the proper water aisles to be chosen, in itself a most difficult task to one who was not familiar with his surroundings. In building the swamp nature had not followed an orderly system, for the many channels, weaving around innumerable islands, were intersected by other channels that ran off at deceptive tangents or ended in cross channels that, should a boatman lose his sense of direction for an instant, would lead him back the way he had come. Where Arkansaw poled his punt along there were no distinguishing landmarks by which he could set a course. In every direction were walls of cypress draped with Spanish moss, the drooping fronds of the trees touching the water, the lacy veils curtaining the sky, shutting out the light, creating gloomy green-and-gray caverns which even the sunlight could not penetrate.

Finding the water channels that would take him and his burden to Chandler was not Arkansaw's only problem. He must avoid the main channels for fear of meeting any of the regular swamp denizens who might be traversing them, for all the swamp people knew that Clara Burleigh had been taken by Vauchain, and any of them, meeting Arkansaw or seeing him, would be suspicious of the bulky bundle of bedclothing in the bow of the punt. He had to be careful to avoid the island shacks which appeared here and there; nor could he apply to any of the swamp people for the food which Clara Burleigh and he would require.

While the daylight lasted he poled the craft cautiously, but when night came on he sent it skimming over the water swiftly and vigorously. Yet while darkness aided him in avoiding the swamp people, it presented some distinct difficulties. It shortened his view of the swamp ahead of the punt, and several times he found the craft pocketed and had to pole backwards to seek another channel. Then a heavy mist, thicker than fog, oozing dampness and cold, descended, blotting out everything except the moonlight. And the moonlight, filtering down, created an impenetrable silvery radiance of dazzling brilliance, billowy and translucent, with pendant writhing wisps that trailed off into the contrasting gloom.

Twice in the interval between dusk and midnight Clara Burleigh stirred. Then, evidently dreaming, or in the delirium of fever, which Arkansaw suspected had not entirely left her, she talked. And what she said Arkansaw never repeated, and afterward tried to forget, though he clenched his teeth, and his sinewy muscles stiffened so that the stout pole with which he propelled the craft seemed to bend in his grasp. And once, hearing her sighing, he shipped the pole and crept forward, parting the bedclothing over her face to whisper to her.

"Are you all right, Miss Burleigh?"

"Yes. I was wondering though . . ."

"Wondering what?"

"Whether you were still here. I thought it might be all a dream. But you *are* here, aren't you? And you won't ever let that man———"

"Hush; he's dead."

She sighed with relief. "Back there—somewhere—you spoke of Father—didn't you? They didn't . . ."

"No. He's in the Planters' House, in Chandler, getting well. Waiting for you."

He returned to the stern of the boat and resumed poling the craft, but presently he heard her voice again, clear in the silence and stronger.

"Who are you?"

"I'm Arkansaw—one of Captain Weldon's Riders. We organized to drive the river pirates out of the swamp."

"Arkansaw," she said. "That's a nickname. What is your real name?"

"I'm Dean Hiller, from down Greenville way. You shouldn't talk. You're powerful weak."

"It's been so long since I could talk to anyone—to anyone I wanted to talk to," she protested. "Please. There are so many things I want to talk about."

So they talked while Arkansaw—which name she used in spite of the new one he had given her—poled the craft through the night blindly, shaping his course as well as he might by the moon.

Her talk was mostly of her father, of the river pirates and of Arkansaw himself, in whom she was frankly interested; and of Stoddard, after Arkansaw had told her about him and about how he had inaugurated the campaign against the river pirates by killing Asa Calder and exhibiting his boots on the courthouse fence. Arkansaw had seen Stoddard several times, had talked with him, and admired him.

Twice during the night the craft grounded, and each time Arkansaw, risking poisonous reptiles, was forced to get out and release it, to clamber aboard, wet to the hips and covered with slime. They lost an hour when the punt veered from a channel into a bed of rasping rushes and penetrated deep into some heavy overhanging briars that scraped the bedclothing off Clara, became entangled and held the boat fast until Arkansaw released it.

"Thank you, Arkansaw," she said when he tucked the bedclothing around her again. It had become dampened from the mist, but Clara assured him she was comfortable.

At dawn, weary but cheerful, they found themselves on a small bayou which was enclosed upon three sides by towering cypress trees which grew in a mass so dense that the daylight could not enter. There was no outlet. Again they had entered a pocket, and, as there was only one channel, Arkansaw poled the craft through it and scanned the swamp with anxious eyes. He tightened his belt, rested his tired arms by letting them hang limply at his sides, and tried, by peering here and there, to gain some idea of direction. Clara had gone to sleep apparently, for she made no sound, and for the next hour or so, following a shallow channel which he hoped might lead to one of the broader water lanes, he was glad she was not awake to look at him. For even when the sun came up he could not be sure of his sense of direction. During the night he had lost it. But doggedly he poled the craft on, knowing his course was southwestward, thinking that before sundown he would come upon a familiar section, some landmark, or some remembered channel he could follow to Chandler.

CHAPTER THIRTY-FIVE

When morning came, the people of Chandler went about their usual tasks in a subdued and thoughtful manner. All night little groups of citizens had crowded the water front, there to wait and watch and listen. The crisis, which had been impending, and which the people had felt without having been informed of the details of the Riders' movements, was upon them. For a day and a night the swamp had writhed with unusual violence, which, unseen by the people of the town, was none the less terrifying. In solemn expectancy the town waited. And while Arkansaw, tired but still stubbornly poling his craft, was seeking a course out of the puzzling green labyrinth; and Weldon, accompanied by Jeff and the group of Riders who had brought Stoddard's boots to the Marston house, were somewhere in the swamp searching for Allie Tuttle's father, Marie and Anne and the judge and Allie Tuttle also waited.

Through the dragging hours of the night the girls had kept constant vigil at the window of Marie's room. A score of times Judge Marston had walked from his den to the end of the veranda to hopefully watch and listen. The veranda lights were still burning, and Stoddard's boots were still where they had been placed; and many times, on his trips to and from the veranda, the judge lingered near them.

The Planters' House carriage had been sent back by Marie, and Allie Tuttle was with Anne and Marie, in Marie's room, for Marie, struck by the despairing loneliness of the swamp girl's manner as she turned to leave the room after confessing her love for Stoddard, had followed her down the hall to the head of the stairs, where she had immediately hugged her, with Anne, standing in the doorway of Marie's room, watching, smiling.

"I ain't fitten," protested Allie.

"You're a brave girl, Allie. Braver than I have been. I've been a fool."

Allie shook her head, studying Marie's face in the light from the hall lamp below.

"Yo' air beautiful," she said—meaning it. "I reckon he couldn't help forgettin' I was alive. Wantin' things too hard makes folks fergit they ain't worth what they're wantin'."

Shortly after daylight, at her own request, Allie was taken back to the Planters' House in the Marston carriage, the judge seated beside her. During the night, in Marie's room, Allie had completely changed her opinion of quality folks. "Yo'-all air got smarter feelin's than common folks," she said; "and yo' air got more sense. Them thet runs yo' down is jest envious and jealous."

"That may be true, Allie," said the judge. "If it is, it's a matter of training and environment, and time."

"And watchin'," she supplemented. "I air goin' to watch quality folks and learn how to act like they do, and be what they are. I air goin' to be a lady."

"You're a lady now, my dear; and Colonel Burleigh loves you."

He patted Allie's head affectionately as they both descended from the carriage in front of the Planters' House, and the judge went up to call upon Colonel Burleigh, and the colonel listened to the story of the finding of Stoddard's boots and sat in his chair with hanging head when at last the judge left him.

When the judge reached home the girls were nowhere to be seen, so he gently took up Stoddard's boots and the placard, carried them into his den and placed them in a corner. Then, exhausted, he dropped into an easy chair and went to sleep. Awakening, he breakfasted with the girls in silence. There was nothing that any of them cared to talk about. They did not mention Stoddard's name. Marie's eyes were red, as were Anne's, but Marie's were still swimming with tears while Anne's were dry.

The philosophy of enduring patience built up in Hatfield Stillwell—Oran Stillwell's father—by his son's helplessness included a willingness to listen and an ability to understand. So when he saw the Marston carriage coming just before noon, the judge and Marie and Anne in it, he asked no questions that might have embarrassed them but greeted them warmly as friends and neighbors making a surprise visit. He knew, though, why they had come, and while he laughed and talked with them, leading them into the house to be received by Mrs Stillwell, where they were instantly made comfortable, he was thinking of how it had been with his wife and himself in that time of awful suspense when Oran, invalided home, was on his way. The house had been strange and dismal and filled with an aching emptiness which would have been permanent had Oran died. To be sure, Stoddard was not a member of the judge's family, but Marie loved him (Anne had told Mrs Stillwell so, and she had told Hatfield) and was enduring the torture of uncertainty, a phase of which was nervous restlessness and lack of interest in familiar places and scenes.

"My house is like a tomb," the judge told Hatfield. "We simply could not endure it any longer. We had to get away. It's the uncertainty that hurts most. When they first brought his boots in I felt it was all over. But now I'm not so sure."

Hatfield said gravely: "Some of the Riders brought us word about it last night. He's got the reputation of being a fighting man, and I wouldn't be too sure that they've killed him."

In a like manner Mrs Stillwell tried to comfort Marie and sought to interest her in her needlework and in some new cooking recipes which she had tried, finding them perfect. But Marie did not respond, and though she praised the bounteous dinner that Mrs Stillwell spread before her guests, she ate very little. For a while in the afternoon she sat beside Oran—who for once did not talk about the war—but she said very little, and several times Anne found her alone on the veranda, staring into the swamp.

CHAPTER THIRTY-SIX

At sundown Arkansaw slowly lifted the pole into the boat, laid it down gently, so that he would not disturb Clara, and slumped forward, his head bent, his arms limp, his face drawn and white. Tricked by several deceptive channels, which were shallow, foul with repulsive growth and the thick green slime of stagnating water, he was in an unfamiliar section of the swamp. All day it had been unfamiliar. Steadfastly he had held to a southwestwardly course, following the sun, and now over him had stolen the disheartening conviction that he was lost. Moreover, hunger and more than twenty-four hours of steady poling had stolen the strength from his sinewy muscles, had deadened them until there was no more strength left in them. Now, anxiously watching the sky, he saw it slowly blotted out by low black clouds.

Twice during the day he had disembarked upon small islands where there had been small shacks belonging to the swamp people. He had approached these with caution which later he found had not been necessary, for the shacks were deserted, and denuded of the food he sought. Each time he had welcomed the opportunity to rest and had carried Clara with him, leaving her while he searched the islands, to return empty handed and disappointed. The marvel of it was that Clara seemed to be growing stronger, and she did not complain of hunger, telling him that the thought of food was far from her, that her only concern was to reach her father.

Now she slept, and Arkansaw had slumped to the bottom of the boat and was also asleep. When he awakened he was immersed in a pitch-blackness that had descended upon him. He started to creep toward the bow of the boat to see if all was well with Clara, when, evidently hearing him as he moved, she spoke. Her voice sounded clear, and he got the startling impression that she was sitting up in the boat.

"Arkansaw!" she said.

"Yes," he answered. "Is anything wrong?"

"I don't know. Nothing is wrong with me, if that's what you mean. I feel much better. I'd feel still better if it weren't for this horrible darkness. It's like it was the night the river pirates burned the Clara Belle. Only, somehow, it's more sinister. Something is happening out there—all around us, it seems. I've heard shooting, and in some places the swamp seems to be on fire!"

Stiffly, with lagging muscles, Arkansaw stood up in the punt, listening, peering into the surrounding blackness. Faint reports reached him; here and there he saw glowing patches of light.

"You're right," he said. "It's fire and shooting. It seems to be away off. On three sides of us. There's nothing straight ahead of us—behind you."

"What do you think it is, Arkansaw?"

"I know what I hope it is," he said grimly. "I hope it's the Riders, burning the pirates out. I thought it would have to come to that. Something must have happened to stir Weldon up." He sat down on the stern seat of the punt and took up the pole, drawing a deep breath into his aching lungs.

"Arkansaw, you're terribly tired," said Clara.

"I reckon I don't feel as fresh as I did," he laughed.

"And you're awfully hungry."

"I hadn't noticed it—much," he lied, although he was so weak that the pole almost dropped from his hands as he set an end of it against the mud bottom of the shallow channel and drove the craft slowly forward toward the banked darkness in which there were no patches of light. For a time he pushed the craft ahead while both of them were silent, hearing an occasional report above the creaking and swishing of the swamp growth against the sides of the boat, watching the distant patches of flame.

"We're lost, Arkansaw," Clara finally said.

"A while ago—yes. Now we're only half lost. I'm pretty certain Weldon has turned the Riders loose. If that's so, then the fires mean that the Riders are burning the shacks in the swamp. The fires are on three sides of us. That would mean that the shore is somewhere ahead in that dark patch, into which we're heading. I don't know how far it is, but I hope we'll make it. One thing is certain, we've got to stay away from any fires or any men we might see. You huddle down low," he warned, "so you won't be knocked overboard by the knee of a cypress or get pulled out by briars. And that moss is dripping wet."

Clara obeyed and, wrapped in the bedclothing, listened to the regular thudding of the pole against the gunwale of the punt and felt the gentle heaving of the craft as it moved onward. Steadily Arkansaw worked with the pole, hour after hour, heading through the black wall of darkness. Occasionally he ceased poling and sat with closed eyes in a welcome, soothing blankness; only to awaken, startled, as the pole dropped from his sleep-loosened fingers. He had to search for the pole in the slime which instantly covered it, and each time he vowed he would sleep no more. And thereafter, feeling drowsiness stealing over him, he shipped the pole until he became conscious again.

The human body may be driven until, deadened, it is no longer responsive to feeling. But the brain continues to weave its fantasies and create its thought images. Dominating Arkansaw was a determination to get Clara Burleigh to her father. The punt and the pole were his only means of accomplishing his purpose, and so punt and pole became at last the only real things of the night—material things, with weight and substance, upon which he could concentrate. He could not trust his vision, for that could not penetrate the darkness, nor could he trust his thoughts, which would stray from the task to which he had devoted himself.

The thudding of the pole against the gunwale of the boat kept him from going to sleep. He fell to counting the thuds, thinking this occupation would keep him awake. Also he could reckon time by counting the thuds. But he found that after he had counted up to several hundred he lost track of the number and had to begin all over again. He tried to space the strokes so that there would be a certain number of them in a certain time—estimated—but he stopped that when he grounded the punt in a shallow and had to get out and shove it off. When he tried to get back into the boat he took a long time at it, and for some minutes after getting in he lay motionless, so tired he could not move.

Clara's voice awakened him. "Are you all right, Arkansaw?"

"Sure," he answered sleepily. "Got stuck in the mud when I shoved off back there. Bushed me, sort of. I'm all right now."

It was strange how his will could conquer physical weariness, and how pangs of hunger could be assuaged by not thinking about hunger and by tightening his belt until it seemed like an iron ring around his waist, even though it kept reminding him of his emptiness. One thing you could do, if you kept your mind on it—you could pole a punt automatically, by force of habit, even if your arms were a dead weight, and your shoulders ached agonizingly, and your head was so heavy you couldn't lift it. And so, almost asleep, Arkansaw poled on, while the hours dragged endlessly, and the dawn came with no sun to set a course by, and a white-faced girl, swathed in damp bedclothing, was sitting in the bow of the punt, watching him with anxious and pitying eyes. It was daylight, or hours after daylight. Arkansaw did not know. The dark clouds above and the dripping mists floating through the lacy veils of Spanish moss created semi-gloom in which time was lost and in which all objects assumed grotesque shapes.

Now, forcing the punt through some drooping cypress fronds that touched the water and showered Clara and himself with dewy drops of moisture, Arkansaw was certain that far ahead of them, beyond a tangle of swamp growth, upon a hummocky island, green with rank grass and slimy pools, he saw something moving. The punt drifted as he stared, and Clara, awake, watching him, asked what he saw.

"Nothing, I reckon." He still stared, and his eyes, red and heavy, were hooded with something dark and guarded. Startled, Clara turned and looked.

At first she saw nothing but the now-familiar tangle of swamp growth, the green slime, the curtains of Spanish moss and the towering cypress. But presently she, too, saw something moving, saw something fall, lie motionless for an instant, to rise and move again.

"It's a man!" she whispered.

Swaying, a bright cold glint coming into his heavy-lidded eyes, Arkansaw shipped the pole into the punt, reached down and drew a huge pistol from the bottom of the boat—the pistol he had used in killing Snakehead—and examined it, twirled the cylinder, cocked it and stuck it into the waistband of his trousers. Sleep had gone from him, but not his weariness or his courage. The cold brightness in his eyes became mockery.

"It's a man, sure enough—walking, wading. Where's his boat? A swamp man, I reckon. Well, if the Riders are wiping them out I might as well take a hand in it." He seized the pole and worked the punt through some tall rushes, and out into a shallow channel that ran along the edge of the island. The punt moved slowly, for Arkansaw was watching the swamp man, who, partially concealed by some filmy willows, was making his way toward them, though still some hundreds of feet distant.

The man's figure was indistinct; a shape, nothing more. Mists swirled around him, parted as he lunged into them, eddying behind him. He came on, and to Clara, watching him intently, he seemed to stagger and sway drunkenly. And now, each moment seeing him more distinctly, she gasped as he fell face down and for several seconds did not move. When he got up again he almost fell a second time, and with bending knees and dragging feet he swayed in a circle to keep himself erect; and Clara saw that in his right hand was a heavy club and in his left a gun similar to the one Arkansaw carried in the waistband of his trousers. A warlike figure, drunk, menacing.

Arkansaw had ceased working the pole. He laid it in the boat and drew the heavy pistol, holding it in his right hand.

"Arkansaw," breathed Clara, "he's a swamp man; he's drunk and armed!"

"Yes," answered Arkansaw, "I see." Some quality in Arkansaw's voice—a smothered note—made her look quickly at him, and she saw that his eyes were widening, filled with doubt and growing amazement as he stared hard at the swamp man, who, now not more than a score of feet distant, a filmy mist enwrapping him, had come to a pause and was standing there, swaying back and forth. His feet were bare, his trousers, plastered with mud and slime, were in tatters, but around his waist was a heavy cartridge belt, studded with cartridges, and suspended from the belt was a great leather holster, obviously designed for the gun he carried now in his right hand, its muzzle irregularly weaving in the direction of the punt. He was naked from the waist up, and his skin, except for the splotches of muck and green slime upon it, was white but crisscrossed with scratches from briers through which appeared numerous large purple welts. High on his right shoulder was a bullet wound out of which blood ran in a tiny stream. But his face, unmarked except for some scratches on his forehead which ran into the wet and matted hair above it, was one that Arkansaw had seen before; and he was striving, even as the man spoke to him through writhing, mocking lips, to remember him.

"I want your boat!"

"Good Lord!" gasped Arkansaw, rising to his feet to stare in amazed bewilderment. "It's Stoddard!"

Arkansaw's excitement brought Clara to her feet, and for the first time, it seemed, Stoddard noticed that the punt had a second occupant. He tried to bow to her but swayed backward, kept his feet with a supreme effort, and stared hard at them, the big gun slowly drooping.

"You're not a swamp man," he said.

"No," almost yelled Arkansaw. "I'm Arkansaw, one of Captain Weldon's Riders! And look, Stoddard; I've got Clara Burleigh with me!"

Stoddard swayed there, trying again to bow to the lady, a weary smile tugging at his lips, his eyes gleaming with pleasure through the agony in them.

"Mr Arkansaw, I'm glad to meet you," he said. "And I'm delighted to find Miss Burleigh with you. And would you have room for another passenger? You see, I'm tired of this swamp."

"My God—yes!" exclaimed Arkansaw quickly. He steadied the punt by driving an end of the pole deep into the mud of the channel and pulling its top tightly against the outside gunwale.

Stoddard dropped the club, slid the gun into its holster and tried to get into the punt, which lurched perilously as he put one foot in it. Finally, with Arkansaw's help, he was placed in a sitting position upon the bottom of the punt, facing Clara.

For a time Stoddard, sitting there, gave no sign that he knew the punt was moving; or that Clara, erect in the bow, her face ashen, was watching him; or that Arkansaw, pushing the craft through the water, was stirred to abysmal rage as he inspected the welts on his body and noted that the bullet which had gone into his chest had come out above the shoulder blade. The wound had discolored the flesh and was bleeding again because of the swamp water that had seeped into it, but it was not a fresh wound, for around it blood had congealed. The network of scratches was from the long spikes of the briers into which he had plunged in making his escape from his enemies. Enemies, of course. Friends don't whip you, nor do friends lash your wrists together so tightly that two or three days later you may plainly see the rope burns. Ankles too. Tied and whipped with a heavy lash. And shot. The bullet wound days old. How many days? Two or three, Arkansaw estimated. He looked at Clara, who stared at him with streaming eyes and shook her head slowly from side to side pityingly. Arkansaw gulped and had to set his teeth to keep from doing what Clara was doing.

Stoddard was holding to the gunwale of the punt as if to steady himself. His head was turned slightly to the right and he seemed to be gazing beyond the island into the dismal distance. Clara saw his lips curve mockingly, and he lifted a hand and waved it in ironic farewell.

"Good-by, Willows," he said and looked straight at Clara, the smile on his lips deepening.

"The Willows?" exclaimed Arkansaw, startled. "Did you come from the Willows, Stoddard?"

"That's what the 'capting' called it," he said and smiled again, this time with wearied derision.

"The 'capting'?" echoed Arkansaw.

"Aye, blimme—the 'capting.' A bloomin' bloke with a cap pistol and a Cockney accent. He shot me—here." He pointed to the wound in his shoulder. "Craftkin," he added. He rocked back and forth in silent laughter, and Clara saw that his eyes, though clear and blue, were agleam with gargantuan mirth, ironic, repressed.

"I know where we are now," said Arkansaw suddenly. For Clara's benefit he added: "The Willows is an island. It's over there." He pointed. "Craftkin's island." With renewed courage and energy he poled the punt forward, while Stoddard, the slime and mud on his body slowly drying, sat there swaying, trying to steady himself, fighting off a great weariness.

His teeth clamped with mingled admiration and concern, Arkansaw worked with the pole. This man—wounded, beaten, lost—was contemptuous of the weakness of his body. Ready to drop, he had retained the poise, the gentleness and the courage which made him what he was—a gentleman. There had been no word of complaint, no appeal for sympathy, and, even now, no mention of his wound, except his jocular reference about the "capting" having inflicted it.

Arkansaw wanted to learn what had happened to Stoddard, wanted to learn the identity of the men who had wrought this monstrous punishment, so that, if Stoddard should die, he would be able to give Captain Weldon their names. But he forebore to question Stoddard, fearing the effort to talk would weaken him—for Stoddard was breathing heavily, and now his eyes were closed. But he still sat erect, bracing himself, disdaining to surrender to his weakness. Clara, watching him, wanted to bathe his wound and the angry welts with clear cool water, to remove the mud and slime with which he was splattered; particularly she wanted to brush the matted hair out of his eyes—hair which was now drying to a rich glinting brown, but so stiff with slime that it looked like a tight-fitting cap. But there was no cool pure water at hand, and she remembered that she was clad only in the bedclothing.

So they did nothing, said nothing, as with powerful sweeps of the pole Arkansaw sent the craft on; not blindly, as before, but with knowledge of his course and a determination to get Stoddard to a doctor before it was too late.

They were still far from the shore line. And now Arkansaw's strength, miraculously restored by the excitement of finding Stoddard, was slowly ebbing. Once more the act of poling grew laborious, painful, slow. Yet Arkansaw was satisfied. Clara Burleigh was stronger; and Stoddard had not collapsed, as Arkansaw had feared he would. A strange man. Not a whimper out of him, nor a groan. Those great long welts must be agonizingly painful; even the brier scratches must burn with a torturing fire; the bullet wound certainly had weakened him, while hunger and exhaustion had exacted their inevitable toll. Yet so far he had spoken no word to tell of his suffering. He seemed not to be conscious of his wounds; and several times as he sat there, still bracing himself with arms extended against the gunwale, he shook with silent laughter.

"The 'capting'," he chuckled, and Arkansaw knew he was referring to Craftkin—perhaps seeing him—which would be his mind re-enacting something that had happened to him, straying from the present to the past. "Oh, there you are!" he added, and his right hand came up from the gunwale and the arm was drawn back so that the elbow snuggled his side. The forefinger of the hand moved as if it pressed a trigger. "Hurts as much as the lash, eh, 'Capting'?" he mocked. "But it's effect is more permanent. You shouldn't have brought the Peacemaker along, Craftkin, and once it was here you should not have been so careless in leaving it where I could get hold of it."

"The Peacemaker?" whispered Clara.

"His gun," Arkansaw explained. "He called it that when he fought Asa Calder."

Stoddard was occupied with the re-enacting of his experiences—a fragmentary review, apparently, with long pauses between, and the derision in his voice was so sincere and spontaneous that it brought sympathetic smiles to the grave faces of Arkansaw and Clara. They gathered from his talk that there were three other men besides the "capting" who had carried him to the island, bound, his boots missing—there to strip him and whip him—and that, after the beating had been administered, the "capting" had shot him, leaving him where he had fallen into the water at the edge of the island, thinking him dead. Two of the men had then gone away in the only boat, and Craftkin and the remaining man had gone into Craftkin's shack. And Stoddard, not having been seriously hurt, and still strong, had found his gun and cartridge belt, and, appearing suddenly in the door of the shack, had shot them down one after the other, saving Craftkin for the last. It seemed a certain expression upon Craftkin's face at the end had amused him, and still amused him as his thoughts dwelt upon it. Clara and Arkansaw could easily imagine the scene. Craftkin, confronted by Stoddard, gun in hand, after having abandoned him as dead; staring at the man who had been his victim—now half naked, dripping, gun in hand, laughing—as he now laughed—as he killed, perhaps watching the "capting" as he writhed, mocking him with the words: "Hurts as much as the lash, eh, 'Capting'?"

A grisly scene. A man to remember.

CHAPTER THIRTY-SEVEN

A change of scene will provide temporary escape from one's thoughts, but as soon as the new environment is established in one's senses, and its novelty is no longer an attraction, the thoughts return more vivid than ever. And so for a few hours the judge and Marie and Anne, entertained by the Stillwells, had a respite from the tragic experiences of the night. Age, with most of its hopes behind, has neither the spirit nor the resistance of youth, and so early in the afternoon the judge was asleep in the big living room, near Oran Stillwell, who was also asleep, while Hatfield Stillwell, with David, Oran's brother, and a plantation laborer, was somewhere in a field behind the stables, and Marie and Anne were in the kitchen with Mrs Stillwell. The clouds that had formed during the night were dispersing and the sun was breaking through, and a slight breeze, strong with the scent of new-growing cypress, swept through the house.

All afternoon Marie had been waiting for Weldon or for news of him. She had left word with the judge's servant, so that Weldon, returning to the Marston home, would know where to find her; but as the hours went by and no word came from Weldon her hopes that, after all, Stoddard might be rescued, had died. And now her expectation of seeing Stoddard again, never high after the men had brought his boots to the Marston house, deserted her. She wanted to cry, but she could not cry here, with all of them watching her, expecting her to cry. She wanted to be in her own room, alone, where the humbling of her stubborn pride would be known only to herself; where she could confess to herself and to God that despite her treatment of Stoddard she loved him—despite the fact that he was a Yankee—of all persons the most detestable until now. She had loved him since that night, on the veranda of the judge's house, when she had first seen him.

She got up from the chair in which she had been sitting and stood there very erect, very pale.

"I'm going home," she said to Anne. "Alone, please. You and Judge Marston may stay until Mr Weldon comes. I'll send the carriage back."

Mrs Stillwell fluttered toward her, politely protesting, but Anne, with greater knowledge of her friend, put an arm around her and held her close.

"Of course, honey. I'm so sorry. I think God is mean to treat you this way—just when——"

"When I have been mean to Mr Stoddard," said Marie. She was very quiet. Her eyes were steady, dry; and bravely she tried to smile.

"Don't pity me, Anne—please. I don't deserve it. I loved him, and I was too mean to tell him so."

"I know you loved him, honey. I think we all knew it."

"And treated him abominably. I wanted to hurt him because—because he knew I loved him, that I—I couldn't help loving him."

"Don't blame yourself, honey," consoled Mrs Stillwell. "If he had lived, you wouldn't feel like that about it. Things like that seem trivial, looking back on them. It's because . . ."

A faint tapping at the outside kitchen door made her turn to see a tall bearded man standing on the stoop, attempting to peer in. He was gaunt, pale, sagging with weariness; his shirt and trousers were soiled with mud and slime, but though the girls and Mrs Stillwell were startled and stood there curiously watching him, they knew by the excitement in his eyes, by a faint smile that tugged at his lips, by something gentle and eager in his manner, that he was the bearer of news which they would welcome. In Marie the feeling was so strong that it sent her to the door to stare at the man, a sudden wild hope stealing her breath; with Anne, close to her, also breathless with anticipation. Mrs Stillwell, her hands trembling, her voice quavering, said:

"Oh!" recognizing the man. "You're Arkansaw."

"Yes ma'am. I've just come in from the swamp, and I've got Clara Burleigh and Stoddard with me. They're in a boat just at the edge of the swamp, and I want to get Hatfield to help me carry them in. Miss Burleigh is sick, and Stoddard is hurt."

Marie saw only one thing—Arkansaw's face. He was the bearer of good news, and the look in his eyes as they met hers flashed a message of hope to her, of wearied delight for the part he had played, of consciousness of duty well done. His haggard face, his hair and beard, stained and splotched from contact with the low-hanging swamp vegetation through which he had passed, were beautiful to her—beautiful then, and more beautiful afterward in her memory. These were the only things she saw—Arkansaw's face and her vision of Stoddard, hurt so badly that he had to be carried. The commotion created by Arkansaw's words she did not hear or feel. But when, an instant later, she stood on the front veranda, without knowing how she had got there, shading her eyes with her hands to gaze out into the swamp, she saw a boat out there, at the shore end of a channel, with perhaps two or three hundred feet of shallow water and marsh intervening, through which a boat could not be forced; and saw that the boat contained two persons—one sitting motionless in the bow, swathed and bundled in what seemed to be sodden rags; the other bending over, stepping out of the boat—she knew it was true—that the man getting out of the boat was Stoddard. She began to run toward him, down the veranda steps and over the grassy slope that led to the marshy ground, not looking at the ground at all, not even caring about the water and slime that swished around her ankles as she got into the marsh—seeing only Stoddard as, knee deep in the tangled vegetation and the black water, he staggered and swayed with rocking head and drooping shoulders, trying to move shoreward, making no progress. She was afraid he would fall before she could reach him, and so as she made her way toward him, sinking deeper into the water at each step until it was above her knees and her skirts were dragging heavily, weighted and soiled, she got within a dozen feet of him and called encouragingly to him, knowing that he did not see her. His legs braced, his head bowed, he was staring downward, his eyes closed.

"Here, dear!" she gasped as she struggled to get nearer. And then, when she saw the huge welts on his naked skin and the bullet wound in his shoulder, she cried wildly: "Oh! What have they done to you!"

At the sound of her voice he turned a little and stared at her wonderingly, and she saw he was not certain that what he saw was real. It was as if, awakening suddenly, he was surprised to find he was not asleep. He peered intently at her, swaying back and forth, and smiled disbelievingly, shaking his head from side to side in silent derision. Divining his condition, sick with horror and pity, she fought her way to his side and threw both arms around him in anguished sympathy, while at the touch of her he started and stared at her incredulously—first at her face and then at her hands, white against his tanned and lacerated skin. She saw his bewilderment, knew that his senses, stupefied by his experiences, were vainly groping in a fog of unreality but that he dimly recognized her. And presently, when her arms went around his neck and drew his head down, and she kissed him hungrily, thankfully—disregarding mud and slime—crying: "You poor dear!" over and over, holding him as if she would never let him go, he smiled in solemn disbelief and watched her curiously as at last she took him by an arm and began to lead him slowly toward the shore.

He was almost certain he had seen Marie Villers and that she had kissed him; but that of course was merely another of his delusions, one of the many fantasies that had been puzzling him for an interminable length of time; just as all the people around him now were unreal and not living persons. They were staring at him, splashing through the water, shouting excitedly, but they were not more real than Clara Burleigh and Arkansaw, with whom he thought he had been drifting in a boat somewhere in the swamp. So he went forward as best he could, staggering, swaying, his knees buckling under him time after time, and only a tugging at his arm roused him to further effort and kept him from staying where he had fallen—the tugging, and a voice, strangely like Marie's, calling to him from somewhere in endearing terms, pleading with him. And occasionally a hand patting his cheek, brushing the damp hair out of his eyes.

It was a long, long way to the shore, even with Marie walking by his side, helping him, sometimes bearing almost his entire weight. And he was thankful that the illusion of her presence was so vivid, for thoughts of her gave him renewed strength. But when he felt someone on the other side of him, holding his arm, supporting him, he resisted, braced his legs in the shallowing water and muck, shook both supporting hands off and tried to draw the heavy revolver from the holster at his hip. The hand was stayed before the gun could come out, and a voice calmed him: "There, there, old man. It's Evan Weldon. You're all right now."

"Weldon, eh?" he mumbled and permitted their hands to help him again. "I thought it was the 'capting'." Now he laughed mockingly, for of course Weldon was an imaginary figure too. Just as imaginary as Marie Villers, whose kisses he still felt. Again, through endless time, he staggered forward, with arms sustaining him, with a light hand patting his shoulder, seeming to caress it. Reeling in his vision was a white house, some horses and a number of people. And at last firm ground under his feet. And now half a dozen hands were supporting him while leading him upward to some steps, across a floor, which he thought was real, into the house he thought he had seen, and into a room to a bed, upon which they placed him, while Marie—he thought—sank down on her knees beside him, and hugged him, and patted his cheeks, and ran her fingers through his hair, and kissed him, and cried, and begged him to live, because she loved him.

CHAPTER THIRTY-EIGHT

So Stoddard came to Stillwell's, to peace and quiet and a soothing tranquillity. He came to lie between cool sheets, upon a soft pillow, to feel the cool breezes that swept into the windows. At first he was not certain about it all, and felt he would never be certain, for at times the white ceiling of the room was crisscrossed with green branches and weaving fronds and drooping Spanish moss, and the bed became a boat in which he floated and drifted, while he could hear the swamp water lapping and gurgling all around him. During these times he talked to Craftkin, always referring to him as the "capting" in mockery. At first he was continually in the swamp, but after a long while—and then only for infrequent intervals—the swamp became a room with people in it, looking at him. He was puzzled, and at times he talked to them, thinking they were in the swamp with him. He couldn't hold the room steady in his vision, because he knew it was another of his delusions and not real, as he sometimes thought.

The faces of the people he saw interested him most. He smiled at the ones he recognized—Evan Weldon, Arkansaw—and once Clara Burleigh, dressed in white, saying something to him. He smiled at her, too, thinking of the bedclothing in which she had been wrapped while he had been with her in the punt. He saw Allie Tuttle; heard her voice saying: "The damned devils!" Even Colonel Burleigh, and Galt and Judge Marston, and many others were in the room. What he could not understand was why all the faces should be so full of concern. Two faces he saw very often—Marie's and Dr Buchanan's. Marie's more frequently than the doctor's. It seemed Marie was always near: moving about the room—when the room became a room, as it did more often now—or sitting in a chair near him, looking at him, or on the edge of the bed speaking softly to him, and bathing his face and temples with something cool and damp. She wasn't real of course. He knew that, but sometimes he talked to her just as if she were real, to complete the absurdity.

"You're really not here," he said, "but I like to believe you are."

"I am here."

He wagged his head at her, smiling wryly.

"There wouldn't be any reason for it," he continued. "You don't like me." And now he smiled complacently with a gleam of triumph in his eyes. "I dreamed you kissed me," he said. "That you came out into the swamp after me. So you see, dreams are better than real life." He was amazed to see a crimson tide surge into her cheeks, but before he could call her attention to the phenomenon she had vanished and he was in the swamp again, talking to the "capting." "Trying to knock the pride out of me," he said. And added mockingly: "It can't be done, 'Capting'."

Of course, being again in the swamp, he did not see Marie sitting there watching him. Dry eyed, shuddering, she was thinking of him as he had appeared that day on the lowland road when she had spoken so bitterly to him; and as he had appeared to her when, reaching his side at the edge of the swamp, she had helped him shoreward. So that was what he had been thinking of while they had been whipping him. Thinking of her. She would never forget that.

* * * *

The people whose faces Stoddard had seen could usually be found upon the big veranda of the Stillwell house. Some of them spent a good deal of time there, others came often and stayed long, while still others—a great many of them—paused there only momentarily to inquire about Dr Buchanan's patient, who, they were told, was doing very well and would soon reach the convalescent stage. Already the story of the exodus of the swamp pirates was history, but there still remained in the memories of Judge Marston and Evan Weldon incidents which seemed to them to deserve repetition, and the judge, particularly, since he was often on the Stillwell veranda—his ward having moved, bag and baggage, to the Stillwell house—recited one incident to every visitor who would listen.

"It was the second day after Mr Stoddard came out of the swamp," said the judge. "After Doctor Buchanan had told us that although Mr Stoddard had been used up pretty well it wouldn't be long before he would be out again as well as he'd ever been. Even better," he added, smiling fondly, "if my ward can manage it. Egad, she hovers over him like a mother!" At this point the judge would invariably clear his throat and permit himself an amused chuckle. "I'd gone home from here for some lawbooks. I'd got into the habit of doing my reading here, so that I'd be near when Marie wanted me to run errands for her. I got the books, then I saw Mr Stoddard's boots standing in the corner of my study, where I'd left them after they had been brought to the house by Weldon's men. I put them into the carriage along with the books, and then I decided I'd go to Chandler to see Colonel Burleigh and his daughter, who were still at the Planters' House and happy as larks. Clara Burleigh was even happier than the colonel said, because Arkansaw was always hanging around there. He'd shaved and slicked up a bit, and Clara had got to liking him. I showed Stoddard's boots to Colonel Burleigh, and he said if they didn't go back to Mr Stoddard there wouldn't be another man in the country who could fill them. After I left Colonel Burleigh I went down to the Planters' House bar for a julep, setting the boots on top of the bar while I waited for my drink to be mixed. I heard somebody gasp, and I turned to see that fellow Forbush standing behind me, staring at the boots. I hadn't heard him come in, but afterward the barkeeper told me he had a room there. I forgot to tell you that I'd brought that bit of cardboard along which had been found with Mr Stoddard's boots. Printed on the card were the words—'Stoddard. His boots.' Forbush's face was whiter than his shirt bosom.

" 'My God! What are you going to do with those?' he said.

" 'I'm taking them to Mr Stoddard,' I told him.

" 'Is Stoddard alive?' he whispered. 'I thought he was dead!'

" 'He'll be back in his boots tomorrow,' I said, permitting myself to anticipate a few weeks.

"Forbush said no more. Before I half finished my julep I heard somebody running down the front stairs with two niggers carrying his baggage. It was Forbush. He was in a powerful hurry to catch a packet which was about to leave the dock. And, egad! Before I could finish my julep the packet had pulled away from the dock with Forbush on it. Remarkable how a pair of empty boots could scare a man so."

Still another story about boots was related by Evan Weldon, who, upon occasion, while gazing meditatively into the swamp from the Stillwell veranda—especially when there were visitors to listen to him—indulged in grim ironic laughter in the midst of which he would pause and permit his voice to linger with sarcastic emphasis upon the words: "The 'capting.' " Pressed for elucidation, he would relate the story of finding Stoddard's boots, adding: "After Stoddard disappeared we got word that he had been taken to the Willows. Of course we knew Craftkin had taken him there. We found Craftkin's island—the Willows," he went on. "We found the swamp sweetheart there and destroyed it. They hadn't used it on him because it was rusted to uselessness. We don't know how many men were on the island when they whipped him, but there were more than two, because there were no boats there, and somebody must have taken the boats away. Evidently they intended coming back for Craftkin and the other man we found there. We found the whip they had used on him—a blacksnake—and Craftkin's gun. And we found something else—Craftkin himself, and the swamp man who was with him on the island. The swamp man had been shot through the heart with a bullet from Stoddard's gun. Craftkin was not so fortunate, for he had been shot in the stomach and in the heart. Both men were lying against the wall of Craftkin's shack. Above them, on the wall of the shack, evidently printed there by Stoddard's finger, dipped in the black mud of a near-by pool, was the inscription: 'The "capting." His boots. Stoddard.' He didn't bother to print an inscription for the other man."

* * * *

One thing Stoddard had noticed—that, as clarity gradually returned to him, there was also a gradual change in Marie's manner toward him. In those times—now occurring less frequently—when the room turned into a swamp, Marie always seemed nearer and often sat on the edge of the bed—which during those times was not a bed at all—and whispered to him soothingly. But whenever the room assumed its proper shape and proportions and his mind was clear as to details, and he became aware that his thinking was normal, she would always be standing at a little distance from him, or would be sitting in a rocker with a sewing basket in her lap, or would be standing at one of the windows gazing out into the grounds. He regretted the disappearance of his swamp visions because they had always brought her close to him. Now, although she was in the room with him a great deal, she was strangely quiet and shy and reserved. And often she went away altogether, her place being taken by Mrs Stillwell, or by Stillwell himself, and occasionally by Anne Randolph, who always smiled at him, her eyes glowing with secret knowledge.

On the day Dr Buchanan told him he might get up, and helped him to dress, and led him out upon the big veranda to bask in the morning sunshine, he did not see Marie at all. Mrs Stillwell told him she had gone home and would not return that day. And so, solemn and taciturn, he spent a lonesome time sitting there gazing out into the swamp, vainly striving to remember what had happened on the day Arkansaw had brought him in. His mental images of what had happened to him might have been actual occurrences. And they might have been dreams. He did not know, and his thoughtful application to the problem brought him no enlightenment. He could not determine where the dreams ended and where reality began. Above all, he must know the truth about his vision of Marie coming out into the swamp after him. It had been very clear to him then and was clear now. Every detail. The concern and anxiety and terror in her eyes; the whiteness of her face; the resolute tightness of her lips as she had waded toward him, her skirts dragging, splashed with mud and water; her soft hands upon his shoulders and his neck; her kisses upon his lips; her body supporting him; her voice encouraging him. And then, afterward, her constant attendance at his bedside and her caresses. If these were dreams he wished he had never awakened from them.

The next day, his body stronger, his mind clear, he was again upon the veranda, seated there, having given her up—for it was late afternoon, and he had waited all day—when he saw the Marston carriage, bearing her and the judge, pull up at the side of the house. Having impatiently waited for her, he now pretended he did not see her until, pausing in front of him, she spoke to him, telling him that he looked very well and that Dr Buchanan had told her yesterday that he was up. She wondered if he were strong enough, and looked at him critically, and drew a chair close to his, so that she could look at him without his seeing her, to note a little smile—quirk which always created a dimple in his cheek when he was amused; to watch the thought-wrinkles that appeared around his eyes whenever he was puzzled—which had happened very frequently; to look at his hair—which she had always liked—and to feel something indescribable and thrilling—his personality, the magnetism of him. And while she spoke to him and settled herself near him, he was thinking what a fool he was to expect that a girl so beautiful and wonderful could do the things she had done in his foolish dreams. However, he was certainly not dreaming now, and he had not been dreaming during a great many days when he had felt her near him, when he had seen her, as he was now seeing her. And therefore, though he may have had foolish and improbable dreams, there was no doubt that somehow her feelings toward him had changed—had changed from bitterness and contempt to gentle concern and interest. He had no explanation for it and no way to measure the enchanting thrill of her presence near him.

He frowned now, thinking about his dreams, which day by day were retreating from his memory, except the one in which she appeared. And so he wondered if, after all, it might be a reality. If he had dreamed that she had kissed him, he could relegate the incident to the limbo of the fantastic and improbable; but if she had really kissed him, he must find some way—some oblique way—to let her know that he knew.

He began by thanking her for doing so many things for him while the fever raged, not even mentioning how surprised he had been to find her there—an omission which she appreciated, for she nodded and smiled at his hair, which was again tousled. He did not see the smile.

"I was out of my head a great many times," he said.

"Yes. It was the fever."

"A great many of the things I dreamed about never happened."

"I suppose so. You see, dreams are imaginary, or they would be memories."

"Yes." He frowned. "That's the difficulty." He was silent—thinking.

She had to prompt him. "What is difficult?" she said. She was eager. Her eyes were dancing.

"It's difficult to separate our memories from our dreams, and it's just as difficult to determine where dreams stop and memories begin. I've not been able to untangle mine."

"Perhaps I can help you," she suggested and saw his cheeks flood with sudden color, at which singular sight she smiled at the back of his head while he was studying the veranda floor.

"Perhaps you could," he said resolutely. "Up to the time I got into Arkansaw's boat things were pretty clear. I could remember. But everything began to get jumbled, and from then on I couldn't be sure of what was happening. Things happened that were absurd."

"Oh, absurd? Of course. Yes?"

"After a long period of drifting about in the swamp, I thought I saw Arkansaw get out of the boat. He walked away, and that's the last I saw of him. Then I waited a long time and finally got out of the boat, too, thinking I would follow Arkansaw. Then I saw you coming toward me through the swamp. At first I thought I was dead and was looking at an angel. Then I saw that your dress was all splashed with slime and water, and I knew you weren't an angel. But you looked like an angel anyway," he added at her smile.

"I wanted to call to you, to tell you to go back, but I couldn't talk just then. It seemed pretty real to me, and I was startled to see you. But of course it wasn't you after all. That's where my dreams began."

"Not me, of course," she said and wagged her head at him.

Not seeing the movement, he went on: "Then you threw your arms around my neck and kissed me." Once more as he paused in the telling a tide of color surged into his cheeks, whereat her eyes danced knowingly and she leaned toward him to whisper, pretending to be severe:

"And did you return my kisses, sir!"

Her face was now close to his, and her eyes were alight with mischief.

"You didn't," she said, "and I want them, Brent—now, dear."

And got them. And others. And then as she sat on his lap, holding him close, not knowing or caring if anyone saw them, he told her that while some dreams are beautiful they can never be as satisfying as reality.

THE END

www.ingramcontent.com/pod-product-compliance
Lightning Source LLC
Chambersburg PA
CBHW022152260626
47155CB00017B/1851

* 9 781479 457755 *